Praise

B.J. DANIELS

"B.J. Daniels doesn't fail her readers in this thrill ride of a tale, in which romance blossoms between childhood friends."
—*Romantic Times BOOKreviews* on
Keeping Christmas

"Daniels has more than an intriguing suspense story; she has put together an explosive tale of love, trust and the twisted ties among an embattled family."
—*Romantic Times BOOKreviews* on
Crime Scene at Cardwell Ranch

"B.J. Daniels weaves together past and present secrets to create intense suspense and a wonderful, twisting plot."
—*Romantic Times BOOKreviews* on
High-Caliber Cowboy

"B.J. Daniels treats readers to her signature bad guys, an intense, heart-stopping story and an electric romance between two special characters."
—*Romantic Times BOOKreviews* on *The Masked Man*

"A suspenseful tale, blended artfully with a romance that will warm your heart. Fans of romantic suspense won't be able to put down this page-turner. Definitely a keeper!"
—*Romantic Times BOOKreviews* on
Premeditated Marriage

B.J. DANIELS

A former award-winning journalist, B.J. had thirty-six short stories published before her first romantic suspense, *Odd Man Out*, came out in 1995. Her book *Premeditated Marriage* won *Romantic Times BOOKreviews* Best Intrigue award for 2002 and she received a Career Achievement award for romantic suspense. B.J. lives in Montana with her husband, Parker, three springer spaniels—Zoey, Scout and Spot—and a temperamental tomcat named Jeff. She is a member of Kiss of Death, the Bozeman Writer's Group and Romance Writers of America. When she isn't writing, she snowboards in the winter and camps, water-skis and plays tennis in the summer. To contact her, write to: P.O. Box 183, Bozeman, MT 59771 or look for her online at www.bjdaniels.com.

SHADOW LAKE

B.J. DANIELS

HARLEQUIN®

TORONTO • NEW YORK • LONDON
AMSTERDAM • PARIS • SYDNEY • HAMBURG
STOCKHOLM • ATHENS • TOKYO • MILAN • MADRID
PRAGUE • WARSAW • BUDAPEST • AUCKLAND

ISBN-13: 978-0-373-19891-7
ISBN-10:   0-373-19891-4

SHADOW LAKE

CHAPTER ONE

LIKE THE OTHER GREAT tragedy in her life, Anna Collins never saw this one coming.

Just minutes before midnight, a deer bounded out of the rain and darkness onto the isolated two-lane highway directly into her path.

She'd been driving too fast, terrified and already out of control in her panicked state. So when she saw the deer, all she'd been able to do was react instinctively.

She slammed on the brakes and cranked the wheel. Through the driving rain and slap of the wipers the doe's huge eyes caught for an instant in the headlights, then it bolted, disappearing in the pines lining the road as the car skidded across the wet blacktop.

Anna turned the wheel hard, overcorrecting, sending up a shower of puddled rainwater. She caught the blur of pines and the steep face of a rocky cliff an instant before the large, heavy car left the pavement on the opposite side of the road, and plunged down the mountainside.

Mute with terror, she didn't have time to scream even if she could have made a sound. Nor would that scream have been heard over the crash of the car as it plummeted downward. Branches snapped off, the sound like gunshots, as leaves and bark pelted the windshield, the car gaining momentum.

A limb slapped the windshield an instant after she saw something dark and deep beyond the glow of her headlights.

Water.

The lake came into view a heartbeat before the car went airborne. The tires crashed down hard, the undercarriage shrieking in a scream of metal on rock before the vehicle hit the rain-dimpled black surface of the water.

At some point the air bag had exploded in her face. Before that, her head had slammed hard against the side window. Now everything glittered before going black, then gray as the front of the car pitched forward, inky liquid lapping up over the hood.

Dazed, Anna lifted her head and touched her temple, her fingers coming away sticky with blood. She stared in confusion. Icy water lapped over her feet, quickly filling the floorboard as the car nosed forward at a steep angle, her seat belt cutting into her breasts.

She could hear static coming from the in-car emergency system just before it shorted out in a flash of orange as the car began to sink. Water gushed over the hood to lap against the windshield.

She tried to open the door but it wouldn't budge against the water already up to the side mirror.

She could hear the motor gurgling and realized it was still running. Would the electric windows still work? Frantically she hit the button as she fumbled with tremulous fingers to unlatch her seat belt.

Her side window hummed down. Ice cold water rushed in. She gasped as the water cascaded over her, filling her lap. The car pitched farther forward, the seat belt tightening painfully as the weight of her body pressed into it.

Hurriedly, she hit the window button. The glass began to whir back up, but a few inches from the top, it stopped. She pushed harder on the button as water cascaded over the top of the window, but the water had shorted out the rest of the electrical system.

Frantic, she grappled again to unlatch the seat belt as the breath-stealing cold water rose higher. The belt *wouldn't* unlatch. She tried again and again but it was useless. The seat belt was jammed. The weight of her body seemingly binding it.

The freezing water splashed over her chest to her neck as the car steadily sank. She was going to drown. She gasped, now panicked and choking on the foul-smelling water that flooded her mouth and nose.

She fought to keep her head above water, but it was impossible. The car was sinking too quickly. The interior was almost completely full now, the water only inches from the headliner.

She closed her eyes and sucked in one last breath as the car completed its slow somersault to land on its top with a jarring thud on the bottom of the lake.

For a second, nothing moved. Anna hung upside down, suspended in the icy water by the seat belt, all sense of direction lost. She opened her eyes, still holding the last breath she'd taken. Her gaze followed the eerie dim path the headlights cut through the murky water.

Lungs bursting, mind starting to drift like her hair now floating around her face, she tried the seat belt release one more time even though she knew it was futile.

Her body cried out for oxygen. She had to take a breath. She couldn't hold out any longer.

A tap at the side window.

Startled, she turned her head as if in slow motion and let out a cry, her last breath rushing from her lips at what she saw pressed against the glass.

CHAPTER TWO

GENE BRUBAKER BOLTED upright in bed. His chest heaved as he gasped for breath and frantically searched the room for whatever had awakened him.

The room was black except for the sliver of moonlight that knifed across the end of his bed through a crack in the drapes. He drew back from the light as fearful of it as the darkness.

He was sweating, his heart pounding too hard, his mouth dry. Another nightmare. The same nightmare. He was left with a cloying sense of dread that clung to his skin.

Lying back, he closed his eyes, opened them again, fearful of sleep. The clock on the bedside table read 11:57 p.m.

Throwing back the covers, he swung his legs over the side of the bed, but had to take a moment before he could stand. He cursed the body that was letting him down. He didn't feel his age, could hardly remember it, but he recalled looking in the mirror one day and being shocked to see a deeply wrinkled gray-haired man squinting back at him.

Stiffly, he finally rose. The floor felt cold on his bare feet as he padded over to the window. He still felt shaken, his legs weaker than usual, as he drew back the drapes. The rain had stopped. He could see the lake through the trees. The water shimmered in the moonlight, the surface burnished silver.

He lifted the window with some effort and took a deep breath of the cold spring night air, letting it fill his lungs. As if anything could chase away the nightmare. He let the breath out slowly as he looked past the trees along the shore of the lake to the expanse of open water beyond.

The night air chilled his clammy skin. He slammed the window and had started to pull the drapes closed again when he noticed a light up the block.

Although nearing midnight, it appeared someone was still up at the church.

He stared at the light, surprised by the sudden ache of need that overcame him. He'd avoided church since Gladys's funeral and truthfully only attended before that to please his wife.

He glanced back at the huge bed, the crumpled sheets on only the one side. The ache of emptiness wasn't new. Nor was the loneliness—or the guilt. He reached for his pants.

Gene Brubaker wasn't a man who believed in omens. In fact, he wasn't sure *what* if anything he believed in anymore. That's why he didn't stop to consider what he was doing as he left the house and walked the block down the street to the Holy Rosary Catholic Church.

He walked past the church every day, aware that for the past few months he'd moved to the other side of the street.

Now when he neared the church, the street deserted, his jacket pulled around him as he huddled against the cold, he wondered what he was doing. Possibly just taking a walk to clear his head. The rain had left the night air damp and filled with the smell of the wet street, and he was struck with the thought that it was too cold for late April even for a town in the Northern Cascades of Washington.

Fortunately, there was no one around this time of the night. Or this time of the year in the town of Shadow Lake. Still too early for tourists with Memorial Day weeks away.

The town's only stoplight flashed yellow down the street as he climbed the broad stone steps to the front entrance of the church, half-hoping to find the door locked. Not that there was much chance of that. Shadow Lake was so small and isolated from the real world that there was no need for anybody to lock their doors. Especially churches.

The door was heavier than he remembered it. But then again he was getting weaker each day. He had to push hard to get it to swing open and when it did, he hesitated. This was crazy. Wasn't this the last place he should be?

A dim light burned inside. What was it he thought he'd find here? he wondered now. Salvation? Or redemption?

He had started to turn to leave when he heard the rustle of clothing and saw an elderly priest rise awkwardly from one of the pews up front and turn toward him.

Father Tom Bertonelli met his gaze. With the flick of the priest's arthritic fingers, his old friend motioned him inside.

Brubaker let the church door close behind him, the smell of the rain and night quickly replaced by the familiar scents of his thirty-eight-year marriage. It evoked both longing and sadness. A lump formed in his throat and he felt close to tears again. Christ, he needed to get some sleep. These nightmares were killing him. His life was killing him.

He wanted to laugh at the irony of that as he glanced toward the confessionals, the church feeling too large, too vacuous. The priest gave a faint nod. Like a sleepwalker, Gene moved toward the polished wood of the confessional, his footsteps echoing across the marble floor.

He was glad when the confessional door closed behind him and he was sitting on the worn seat in the dark, the seclusion giving him a sense of safety if not peace.

Tom Bertonelli had been his friend for years. They'd fished together, shared meals up at the house, talked politics. But that had been before Gladys died, before Gene Brubaker had lost all faith.

Leaning back in the shadowy darkness, he closed his eyes as he heard the door to the adjacent confessional open, then close softly as the priest arranged his robes.

Brubaker didn't open his eyes.

"What troubles you?" Tom asked in a voice dry as parchment.

The lump rose in his throat again. He swallowed. "Father, I have sinned."

JUST BEFORE MIDNIGHT, ROB Nash parked under the wide branches of a large old pine tree along the quiet street next to a pile of dirty snow. Cutting his headlights and engine, he settled in to wait.

Rain dimpled the mud puddles along the unpaved back street. All the houses were dark except for one. The other houses were mostly summer cabins, boarded up for the winter. The seasonal residents wouldn't be returning until Memorial Day weekend and it was only April.

A drenched cat crept across the muddy street and disappeared into a honeysuckle hedge. Somewhere in the distance, a dog barked.

It was Tuesday, a notoriously slow night of the week in Shadow Lake, Washington, in the Northern Cascades. Not that there was much trouble in the town this time of year, given that few people wintered-in. The number of residents dropped drastically during the cold months.

It was another story in the summer, though. Tourists flocked to the lake to boat and fish and shop for antiques and curios, causing traffic problems and all the disturbances that came with the increase in population.

Nash hated summers. The town got too hectic, too crowded. That was one reason he wasn't looking forward to another busy season and wondered if it wasn't time for him to retire. He had a new bride to think about.

He'd put in thirty-five years and yet he was still young. Relatively. Fifty-five wasn't that old anymore. He could spend more time fishing. Spend more time with Lucinda, something he wished he had done more of lately.

Headlights flashed at the other end of the street as a car turned and headed toward him. Nash slid down a little in his seat and picked up his binoculars to watch through the half circle in the steering wheel and the low-slung branches of the thick pine he'd pulled under.

He felt like a fool. Worse, he felt disloyal. He'd made a point of letting everyone believe he would be in Pilot's Cove for a couple of days. He hated this kind of deception and had always believed he was a better man than that. Right now he wished both were true.

The approaching car's headlights went out just before the vehicle pulled into the driveway of the only house with lights on down the street, a single-level white brick rancher with a two-car attached garage. Nash felt a jolt as he recognized the car—and the driver.

The front door opened and a young, slim woman rushed out of the house. She'd obviously been expecting her visitor because she wore her red raincoat, the one Nash had bought her for her birthday.

Nash saw her face and the driver's for only an instant as she opened the car door, the dome light coming on. Lucinda Nash slid into the passenger seat. The door closed and the dome light shut off.

Son of a bitch. Nash sat up with a jerk, throwing open the patrol-car door as he drew his weapon. And just moments before, he'd felt bad for being suspicious and deceitful. Apparently he'd had every reason. Hadn't he known something was going on with his wife?

His mind racing, he tried to come up with a reason other than the obvious one for why she would have gone out this time of the night—let alone with that particular man.

Nash had witnessed his share of affairs over the years. It's what a man got for spending a good part of his life on dark streets when good people were in bed asleep. He was no

stranger to the uglier side of humankind. He'd seen things he
hadn't wanted to see, the kind of things that left him with a
nasty taste in his mouth and a shitty impression of humanity
in general.

Now he tried to catch his breath, to still the trembling in
his limbs. His radio squawked. He ignored it. He stumbled
out into the muddy street, the rain pounding out a staccato
beat on the car's roof as he slammed his door behind him.
Fuck retirement. He was going to kill the bastard. Kill them
both.

The car in front of his house backed out slowly. Nash
stopped and gripped the weapon in both hands, willing the
driver of the car to turn down the street toward him.

But the driver turned back the way he'd come, keeping to
the dark pines along the edge of town.

Nash raised the gun as the car took off, the taillights disappearing in the rain and darkness before he could get off a shot.

He took a couple of steps after the retreating car before
staggering back under the weight of his discovery. His palm
came down on the warm wet hood of the patrol car as he
caught himself to keep from falling.

For a moment he thought he was having a heart attack. He
fought to breathe, his chest heaving. His stomach convulsed.
Launching himself toward the dried weeds under the tree, he
retched until he was almost too empty to stand.

Behind him, his radio continued to squawk. He caught
only snatches of what was being said. The operator from one
of those fancy in-car emergency systems had called about an
accident on the way into town.

Leaning against the car, Police Chief Rob Nash wiped his
eyes, then slowly holstered his weapon before stumbling back
to drop into the front seat of his patrol car. He had started to
reach for the radio when he heard his second in command take
the call.

CHAPTER THREE

ANNA COLLINS TRIED to open her eyes, the weight of her lids like concrete shutters. Light filtered in at the edge of her vision, growing brighter.

"She's awake, Doctor," a female voice said nearby.

The room swam in a sea of green and white. She focused on a nurse standing at the end of the bed. A hospital room?

Head pounding, she blinked in confusion, time and sense of place lost, leaving only one thought: She'd been here before. Or had she? She closed her eyes again, preferring the darkness.

"How are you feeling?" said a deep, older male voice next to her.

She forced her eyes all the way open. An elderly man stood beside her bed. His thick gray hair was rumpled as if he'd just gotten out of bed. His face was deeply wrinkled, skin weathered as if from the sun and wind. He wore canvas hunting pants and a flannel shirt beneath the white lab coat that flapped open as he moved closer. He smelled of cinnamon.

She watched him move something around in his mouth. He made a smacking sound, then pushed what appeared to be a round candy into his cheek as he eyed her with pale blue eyes faded by age.

Although he had a stethoscope around his neck, he looked nothing like any doctor she'd ever seen.

"Hello," he said, giving her a smile, the candy making his cheek protrude on the one side. "I'm Dr. Gene Brubaker."

She *was* in a hospital. Anna wet her dry lips as she glanced around the room, her thoughts jumbled, her head aching. The drapes were drawn on the window, but she could see through a slim opening. It was dark out.

She glanced at her wrist. No watch. Instead, she found that her arm was hooked up to an IV. "What…time…"

"Almost three—a.m.," he said.

She nodded, time meaning absolutely nothing right now.

The doctor handed her a glass of water from the nightstand beside her bed and waited while she drank greedily.

"Easy," he warned as she choked on the water. "You're in a hospital, miss. You've had a car accident."

She blinked. A car accident? Her heart began to race. "My son. Tell me my son is all right."

He frowned, his thick gray eyebrows beetling together. "Your son?"

"Tyler. Where is Tyler?" She tried to sit up, but he rested a heavy hand on her shoulder as he took the empty cup from her.

"Easy now. Let's just take it a step at a time. Can you tell me your name?"

"Anna…" For a moment, she couldn't think of her last name. She swallowed, her throat raw, the headache blinding. "Collins. Please, I have to see my son." Her voice broke. "Tell me he's all right. Tell me he made it."

"Try to remain calm," he said, frowning down at her with grandfatherly concern. "Your son was in the car with you? How old is your son?"

"Tyler's four. You have to help him!" Her voice rose and she began to sob as she clutched at one edge of his white lab coat. "Just tell me he's alive. *Please.*"

She was hysterical now, sobbing and gripping at his coat, crying, "Save my son. Please save my son."

"Sheila," the doctor said, and the nurse she'd seen before

moved into her line of vision. Anna felt something prick her skin. Darkness moved along the edge of her vision again, that silent black emptiness calling her back.

She'd been in the dark too long. She clutched tighter at the doctor's white lab coat. "My son. *Please.*" Her voice rasped as the heavy weight of the drug worked to pull her under.

Dr. Brubaker nodded. "Don't you worry now. We'll take care of it."

Her fingers loosened on his coat, her arm dropping back to the bed. Her eyes fluttered. She felt the dead weight of her body as she was dragged down, back into that dark nothingness.

OFFICER D.C. WALKER SHOOK the rain off like a duck as he entered the small, quiet hospital. He caught his reflection in the window as he passed the empty nurses' station. He looked like hell. But he felt worse as he pushed open the door to the doctors' lounge.

Doc Brubaker glanced up from the chair where he was sprawled. It gave Walker little comfort that Doc looked worse than he did.

"Any luck finding the boy?" Doc asked anxiously.

Walker shook his head as he shrugged out of his rain jacket and tossed it onto one of the orange plastic chairs. He helped himself to a stale doughnut.

Without asking, Doc reached for the coffeepot and poured him a cup, then refilled his own.

"Thanks," Walker said as he took the coffee and plopped down in an empty chair. The coffee looked like black sludge, but as long as it contained caffeine and was hot, he wasn't about to complain. He couldn't remember a longer night and it still wasn't over.

"I called out Search and Rescue," he said, between bites of the doughnut. "They've combed the shoreline and the woods, but so far nothing. It's so damned steep where the car went off. Water's deep there and with the spring runoff, real murky. The dive team's gearing up to go down."

Doc shook his head. "I hate to think of a four-year-old out there, as cold as it is. I suppose he could still be in the car."

"If he was strapped in a car seat in back, she might not have been able to get him out."

Dr. Brubaker rubbed a hand over his face. "The only way the boy might have survived is if there's a trapped air bubble. Stranger things have happened."

Walker studied him for a long moment wondering if the doc really put much store in that. "Mac's gonna get his biggest tow truck up there at soon as it gets light. He's not sure he has enough cable to pull the car out though. Might have to borrow a newer towing rig from one of the large towns. Your patient say anything else?"

Doc shook his head. He definitely looked older since his wife had died. Walker thought about the rumors he'd heard that Doc was dying. He didn't put much stock in them though. Rumors were always circulating in Shadow Lake. And just because Doc was getting his affairs in order, so what?

Like the rumor going around about Police Chief Nash's pretty young wife, Lucinda. But who the hell married a woman half his age and thought she'd be faithful? Walker had learned the hard way about infidelity during his one and only marriage. Not that he was bitter. Much.

Shadow Lake was a hotbed for affairs, especially during the long cold winter months when the population dropped. There was a standing joke that the residents who wintered-in here switched wives and girlfriends and then held a roundup in the spring to divvy up the kids. He used to think that was funny.

"Were you able to reach her husband?" Doc asked. He sounded tired and he certainly hadn't been looking well lately. But Walker figured that was to be expected given how many years he and Gladys had been together. He imagined it must have been hell for Doc to watch his wife waste away like that and in so much pain.

"No answer at the husband's house," Walker said. "I left a message, but for all we know the husband was in the car too. Hell, he might have been the one driving."

"I hadn't thought of that," Doc said. "All I could think about was the little boy."

It was too bad Doc had never had any kids of his own, Walker thought.

Fortunately Anna Collins had been in a vehicle with an in-car emergency system that had notified the police department the minute her air bag deployed and tried to raise the car's occupant on the built-in cell phone.

When no one responded, the operator had given the police dispatcher the location of the car via the in-car global-positioning system and the Shadow Lake dispatcher had radioed the police department where Walker had taken the call.

Walker pulled his pencil from behind his ear, touched the tip of it to his tongue and opened his small notebook. "You said she just stumbled up to the hospital?"

Dr. Brubaker nodded. "Half drowned, good-size knot on her left temple. Sheila was on duty and heard the alarm go off, looked up and saw her collapse just inside the front door. She said the woman regained consciousness, mumbled something about her car crashing into the lake before she passed out again.

"That's when Sheila beeped me," Doc said in an exhausted voice. "I called you right away and was told you'd gone out to the crash site."

Walker had been taken aback when he'd seen where the woman's car had left the road. "No way could she climb back up to the highway, so I guess it makes sense that she would come out on the beach. That would have put her out with the hospital being the closest building."

"That's probably what had saved her life," Doc said. "Given the temperature of the air and the water, if she'd been out there any longer she wouldn't have made it. She was already hypothermic when she reached us."

"Did she mention her son when Sheila found her?"

"No." The doctor poured himself more coffee. "She was confused and scared."

Walker nodded. "I called her in-car emergency provider. The car is a blue Coupe de Ville Cadillac registered to her and a—" he consulted his notes "—Marc Collins, presumably her husband. The address is Seattle. No answer at the primary residence, but I had a black-and-white go over to see if anyone was home. She said her son's name was Tyler, right?"

Brubaker nodded. "She became so hysterical I had Sheila give her a sedative to calm her down. Anything I'd have said would have only upset her more. She just assumed that her son was here at the hospital."

"You can't miss the spot where her car went off the road," Walker said. "Right there by the cliffs. No sign of the vehicle. But lots of small trees down. Couldn't have gone off at a worse place if she'd planned it."

Doc looked up. "You don't think she—"

"Purposely drove off there?" Walker shrugged. He'd long ago given up trying to guess what a woman might do. "There weren't any skid marks that I could see. But it was raining, so I couldn't tell if she tried to brake."

Doc shook his head and closed his eyes as he leaned back in the chair. "I'm sure it was just an accident."

Walker was never sure of anything. "She didn't say what she was doing driving up here at that hour of the night?"

"No. She should sleep for a while. I'm hoping her son is

found and I will have good news for her by the time she wakes up."

"I wouldn't count on that," Walker said, studying the doctor again. Since his wife's death, Doc Brubaker had been trying to find a doctor for the town. Few doctors wanted to live in such an isolated town, let alone make so little money and work such long hours. Along with being on call for the town, the local doctor saw to the small nursing home facility attached to the hospital.

Doc hired young interns for the summer months to give him a break, but none of them had shown any interest in staying once the first snowflake fell.

Walker knew Brubaker had talked about retiring even before his wife had died. He figured it wouldn't be long and Shadow Lake would be without a doctor. "You all right?"

Doc opened his eyes, seeming surprised by the question, then uncertain as he glanced toward the darkness beyond the windows. "It couldn't have been a suicide attempt. Not if the boy was in the car with her."

Obviously the doc didn't read the papers. Not having any children of his own, Doc Brubaker had no concept of what parents could do to their children.

Walker stood and noticed he'd left a puddle of rainwater on the floor in front of the chair where he'd been sitting.

"Don't worry about it," Doc said, following his gaze. "I'll get someone to clean it up. Find the boy. I don't want to tell that young woman that her son is out there in that lake."

BRUBAKER CLOSED HIS EYES as Walker left. Sheila would come for him when he was needed.

But he knew he wouldn't sleep. He couldn't remember the last time he'd gotten a decent night's sleep. Well, he thought ruefully, it wouldn't be long and he'd get plenty of rest.

He got up and made another pot of coffee. It was going to

be a long night and making the coffee gave him something to do. Not that it could take his mind off the woman down the hall. He was worried about her. The cold of the lake had caused heart rhythm disturbance. Sheila had said the woman seemed delirious when she'd been found, suffering from hypothermia.

But he suspected that was the least of it. He'd seen a look in Anna Collins's eyes that had been painfully familiar.

He hated to think how many times he'd seen that look in his patients' eyes over the years. More recently, he'd seen it in his wife's. Defeat. Surrender. A lack of will to live.

With Gladys it had been the pain and knowing what the future held for her. He squeezed his eyes shut remembering the feel of his wife's hand in his as she met his eyes that final night.

He shoved away the memory and considered the woman down the hall, bothered by the fact that she couldn't be more than thirty. He realized he could have had a daughter her age if Gladys had been able to carry the baby they'd conceived to term.

Another painful memory to be shoved to the far corner of his heart.

He wondered what had happened to the woman down the hall that had put that look in her eyes.

Most patients were surprised to wake up in a hospital. She hadn't appeared to be. He could only assume it was because she'd been in a hospital, not that long ago, from what he would guess had been a severe head injury given the sizable older scar that ran from her forehead up into her scalp.

And now she had a cut and goose egg on her temple from her car accident tonight, along with water in her lungs.

He could only guess what this woman had been through. Or what she'd been doing on the lake road this time of year, late at night in a rainstorm. He just hoped she'd been alone in the car, and confused due to her two recent head traumas.

Brubaker couldn't stand the thought of what it would do to the woman if her son had been in that car.

WHEN ANNA OPENED HER EYES, she found a man about her age slumped in the chair next to her bed. Her heart began to pound as she saw that he wore the blue uniform of a cop.

He had removed his hat. It now dangled from the fingers of his left hand. His dark hair was too long at the nape and his features were rough, his nose obviously having been broken more than once. And, even though his eyes were closed and his breathing deep in sleep, there was a scowl on his face.

Blinking in confusion, she touched her temple and found a small bandage. A mixture of fear and hope filled her as her fingers quickly rushed to touch her forehead, praying that the horrible scar wouldn't be there.

It was. Tears sprang to her eyes, all hope gone that this was the first time she'd awakened in a hospital, leaving her body like a ghost, her mind and heart again in agony.

As quietly as possible, she turned toward the window, not wanting to rouse the police officer. She'd awakened before with a policeman next to her hospital bed. It had been the worst news of her life. She couldn't imagine how it could be worse this time.

Daylight spilled through the large first-floor window. Beyond the rain-streaked glass, clouds hung in the pines. Past them, she could see more pine trees and what appeared to be rocky cliffs rising out of the rainy mist.

She had no idea where she was. All she knew for certain was that she'd never seen this place before.

She closed her eyes. Earlier she'd fought the bottomless sleep of the dead, thinking there was hope.

Now she knew better and gladly welcomed oblivion.

"Mrs. Collins?"

She squeezed her eyes shut.

"Mrs. Collins, I know you're awake."

She slowly parted her eyelids to find the cop had walked

around the bed and was now standing over her. She hadn't heard him and suspected he'd wanted it that way.

As she looked up into his face, the warm brown eyes startled her. They didn't go with the hard leanness of his face.

"I'm Shadow Lake Police Officer D.C. Walker. I need to ask you a few questions."

She tried to remain calm as she watched him take a small notebook from his breast pocket, pluck a pencil from behind his ear and pull the chair closer to her bed.

He flipped to a page in the notebook and squinted down at it as if he couldn't read his own writing. "Your name is Anna Collins?"

She nodded, then realized her mistake. "No. *Drake*. It's Anna Drake."

He frowned. "You told the doctor it was Collins and your in-car emergency service has the car's primary driver listed as Anna *Collins*." His attention went to her ring finger and the large diamond next to her gold wedding band.

"I *was* Anna Collins. I'm only recently divorced. I just haven't taken off the ring yet or changed my name on the car." She felt her face flame and cringed at the way she sounded. Pathetic. And still wearing the ring. A woman unwilling to accept reality. That was her.

The cop looked as if he would doubt anything she told him after this. "I understand your car went off the road last night and into the lake?"

She felt a jolt. "Is *that* what happened?"

"You don't *remember?*"

She started to shake her head but stopped herself. Any movement caused excruciating pain. She ran the tip of her finger along the scar from her forehead into her hair, then retraced the line as she had a habit of doing whenever she was trying to remember.

"No, I do remember being in the lake." She shuddered as she had a flash of memory—water rising over the hood of the Cadillac.

He studied her, then asked, "Who was in the car with you?"

She swallowed and straightened the covers. "No one."

"What about your son? You told the doctor your son was in the car with you."

Her throat closed. "I was confused. He wasn't in the car." She touched the old scar again then, realizing what she was doing, quickly brushed her bangs back down over it and curled her hands together in her lap to keep them from shaking.

"I just want to make sure you know what you're saying. Ms. Drake?"

She hadn't been Anna Drake for almost ten years. Why had she insisted on taking her name back? She could no more go back to being the woman she'd been before she'd married Marc Collins than she could change the past.

"My son wasn't in the car with me."

"Tyler, right? You're sure he *wasn't* in the car?"

"Yes. I told you I was confused earlier. I thought—" She turned her face away. "I was wrong." Tears burned her eyes. "Please, I'm really tired."

He raked a hand through his hair. "Where were you going when you had your accident last night? Were you headed to Shadow Lake to visit someone?"

She shook her head, the pain almost comforting compared to the fear that quaked through her. History was repeating itself. She couldn't remember last night. Nothing.

"I don't know where I was going. I…I don't remember." She closed her eyes. "Please, I just need to be alone."

"Where is Marc Collins?"

"I don't know. I told you. We're divorced." She squeezed

her eyes tighter, her fingers gripping the sheet until they ached. She heard the cop swear under his breath and could sense him still sitting there watching her. After a few moments, she heard him close his notebook. But he didn't leave. *Please, just go away.*

"Is there someone I can call? Family? A friend?"

"No," she said, without opening her eyes. "There is no one."

She waited until she heard the door close behind him before she let it out, the anguish, the tortured grief. *Tyler. My baby. Oh God, Tyler.*

CHAPTER FOUR

POLICE CHIEF ROB NASH bolted upright in the bed in an unfamiliar motel room, his clothes sweat-soaked to his skin and a cheap synthetic second-rate motel pillow clutched in both fists as if he was trying to strangle it.

His heart raced as last night came back in a wave of nausea. Hands shaking, he threw the pillow across the room and fell back on the bed to stare up at the water-stained ceiling.

It all came back like a swift kick to his gut. His cheating wife. The wild drive to Pilot's Cove. The rain and darkness and falling-down-drunk pity party he'd thrown for himself.

He'd awakened a motel clerk demanding a room sometime after four in the morning and been forced to show his badge to keep the clerk from calling the cops on him for disturbing the peace. Kind of like the run-in he'd had at the Past Time bar and liquor store where he'd gotten the bottle of Jack Daniel's.

The memory made him as sick of the smell of fear and alcohol permeating the motel room.

Nash had heard about men hitting bottom. He'd seen his share that were certainly on their way if not already there. He'd just never thought he'd be one of them as he reached for what was left of the Jack Daniel's and plotted how to kill his wife and her lover.

OFFICER WALKER OPENED the door to the doctors' lounge to find Doc Brubaker nuking a frozen beef burrito. On the way in, he'd passed Sheila leaving. She'd gone off duty, leaving the elderly Connie Danvers at the nurses' station monitoring the small hospital's only patient.

"I thought doctors ate better than that," Walker said as he helped himself to a cup of coffee.

Doc shrugged. "She told you?"

He nodded. "She swears she was confused when she woke up earlier and thought her son was in the car with her, but that he wasn't."

"You don't believe her?"

Walker shrugged. "Who the hell knows? I'm not even sure *she* knows."

"Which wouldn't be unusual given her head trauma."

"Which is why I haven't called off the search." He pulled out a chair and dropped into it. "I called the Seattle Police. They're canvassing her neighborhood to see if they can get some information. But it's one of those neighborhoods where the houses are a quarter mile apart and the neighbors don't know each other. I'm also trying to find out if maybe there was a custody problem with the kid. So far nothing. I'm afraid her son is out there somewhere in that lake and she knows it and just doesn't want to face it."

"Understandable. That's a hell of a thing to have to face."

"Especially if she panicked and left him down there to drown."

The doctor grimaced. "Maybe she couldn't get him out of his car seat. Or maybe he's with family or friends or even his father, alive and well, and nowhere near Shadow Lake." He sighed. "Let's hope that's the case."

Walker glanced out the window toward the cliffs, unable to shake the bad feeling he had. "What I'd like to know is what the hell she was doing on that road at that time of the night. The divers found the car, but the water down there is so murky they couldn't see shit. Even if the kid's car seat is in the back, it doesn't prove he was with her—or that he was even strapped in."

"Still no luck reaching the husband?"

"Ex-husband. She says they recently divorced." Walker took a sip of the horrible coffee. If anything the coffee was worse than the cup he'd had earlier, and the smell of the burrito as the microwave dinged was enough to make him sick to his stomach.

"She's still wearing the ring though," he said. "There's something there that's not right. Did she say how she got that awful scar?"

"I haven't asked. But I think whatever pain the woman is in isn't necessarily visible," Doc said.

"Yeah? Well, we're all in pain, aren't we." He finished what he could of the coffee, needing something to keep him going. As he rose to rinse out his coffee cup, he said, "The towing crew should be getting to the site any time now. See what you can get out of Anna Collins, Drake, whatever. But I gotta tell ya, she's lying about something." His cell phone rang. He apologized and took the call.

DOC BRUBAKER WATCHED WALKER pull out his notebook to jot something down, worried. He felt bleary-eyed. His lack of sleep was starting to hamper his ability to think clearly. Only his concern for his patient was keeping him here.

An added concern was Walker. He'd delivered Walker, had watched him grow up in Shadow Lake, seen him change into the cynical, angry man he'd become after his wife left him and his best friend died.

It saddened Brubaker, even though he knew that life shaped a person. Walker had been through a lot, but nothing more than other people faced every day. Brubaker worried that Walker was taking this case too personally, that he'd seen similarities between his ex-wife and this woman and that ultimately, it would cloud his judgment.

Doc finally got up to retrieve his burrito from the microwave, hoping it would be cool enough to eat. He wasn't hungry, but he knew if he didn't keep something in his stomach, he'd regret it.

Walker snapped his phone shut. "The divers are going back down to hook up the cable from Mac's tow truck. I need to get up there."

"Let me know what you find. As soon as I eat, I'll go down and see our patient."

Walker nodded, frowning. "I'll be at the accident site if you need me."

Doc ate part of the burrito, forcing what he could down before tossing the rest in the trash. When he pushed open the door to Anna's room, he found her awake and staring up at the ceiling, her eyes red and swollen from crying. She didn't seem to hear him come in. He studied her for a moment before approaching her bed.

"How are you feeling?"

She said nothing when she looked at him, her eyes hollow as he drew up a chair.

"Do you remember your car going off the road and into the lake?" For a moment, he thought she wouldn't answer. There was a frightening dullness to her eyes.

"It was raining," she said in a distant tone.

He watched the pupils of her eyes and saw that she was starting to recall the accident.

"I lost control of the car." He could see the fear, hear it in her voice. "Water was coming over the hood, filling the car…" She shuddered. "That's all I remember."

He nodded but wondered if she hadn't remembered more than she was saying, from the way her eyes filled with tears.

"That must have been terrifying." As he put his stethoscope in his ears and moved closer to check her heart and lungs, she brushed back her bangs to run her finger along the old scar on her forehead.

When he was finished, he stepped back and she pulled her hand away from the scar almost guiltily.

"That's a lonely stretch of highway to be traveling, especially that late at night alone," he said. "I doubt there was much traffic with it being off-season and raining. Were you on your way to Shadow Lake or leaving town?"

"I don't know." She looked at him, the admission clearly painful. "I've tried to remember, but…"

"Don't worry about. You'll remember when the time comes." He reached over to brush back her bangs. "How did you get the scar?"

Instantly, she looked self-conscious. "I've been told it was from a car accident eight months ago."

He weighed that information. This wasn't the first time she'd experienced memory loss then. "Were you unconscious for long from the accident?"

"I was in a coma for six months."

He tried not to let his surprise show. Six months was a long time, but probably not for a head injury of that magnitude. He asked, although he already suspected the answer, "And you've never regained your memory of that accident?"

"No." Her tears boiled over. He noticed she had hazel eyes. "I only know what I've been told about it."

He could see the pain of whatever burden she bore in her face and reached for her hand and squeezed it.

She turned her face toward the window but held tightly to his hand, as if anchoring herself for a moment.

He followed her gaze to the window. It was still raining; the dense fog that had enveloped the lake and shore earlier had lifted. Walker would be up on the road with the tow truck getting her car out of the lake. What if the boy was inside the car?

"Do you want me to close the blinds?" Brubaker asked.

She shook her head as she turned back to him and let go of his hand to touch the bandage on her temple. "Is this why I can't remember now?"

"Probably. Because of your earlier head injury, it's possible to have some memory loss even if the second injury wasn't nearly as severe. I would suspect the memory loss this time will only be temporary."

"I will remember *everything* then?" she asked, and his heart fell at the sheer terror he heard in her voice.

IT SURPRISED HER WHEN the doctor didn't leave. She was used to people keeping their distance. Doctors at the hospital, after she'd come out of her coma, had seemed to have little time for her.

Even complete strangers gave her a wide berth, as if they could smell the misery on her. Just as she could smell their fear that if they got too close they might catch it.

She wiped at her tears, surprised that she still had tears to cry. She felt raw inside, but then she had since the moment she'd awakened from her coma two months ago. The memory was like a knife piercing her already bleeding heart.

What was new was the terror whenever she thought of last night. Hadn't the worst that could happen to her already happened? And yet she still felt as if something horrible was going to occur.

"You're fighting to keep your eyes open. Try to get some rest," the doctor said quietly. "You've had quite the ordeal."

He had no idea.

"You've never had memory loss, have you?" She hadn't meant for the words to come out so sharply, and she instantly regretted them. "I'm sorry. It's just…difficult to have huge chunks of missing time. Black holes in which you have no idea what happened to you. What you did. What you could or should have done differently." No, she thought, you just

wake up to the consequences. And to people demanding ex-
planations when you had none.

"No, I haven't," he said quietly. But she could tell he thought
there were worse things than not being able to remember.

"When can I leave the hospital?"

"I want to keep you at least overnight for observation," the
doctor said quickly. "You need to get your strength back."

She closed her eyes, suddenly just wanting to be left alone.
She would have prayed for sleep but she knew her prayers
were no longer answered. Her weakened body and mind were
exhausted. But lately sleep evaded her or was fraught with
pieces of memory that churned in her thoughts giving her no
peace or answers.

She couldn't even remember what had happened last night.
Not that it mattered. Nothing mattered.

So why couldn't she hold back the nagging thought that
she *had* to remember? That there was something she desperately needed to recall?

How could she not be worried? She couldn't imagine why
she'd been on that road last night. She'd never even heard of
Shadow Lake. Why would she come up here at that hour of
the night in a thunderstorm?

What she did remember only made her anxious. The bitter,
numbing cold of the lake water, the bite of the seat belt into
her breasts, the horrible metallic taste of her own fear. Air. Her
lungs had been bursting with a need for air when—

Her eyes flew open. Heart pounding, her mind veered
away from what she told herself couldn't be a memory.

"Are you sure there isn't someone I can call for you?" Dr.
Brubaker asked in concern, surprising her that he was still
in the room.

"Yes." Her voice broke. "I'm sure."

He glanced toward the window again where a sliver of the
lake could be seen through the rain and pines.

"Just ring the call button if you need anything." He seemed hesitant to leave her alone, but finally started toward the door, and, just as quickly, she didn't want to be left alone.

"Where did my car go into the lake?" she asked.

He stopped and came back to point to a spot through the trees in the distance. "See those cliffs up there on the mountain? You went off right before the road drops down into town."

Anna gasped. How had she survived? "How did I get to the hospital?"

"I can only assume that when you surfaced, you swam toward the shore, which would have put you out just down the hill from the hospital," he said. "It's the first building on this side of town. The nurse found you barely inside the door. Given the temperature of the air and water, you were lucky the hospital was so close."

She felt a chill and pulled the blanket up to her shoulders.

"You're safe now. That's all that matters."

Why didn't she believe that?

"Rest. I promise you it's the best thing you can do to regain your strength—and your memory."

Anna glanced out at the lake. How had she survived last night? *Why,* she wondered, as hot tears scalded her cheeks.

The six months in the coma were completely lost to her. The two months since she'd awakened had been a living hell. The panic attacks had started the minute she'd gone home from the hospital. Without warning she wouldn't be able to catch her breath. She would start shaking, her heart pounding so hard she was sure she was having a heart attack. Hoping she would.

Like now when she looked at the lake. Her pulse raced, her mouth went cotton-ball dry. There was something she desperately needed to remember.

DEPUTY WALKER MOVED TO THE edge of the road to watch as the wrecker crew snaked the steel cable down the steep mountainside to the lake.

He'd already been warned that the crew would have to inch the car up the mountainside since they didn't have enough single cable to reach the car and would have to use an extension. The town wrecker was old, the winch outdated.

When he'd reached the site, he'd been informed divers had gone back down to run a strap through the interior of the car. The car had come to rest upside down in about thirty feet of water.

"No sign of any other passenger?" he asked the head of the dive squad on the shore via the tow truck's radio.

"Not in the car."

"Was there a child's car seat in the back?" Walker asked.

"Negative."

"You're sure?"

"Affirmative. There's a suitcase that had been in the backseat but is now resting on the headliner. That's all."

Walker rubbed his jaw. Why wasn't the suitcase in the trunk? "What about the trunk?"

"Don't know. It's resting in the mud."

"Thanks." He handed the radio back to the tow-truck operator.

Where had this woman been headed? he wondered as he waited. He told himself the answer might be in the car.

Walker had the town's two other officers handling traffic. Not that there was much this time of the year. But word had spread and since this was probably the biggest news all spring, the locals had come up to get in the way. Shadow Lake residents, especially those who'd just gone through a long boring winter, weren't about to pass up free entertainment.

As Walker looked down the path the Cadillac had taken, he couldn't help wondering what had happened last night up here on this mountain. Anna was recently divorced. When he'd talked to her she'd been more than a little despondent. Had she purposely driven off here? Panicked once the car hit the water and changed her mind?

Or had she picked this spot, knowing that the hospital was close by, as some ill-conceived plot to get her ex's attention. That's something Walker's ex would have done. If she'd wanted him back, that is.

He hated the bitter taste in his mouth. But he'd noticed some things about Anna Drake Collins that were just like his ex. Anna clearly came from money, lived in Seattle in a posh neighborhood, had that air of privilege about her and was model attractive—just like his ex.

What worried Walker was how far a woman like that would go. And if she really wanted to get back at her ex, Walker feared the kid had been in that car.

"We're ready to bring her up," Mac called from the tow truck. "Did you hear me?"

Walker looked up, startled to find the wrecker operator standing in front of him frowning.

"We're *ready.*"

"So bring her up."

"If I were you, I wouldn't stand there. If that cable should—"

"Just pull her up," Walker snapped, anxious to see what was inside that car.

Below him, the emerald lake lay in the tree-lined basin, the surface dimpled by the drizzling rain. There was no warmth, only wet and cold as the motor on the tow truck revved. He stood next to the wrecker, wanting a clear view when the car broke the surface.

He'd found a business number for Marc Collins and left a message to call the Shadow Lake Police Department.

That the man's ex-wife had been in an automobile accident but was fine.

Walker hoped the boy was with his father, but from the way the mother was acting, he had a bad feeling that wasn't the case, and his cop instincts were seldom wrong.

His cell phone rang. He stepped away from the whine of the wrecker to take the call.

"Walker?"

He almost didn't recognize the voice. "Chief?"

"Just wanted to let you know I won't be back for a few days."

"Is everything all right in Pilot's Cove?"

"Yeah, I just need to take care of some things over here."

Before Walker could tell him what was going on in Shadow Lake, the police chief hung up.

Walker snapped his cell phone shut, telling himself he had to be wrong. The chief had sounded drunk.

As Walker started back toward the tow truck, his phone rang again. This time it was the dispatcher. She had Marc Collins on the line.

"Put him through," Walker said.

"What's this about my wife being in *another* accident?" the man demanded the moment Walker answered.

"Don't you mean *ex*-wife?" Walker asked, instantly irritated with the man's tone.

"Is that what she told you? We're still married."

"Why would she lie?"

"Your guess is as good as mine," Collins said.

Walker explained about Anna's so-called accident. "She was lucky."

"Anna wrecked *another* car? But *she's* fine. Another hit-and-run or can't she remember?" Marc Collins asked with sarcasm. "Isn't it just Anna's *luck*."

Walker bristled. "She almost drowned," he snapped, beyond irritated with the man. Surely Anna Drake hadn't wanted to get back with this man. "Look, I just need to be sure that your son Tyler wasn't with her."

Marc Collins let out a brittle laugh. "Didn't she tell you? She killed Tyler eight months ago."

THE MEMORY CAME IN A RUSH. Rain, the narrow dark highway, in a hurry for some reason, then a sudden movement as something sprang out onto the pavement. A deer? It *had* been a deer, hadn't it?

Anna saw it happening in her mind's eye. Her losing control of the car. Skidding along the highway through the deep puddles, blinded by the spray until...

She felt the start of a panic attack as she remembered crashing down the mountain and into the water. The car had sunk so quickly. She was breathing hard now, remembering the freezing cold water rising around her and the seat belt... There was something...

Her heart pounded harder and harder. She tried to push away the memory that seemed to crush her chest, as she tried to catch her breath.

In a panic, she reached for the nurse's call button, but her fingers were slick and she was shaking so hard it slipped from her fingers. My God, she was dying.

Deep breaths. Think about anything else. Anything but last night.

She flopped back, gasping, tears running down her face. The panic subsided slowly, her rapid pulse roared in her ears.

She'd tried to convince herself that it didn't matter how she'd ended up in a hospital room in Shadow Lake.

But her mind wouldn't let it rest. She hated driving at night, especially in the rain. What had forced her to do it?

Sitting up, she swung her legs over the side of the bed. The movement sent a wave of nausea through her, forcing her to grip the bed until the wooziness passed.

As she stood, she was half surprised to realize she'd completely forgotten about the IV in her arm. She rolled the stand along with her as she shuffled to the closet, practically leaning on the flimsy thing, shocked by how weak she felt.

At the closet, she gripped the door frame, fearing she was going to pass out. She slid open the closet door and drew back in surprise. *This* was what she'd been wearing last night?

Dread filled her as she touched the slinky black dress and lacy black undergarments draped over the hangers, her fingers brushing her good gray wool coat. Where had she been going dressed like *this?*

There was a small puddle of water beneath the still sopping-wet coat. Next to the puddle on the floor was a single strappy black high-heeled sandal. What struck her was that the black dress was Marc's favorite.

Like a splinter under her skin, the thought of why she would have worn it worried at her.

To make matters worse, she could think of no reason she would have driven to Shadow Lake dressed for an evening out. And driving in those shoes? What had she been thinking? No wonder she'd ended up crashing into the lake.

Leaning against the closet door frame for support, she searched a pocket of her coat, hoping for some clue.

Given where the doctor said her car had gone into the lake, how had she been able to get out, let alone swim in what she'd been wearing? Especially in apparently only one high-heeled sandal. Had she literally stumbled out of the lake and into the hospital?

What kind of luck was that?

Unbelievable luck.

A memory tugged at her. She felt another panic attack coming on and quickly shielded herself from the memory.

She stuck her hand in the other pocket. Her hand froze as her fingers found something soggy and hard. She pulled out the contents and frowned down at four balled-up twenty-dollar bills and a credit card with what appeared to be a wet receipt stuck to it and…

Her frown deepened. A folded scrap of paper. It appeared to have some writing on the inside but the ink had run some and the paper was still wet and fragile. She gave up trying to unfold it while it was still wet.

She tried to peel the receipt from the credit card. The thin paper started to tear. It was impossible to read what had been printed on it anyway.

Why had she stuffed all of this into her coat pocket? Where was her purse? Still in the car, no doubt. Just the sight of what she'd found in her coat pocket proved she'd been upset about something. It wasn't like her not to take the time to put her credit card back into her wallet in her purse. Or maybe she'd lost her purse even before she'd crashed into the lake.

That thought made fear quake through her. What in God's name could have happened that she would have lost her purse?

Her body suddenly felt too heavy for her leg muscles to hold her any longer. Dragging the IV cart, she stumbled back to the bed, taking the items she'd found in her coat pocket with her. She dropped everything into the nightstand drawer. Her legs felt like water. It was all she could do to climb onto the bed and draw the covers over her.

Sleep dragged her down like the lake had taken her car to the bottom. On the edge of sleep, she saw herself going into the lake again, the car sinking, panic taking hold of her as she saw herself upside down under the water, trapped in the car.

As exhaustion finally pulled her under, she had one fleeting terrifying thought: There's something out there in the murky water. *Someone.*

CHAPTER FIVE

WITH MORE THAN A little relief, Dr. Brubaker checked his only patient and found her sound asleep. Telling the nurse to beep him when Anna woke again, he left the hospital to go home, shower, shave and change clothes.

As was his routine, he turned in the gate to the cemetery on his walk home and headed for his wife's grave.

Gladys had picked out the two plots, saying she wanted to be able to catch the morning sun. She'd always loved that about her kitchen window. He'd so often see her standing in front of the sink, her face tilted up to catch the morning sun, that sometimes even now when he came into the kitchen he caught glimpses of her for just an instant.

Better to see her there, in the sunlight, rather than the hospital bed where she'd spent the last months of her life. Gladys had wanted to die in their home so he'd moved one of the hospital beds into the living room.

She'd been so small lying there. He'd watched her grow thinner and thinner, disappearing from his life with each passing day. At the end, he'd feared that he would wake from the bed he'd made next to hers and find that she had wasted away to nothing as if she'd never existed.

As it was, she'd been nearly child-size by the time she'd died, way too small for the casket he'd picked out for her.

He recognized the names on the gravestones as he walked through the rain-soaked cemetery. A light drizzle fell, the clouds gray and dark over the lake. He'd known a lot of the people buried here.

Some of them he'd brought into the world, a lot of them he'd kept alive as long as he could before they'd passed on. The thought gave him little comfort.

Through a weathered iron fence and veil of pine boughs, he caught a glimpse of freshly turned earth. The wind must have blown off the green tarp the funeral home used until it quit raining long enough to lay the sod. Or had the tarp come off when Big Jim Fairbanks started rolling in his grave, Brubaker wondered.

Unlike Gladys, Big Jim had fought until the very end. He'd wanted to live and had said he was too damned young to die even though he was older than most, Doc included. Big Jim hadn't gone peacefully. Nor did Doc suspect Big Jim Fairbanks rested easy, either.

Brubaker realized as he stared at Big Jim's grave that he believed in retribution, if nothing else. There was a price to be paid for what was done on this earth. A man had to pay for his sins. And a man like Big Jim Fairbanks would be paying dearly about now.

And soon so would Gene Brubaker, he reminded himself.

Turning, Doc went to spend time with his wife as he had done every day since her death.

"OH DEAR, WHAT HAVE YOU DONE?"

Anna woke with a start as an older gray-haired nurse rushed to her bedside. "Pulled out your IV, have you?" Her name tag read Connie. "Must have really tossed and turned in your sleep to do that."

Anna said nothing as the nurse reattached the IV. She'd lost the scrap of memory she'd had just before she'd been awakened. In frustration, she looked toward the window, saw the lake and closed her eyes to keep from shuddering.

"There, that should hold this time," the nurse said. "How are you feeling?"

Anna could only nod.

The nurse studied her. "You want me to call the doctor?"

"No. I just want to sleep." She really just wanted to be alone, not sure she wanted to call back the memory. She could feel an uneasiness and knew that if she tried to force the memory it would turn to anxiety, then panic.

"I'm fine," she told the nurse and closed her eyes, waiting for her to leave.

The moment the nurse closed the door behind her, Anna sat up, feeling desperate and scared.

Calm down. Calm down. She heard her husband Marc's voice. *Calm down.* Only he was no longer her husband. The divorce was to be final yesterday. Was that true? Only yesterday?

Her hand was shaking as she picked up the phone and dialed. Gillian Sanders had been her friend since college and was now a successful lawyer. Anna knew she wouldn't have made it through the past two months without Gillian.

Gillian's cell phone rang four times and voice mail picked up. "It's me, Anna." Her voice sounded panicky even to her. She considered leaving the hospital number but knew that would scare Gillian. "I'll try back later."

She hung up, disappointed she hadn't reached her. Right now she needed Gillian's logical calming influence. Gillian had a way of seeing to the heart of things. Like when Anna had come to her for advice about Marc.

"Don't fight the divorce, honey," Gillian had advised. "He's a bastard. Have you ever really been happy with him?"

"Yes, when Tyler was born…"

"Come on. You were happy because of Tyler—not Marc. Admit it."

Anna had started to cry. Admitting that her marriage had

been anything but happy from the beginning was devastating.

Gillian had pressed a business card into her hand.

"What is this?" Anna had asked through her tears.

"A damned good divorce attorney. But you didn't get it from me."

"I want *you* as my lawyer."

"Anna, I'm not a divorce lawyer and I know both you and Marc. You want someone who is impartial and tough as nails. Believe me, Marc will get the toughest lawyer money can buy."

"But I want someone who will protect my interests."

"I am, sweetie," Gillian had said, taking her hand. "Divorce the asshole before he can file first. You can do better."

But Anna had waited and let Marc serve the papers on her. The divorce lawyer Gillian had recommended had taken care of everything. All Anna had to do was sign the papers and wait for the dissolution of her marriage to be final. She'd only managed to get through it by pretending it wasn't happening. She'd lost her son. Now her husband.

Coward that she was, she'd also pretended that she didn't know why Marc had wanted the divorce.

As of yesterday, she was no longer Mrs. Marc Collins.

She realized she was still gripping the phone. She needed to talk to someone. If not Gillian, then Mary Ellen. Mary Ellen was a mutual friend of Anna and Gillian's, a college sorority sister. Blond, buxom, a bit scatterbrained, but a talented interior designer, Mary Ellen had gotten through life on "cute" and good taste.

Anna dialed Mary Ellen's number trying to get into the mood to talk to her always bubbly friend. She was tired of calling her friends crying and desperate. She was tired of being depressed and morbid and scared. And she knew they were even more sick of it than she was.

The phone rang four times and Anna was about to hang up when Mary Ellen finally picked up.

"Hello?"

"Hi, it's me."

"Oh, hello."

Anna was momentarily taken aback by Mary Ellen's blasé reaction. This was not like her. "Is everything all right?"

Silence. "Yes, I'm in the middle of something right now. Can I call you back?"

Anna sat up a little straighter in the bed at Mary Ellen's overformal tone. "Okay, I mean, no. I…" She glanced at the phone, unsure of the hospital number. "I'll call you back later."

"That would be fine." Mary Ellen hung up, but not before Anna heard a man's voice in the background.

She stared at the phone as she replaced the receiver. What had *that* been about? The voice she'd heard definitely hadn't been Mary Ellen's husband, David.

The voice had sounded like…

Anna felt a wave of nausea wash over her.

Marc. The voice had sounded like Marc's, but that wasn't possible. Marc didn't like Mary Ellen. He'd never liked any of her friends. But while he made fun of Mary Ellen, he was much harsher when it came to Gillian. He could barely be civil to Gillian—and vice versa.

So it couldn't have been Marc's voice Anna had heard in the background.

She fought her disappointment in not being able to talk to Mary Ellen. She needed to talk to a friend. Gillian and Mary Ellen were the only ones she still saw. The rest of her so-called friends had disappeared.

She thought about calling Marc, just to prove to herself that it hadn't been his voice she'd heard at Mary Ellen's. But she had nothing to say to him. Gillian was right. Tyler had been the reason Anna had stayed with Marc. She'd so desperately wanted Tyler to have a father even if Marc had been a disappointing one. She'd hoped that as Tyler got older, Marc would get better.

Her throat closed at the thought of Tyler, her chest aching as tears again burned her eyes, blurring everything.

You have to stop this, Anna.

Marc's voice again and a memory so clear it hurt. "You have to stop, Anna, before you drive us both crazy. I can't take any more." Possibly his last words to her before he moved out of their house. Or maybe more recently. They'd had so many fights she couldn't remember the last one.

She dried her eyes and dialed Gillian's cell again. Still no answer. She hung up without leaving a message.

Had it only been yesterday that she'd had Gillian and Mary Ellen over for lunch? Mary Ellen and Gillian had made a point of not mentioning the divorce or the fact it was to be final later that day.

Needless to say, the lunch had been strained. Anna frowned as she recalled how distracted Gillian had been. Even Mary Ellen had been unusually quiet. At the time, Anna had thought it was just her pending divorce causing it, but now she recalled she'd picked up an undercurrent. Mary Ellen and Gillian had seemed upset with each other.

Funny she would realize that now. She'd thought she was doing so well yesterday, but apparently she'd been numb to what had been happening around her.

She felt a sliver of anxiety burrow under her skin. Since she'd come out of the coma she'd been picking up weird vibes from everyone, especially Marc. But often Mary Ellen and Gillian, as well. Either they were all walking on eggshells around her, or they were keeping something from her.

When she'd mentioned this to Marc, he'd accused her of thinking everyone was plotting against her—especially him. But she still couldn't shake the feeling that from the moment she'd opened her eyes two months ago in another hospital, her husband and friends *had* some secret they didn't want her to find out about.

She knew that was crazy thinking. No secret was as horrible as the reality of what she'd awakened to.

Closing her eyes, she lay back on the bed. Her head ached and she felt sick to her stomach. She pulled the sheet up to her chin. It felt cool and smelled fresh from the laundry. Her stomach did a slow sickening roll as she recalled her friend's stilted part of the conversation. Mary Ellen hadn't even used Anna's name during the call.

Because Mary Ellen didn't want whoever was there to know it was her?

Marc would say this was just another case of her imagining things. What did she think Mary Ellen and Marc were doing? Plotting against her? It might not even have been Marc's voice she heard.

She was acting irrational. She battled the urge to call Mary Ellen back and demand to know what was going on. She could feel another panic attack coming on. Marc had told her she was delusional enough times. She *felt* delusional.

She tried her friend Gillian's cell phone again. *Still* no answer. Gillian always had her cell phone with her. It wasn't like her not to answer unless she was in court.

Anna didn't leave a message. Instead, she tried Mary Ellen again.

Mary Ellen answered this time on the first ring. *"Anna?"* Apparently she'd been waiting by the phone. "Where are you? Are you all right? We've been worried sick about you."

Hearing the concern in her friend's voice, Anna started to pour out her story about the accident, but she heard herself say *"We?"*

Mary Ellen's voice softened. "Honey, Marc is really worried about you."

Anna closed her eyes. It *had* been Marc's voice she'd heard earlier in the background. Just as she wasn't mistaken about the recrimination she now heard in her friend's voice.

"I'm sure Marc has better things to do than worry about me," she said. "We're divorced. I'm not his concern anymore."

An odd silence then, "Honey, Marc didn't go through with the divorce. The papers were never filed."

"What?" Hadn't that been her hope, her prayer? Losing Marc had made Tyler's death more real somehow. Anna had clung to the marriage because it was all she had.

"He changed his mind," Mary Ellen was saying. "But, honey, I was sure he told you that last night."

"Last *night?*"

AFTER OFFICER D.C. WALKER disconnected his call with Marc Collins, he had started to dial his boss when he noticed Mac was having a problem with the winch. He walked back over to the side of the mountain and saw nothing in the mist but water.

"Hook came undone," the wrecker operator yelled to him. "Divers are down reattaching the cable."

Walker stared at the lake with the rain clouds mirrored in it, still shocked by what he'd learned from Marc Collins. The gloomy gray day did nothing to lift his spirits. Where the hell was spring?

The news he'd received had left him angry and upset. What else was the woman in the hospital keeping from him?

One thing was for sure: he needed to let Chief Nash in on what was going on. He started to call him, but stopped as the divers reappeared below him on the shore and signaled to the wrecker operator that the car was ready again. Mac gave Walker a thumbs-up and the tow motor revved once again.

What worried Walker was how the chief had sounded earlier when he'd called. Was there some kind of trouble in

Pilot's Cove that his boss wasn't telling him about? Or had the chief gone to the county seat to pick up the paperwork before he announced his retirement?

Walker brightened at the thought. He'd been waiting for twelve years for that job to open up. He couldn't stand the suspense. He stepped away from the wrecker to call the Pilot's Cove office.

"I was hoping to catch Chief Nash," he told the woman who answered.

"Chief Nash from Shadow Lake?"

"Is there another Chief Nash I don't know about?" He instantly regretted the sarcasm. "Sorry, it's important I speak with him."

"We haven't seen Chief Nash in about four months," she said, her voice as chilly as the lake below him.

"He was over there yesterday doing something with your department."

"Afraid not. Maybe he was at Dam City or—"

Walker hung up when the engine on the tow truck let out an ear-piercing whine as the cable to the Cadillac began to grow taut again. The huge steel cable hummed.

Walker walked back over to stand next to the wrecker, still a little stunned. Chief Nash had lied. Walker couldn't have been more shocked by that. He had great respect for the man. Nash was from the old school of justice, tough as nails, but fair and straight as an arrow.

There had to be another explanation.

The rear end of the overturned Cadillac broke the surface of the water. It looked like a blue turtle flipped over on its shell.

Walker stared at the path the Cadillac had taken down the mountain, a path of broken saplings, tire tracks and carnage. The same path the car would have to take this time, only on its top.

It was a miracle the woman had gotten out of the lake alive. Since talking to Marc Collins, Walker was even more convinced Anna Drake Collins hadn't planned it that way.

Suddenly the whine of the wrecker's winch intensified and then the cable snapped.

Walker watched the long snaking link of steel shoot like a rubber band back up the mountain—headed straight for him.

DOC STOOD IN THE DRIZZLE, unaffected by the cold and the rain while he talked to his dead wife the way he always did. It didn't seem to matter what he talked about, just that he did.

Today he told Gladys about his latest patient.

"She's pretty. She has hazel eyes that remind me of yours," he said as he bent down to pull a weed that he hadn't noticed before beside his wife's headstone.

"I'm worried about her, but you know me," he said with a laugh. "You always said I took on everyone's worries because I didn't have enough of my own." His eyes misted over for a moment and he had to bite his lip before he could continue.

"Her four-year-old boy might have been in the car with her when it went into the lake. I'm just sick at heart at the thought. I don't think she's strong enough to take that news."

He cleared his throat. "Walker is on the case." Gladys had always been fond of Walker and his friends. She'd made them their favorite cookies and would call the boys up on the porch whenever they passed by. She liked to watch them eat a half-dozen cookies each, washed down by the homemade lemonade she kept for just such a visit. She'd ply the boys with treats in exchange for conversation.

It still hurt that he and Gladys had never been blessed with their own children. Gladys had loved children so. She would have been like a mother hen with Anna. Gladys could sense need in people. Gene had always thought it was one reason she'd married him.

"Walker's afraid the woman tried to kill herself. I don't believe it. Especially if her son was in the car. She wouldn't do that. Not this woman."

He brushed off rainwater that had puddled on top of Gladys's stone. "I miss you." He stopped, unable to continue. There was more he wanted to say, but he couldn't find the words. Just as, for a long time, he hadn't been able to tell Gladys she was dying.

But she'd known. She'd suspected it was cancer. Still, it had been the hardest thing he'd ever had to do, to tell her it was inoperable, to tell her she had only a short time left.

She'd taken it much better than he had. But then that was Gladys. She'd never worried about things she couldn't change. He wished he could be more like her.

He looked down at his wife's grave again. "Can you ever forgive me?" But it wasn't Glady's forgiveness he knew he was seeking. His wife had been the most forgiving person he'd ever known.

He brushed a hand over her headstone, tears blurring his eyes, his nose running. He made a swipe at his eyes, nose, looking to the lake. Summer felt a long way off. Doc had no plans to see it.

He cleared his throat. He needed to get on home. Soon he'd have to return to the hospital and make sure Anna was all right. She needed him. At least for a while.

CHIEF ROB NASH HAD TO take a piss. He'd lost count of the beers he'd drunk in an attempt to fight off last night's hangover. It wasn't working.

But as he passed the bed, he saw that he had another message on his cell phone from Walker. Nash picked up the phone, those old habits so conditioned it took everything in him not to return the call.

Walker could handle whatever it was, he told himself as

he tossed the phone back on the bed and proceeded to the bathroom. He knew Walker wanted his job. And soon, he would get it.

Nash realized he should have retired a long time ago. He was past his prime and clearly couldn't trust his instincts anymore. Marrying Lucinda proved that.

As he stood in front of the toilet, he caught his reflection in the mirror. He looked as if he'd aged overnight.

He was fifty-five years old. Most cops his age had quit a long time ago. He had his years in. He could retire on his pension. He'd worked hard his whole life, saved all his money, never really given retirement much thought. Because he knew he would go crazy within a week.

Standing there bent over the motel-room toilet, sick and tired and hurting like hell, he admitted he didn't know what he was going to do. Which was strange because he couldn't shake the feeling that a decision had been made for him the moment he saw his wife get into that car with that man.

CHAPTER SIX

OFFICER D.C. WALKER didn't have time to see his life flash before him as the wrecker's cable shot upward directly at him.

The cable passed so close he felt the hair rise on his forearms. The steel wrapped around one of the trees behind him, snapping off leaves and limbs like the hurtin' end of a whip, then made a loud popping sound right next to him as the end smacked the hood of the wrecker, leaving one hell of a dent before dropping to the ground as harmless as a dead snake.

Down the mountainside the Cadillac, dragging a piece of frayed broken steel cable, slid back into the lake.

Walker let out a curse as he watched the car disappear below the surface again.

When Mac, the wrecker operator, quit swearing and crossing himself, he gave Walker the bad news. Another wrecker, a newer larger one with a longer cable, would have to be called in. It might have to come from as far away as Seattle, though. That was if Mac could find a towing service that could spare a rig that size.

But one thing was for certain. The car wasn't coming out of the water today. It was too late in the day now to get another wrecker here even if one could be found within a hundred miles.

Walker swore. "Do the best you can and let me know when you find one." He turned, still shaken as he climbed into his patrol car and headed for the hospital. He was on his own with the chief gone. It was time he had a talk with Doc Brubaker's patient.

POLICE CHIEF ROB NASH WOKE to darkness. He stumbled out of bed and into the ratty motel bathroom. His head hurt like hell and his stomach rumbled, the taste of alcohol in his mouth rank enough to make him want to vomit.

He glanced at his watch, shocked to see that he'd lost the entire day. Lucinda was expecting him home tonight. He swore as he turned on the shower, stripped down and stepped under the stinging water.

Lucinda. He tried to force away any thought of her. He'd never known this kind of pain, let alone such fury. It left him light-headed, sent his blood pressure soaring and made him feel as if he was shaking from the inside out. The sensation had him wondering if he wouldn't come apart at the seams. Worse, made him fear he would follow through with his first instinct and kill Lucinda.

It was why he'd called Walker and told him he was taking a few days off. He wasn't firing on all four cylinders and he knew it. A dangerous place, given his feeling.

But Lucinda and what he'd seen last night was like a tooth-ache that wouldn't let him forget it. Eventually he would have to deal with it.

He'd set his wife up.

And she'd taken the bait.

That's what a man his age got for marrying a woman too young and pretty for him, he thought as he stepped from the shower.

Just the thought of facing Lucinda with what he knew made him break into a cold sweat. He clenched his fist, slamming it into the mirror. Glass shards and blood went everywhere.

He wrapped his hand in a towel. There were only a few small cuts. He wouldn't bleed to death.

He stared at his reflection in what was left of the mirror. Hair graying, shoulders slumped, gait shuffling and unsure. Hell, he looked just like his old man right before the poor son of a bitch blew his brains out.

ANNA DIDN'T REMEMBER DROPPING off to sleep after her call to Mary Ellen. She'd been upset and had gotten off the line, promising to call back.

Now she shot straight up in bed and reached for the call button, fumbling with it, afraid she would lose the memory that she'd dragged to the surface. When the nurse named Connie had come hurrying in, Anna asked to see the doctor.

"I'll call him," she said. "Eat some of your dinner while you wait." She sounded worried. "Doc won't be long. He only lives a couple of blocks from here."

Anna looked over at the tray next to her bed. Her stomach growled. She couldn't remember the last time she'd eaten. She vaguely recalled a breakfast and lunch tray, but didn't remember touching either. She hadn't been hungry for so long.

Now, though, she felt ravenous. She dug into the food, not tasting it, but knowing she needed the nourishment. She knew that after Tyler's death, she'd lost her will to live. There didn't seem to be any reason to get out of bed in the mornings. No wonder Marc had felt so abandoned. No wonder he'd wanted a divorce.

Her need to remember what had happened last night was driving her not to fall back into that dark depression. Last night was like a puzzle that she needed to solve. That she could solve. Not like the alleged hit-and-run that had taken her son. The pieces to that puzzle had been lost forever.

But this accident she might be able to unravel, and she still felt as if she desperately needed to.

She was anxious to tell the doctor what she remembered.

Unlike Officer Walker, the doctor seemed to believe her and want to help her remember. She didn't need any more mysteries in her life. Any more secrets.

Her dinner was lukewarm, but she ate the roast beef and mashed potatoes and canned corn as if it was a gourmet meal from her favorite four-star restaurant. She'd downed the glass of milk after polishing off the apple crisp just before Dr. Brubaker stuck his rumpled gray head in her doorway.

She shoved the tray away. "I remember going into the lake," she said excitedly. "I mean I remember being in the water. I remember almost everything."

He smiled, seeming pleased as he pulled up a chair next to her bed and lowered himself into it. "That must be a huge relief to you."

"I swerved to miss a deer and lost control of the car." She could see it now, the darkness, the rain, the deer bolting out of the trees. Her heart began to pound as she saw the car skidding toward the small saplings in her memory, crashing down the mountainside, plunging into the lake.

Oh God, the lake. The water. She shuddered as she recalled the water.

"I couldn't get the seat belt to release." Suddenly her heart was pounding so hard she couldn't catch her breath, but she also couldn't stop. She could feel the panic attack coming on. And then she felt his hand cover hers.

"You're safe *now*. It's all right. It can't hurt you."

She nodded and lay back against the pillows, tears of fear blurring her eyes. "I remember being underwater, thinking I was going to die."

"Do you remember getting out of the car?" he asked.

"No." She made a swipe at her tears with her free hand, not wanting to break contact with the warmth of his hand covering hers. Her mother had died when Anna was nine. Her father when she was seventeen. She'd been so disappointed that neither had lived to see their grandson born. Marc's parents were both still alive but had no apparent interest in grandchildren.

"I was trapped in the car," Anna said, refusing to let the memory slip away again. "I remember thinking I was going to drown. I had to breathe." She stopped, her gaze locking with his. "I heard a sound at my side window." A slice of pure ice cut through her, but she didn't force the memory away. "There was someone in the water."

"Someone else was in the lake?" the doctor asked. "Your son?"

"No," she said quickly. "Tyler is…wasn't there. The person in the water was a man. At least I think it was a man. His face…" Anna shuddered at the memory and heard a sound at her hospital-room door. She looked up with a start to find Officer Walker framed in the doorway.

The expression on his face was almost as terrifying as the memory of being under the water and seeing something—someone—floating on the other side of her window.

"You say there was someone else in the lake?" the cop asked as he stepped into the room, his brow furrowed. "Your memory coming back, Mrs. Collins?"

Was it her imagination, or did the doctor look alarmed by the policeman's tone?

"I need to ask your patient a few more questions," Officer Walker said, never taking his eyes off Anna. "You're welcome to stay, Doc, if you feel it's necessary."

Dr. Brubaker looked from the cop to her. "Do you want me to stay?"

She nodded even though it hurt her head. She didn't trust her voice.

"I talked to your *husband,*" Walker said.

"Marc?" She wasn't sure why the thought of Marc talking to the officer upset her, but it did. "He knows I'm here?"

The cop frowned. "Is that a problem?"

"No. Of course not. I just didn't want him…worried."

"Why would he be worried?" Walker asked.

She said nothing, feeling confused, head aching.

"You are still Mrs. *Collins,* aren't you?"

Anna opened her mouth, closed it, opened it again. "I didn't know Marc hadn't gone through with the divorce until I talked to a friend earlier. I had no idea."

He studied her openly then asked, "You don't remember your husband telling you last night?"

"No." Her voice sounded small, scared.

"But you were just saying that your memory has come back," he reminded her.

"Not all of it." Her fingers went to her scar.

"Why don't you tell the officer what you told me," the doctor suggested.

She swallowed, her throat dry and scratchy. Her head ached and she felt tired again, her earlier excitement about getting back some of her memory replaced by fear.

She told Officer Walker about the deer, losing control of the car, going into the lake and seeing someone on the bottom.

The cop gave her an unbelieving look. "Your husband told me you were upset when you left home last night. Can you tell me what that was about?"

So she *had* seen Marc last night at the house? "No. That is, I don't know. I don't remember seeing my husband last night or what I might have been upset about."

The cop's look said he found that a little too convenient. "Your husband said you might have been upset because he told you he hadn't gone through with the divorce."

She frowned. "Why would I be upset about that?"

"Why don't you tell me," he said.

She shot a look at the doctor. He looked worried as if he feared—as she did—that something had happened to make

Officer Walker more suspicious of her. She knew she didn't have to answer his questions, but she had nothing to hide. At least she hoped that was true. And at this point, Officer Walker seemed to know more than she did about what had happened last night.

"I was the one who didn't want the divorce in the first place," she said.

"You don't recall seeing your husband at all last night?"

She shook her head slowly, a vague memory pulling at her. An ugly argument. But she'd had so many arguments with Marc… "I can't be sure."

Walker sighed and looked at the doctor.

She felt dread settle in the pit of her stomach. Something was wrong. She knew she should stop the police officer now, not answer any more of his questions. But she desperately wanted to know why he was asking them, why his manner was even more suspicious than it had been earlier. "Why are you asking me all these questions?"

"Your husband said he not only saw you last night, but that the two of you argued. When you left, he said, you were threatening to kill someone."

"That's ridiculous," she snapped. "You don't know Marc. He…" She thought of something Gillian had once said about Marc. *He likes drama in his life. It's his drug of choice. He gets high on it. And when he doesn't have enough drama, he makes it. Or forces you to.*

"Marc overreacts sometimes," she said simply.

"Have you been under the care of a psychiatrist?"

"No, I mean, I was but I stopped going."

"Mrs. Collins, did you purposely drive your car into the lake last night?"

"Of course not!"

"Were you even in the car when it went into the lake?" he asked, sounding aggravated with her.

She felt close to tears. "Why would I lie about something like that?"

"You tell me."

She couldn't believe this was happening.

"Maybe for the same reason you threatened to kill someone? To get your husband's attention?"

She wanted to argue that even if she was stupid enough to pull a stunt like that, she no longer cared enough about Marc to even *threaten* to kill herself—let alone try. Nor did she believe Marc would care.

That thought rang so true she was momentarily stunned by it.

"If you're telling the truth, Mrs. Collins, then you don't remember what you did last night, isn't that right?" the cop asked.

She blinked, focusing again on him and his question before she slowly nodded. She'd lost the hours before she'd swerved to miss the deer. Just as she'd lost the reason she was on that highway to begin with.

And the truth was, in the state she'd been in since coming out of the coma, she couldn't swear to what she might have done. Maybe she *had* tried to kill herself last night. But she had to wonder what would have pushed her to that point.

"I suppose you also don't remember being so upset that you forgot about getting a speeding ticket about thirty miles outside of Shadow Lake."

She shook her head.

"Or telling Dr. Brubaker to look for your son?" The cop sounded angry.

"No." A headache was building. "I told you. I was confused when I first woke up. Everything I've told you is the truth."

"Why didn't you tell us, Mrs. Collins, that your son Tyler is dead?" Walker snapped. "That he was killed eight months ago in a hit-and-run accident. The same one that left you in a coma."

CHAPTER SEVEN

DR. BRUBAKER'S GAZE shot to Anna's at the cop's words. The sympathy Anna saw in his eyes made her want to weep. She felt awash in confusion, her emotions running too high.

"Why were you driving to Shadow Lake, Mrs. Collins?" Walker asked.

"I don't know." She heard the hysteria rising in her voice again and tried to tamp it back down, but it was impossible.

"It's her head injury, Walker," the doctor said quietly. "The loss of memory is normal. It's a form of retrograde amnesia. Memory of the traumatic event is not the only thing lost, but often minutes or even hours leading up to the event."

She looked at the doctor with gratitude. Clearly Officer Walker didn't believe her memory loss. Or anything else she'd told him.

The cop glanced at the doctor, then at her, before taking out his notebook. After a moment, he removed the pencil from behind his ear and held it over the paper. His gaze rose again to hers.

"You have a global-tracking device in your car, Mrs. Collins?"

She frowned. "Yes," she said hesitantly.

"When your car went off the road and the air bag deployed, a call went out to the police station here. I talked to your in-car system provider. It seems your last communication to them was a request for a route from Seattle to Shadow Lake."

This town *had* been her destination? "I have no idea why I would have done that." She could hear the apprehension in her voice. "As far as I can remember, I've never even heard of Shadow Lake before."

"There was a suitcase in the backseat of your car," he said.

A suitcase? She had a flicker of memory and saw herself packing furiously. "Maybe I was going on a short vacation." But the clothes hanging in the hospital room closet certainly didn't go with that theory. She feared what she would find in her suitcase.

"It's a little early for a vacation in Shadow Lake," the cop said. "Most of the motels and cabins aren't even open yet."

She sighed, exasperated by his inability to accept that she couldn't remember. "How many times do I have to tell you I don't know?"

"You also asked for directions to the Shadow Lake Police Department," Walker said.

Out of the corner of her eye, Anna saw Dr. Brubaker swing his attention to the cop in surprise.

Anna tried not to let her own shock show. She couldn't imagine any reason she would be interested in where the police department was located in Shadow Lake. Maybe someone had programmed her car. Even as she thought it, she knew how ludicrous that sounded.

For some reason she'd come to Shadow Lake—and thought she was going to need the police.

"I have no idea why I did any of those things. Please, tell me why you're asking me all these questions."

"Why don't you tell *me*, Mrs. Collins?" Walker said. "Why drive up here in the middle of the night?"

"Don't you think I would tell you if I knew?" Anna said, hearing the panic in her voice. "None of this makes any sense to me. You act as if I'm hiding something from you. I'm telling you everything I know."

"But you didn't tell us about your son," he said.

"I think we should give Mrs. Collins a chance to rest," Dr. Brubaker said.

"Just one more question," Walker said, without looking at the doctor. His eyes were locked on Anna. "I want to hear about this person who you say was in the lake with you."

"Not *with* me. In the water outside the car." She swallowed, afraid that when she told him what she'd seen, he really would believe her a liar. She took a breath and let it out slowly, reassuring herself that she'd seen the man. He had to have saved her life. How else had she gotten out of the car?

Maybe more important, the man would be able to back up her story. He must have seen her lose control of the car and go into the lake. He could prove she was telling the truth.

"I saw a man at my side window," she said, knowing her story would be met with more than skepticism. "I couldn't get my seat belt to release. I thought I was going to drown."

The cop was waiting patiently.

"The car was upside down and I was under the water. I remember thinking I couldn't hold my breath any longer. I heard what sounded like someone tap on my side window. I turned and…" She faltered. "I saw a face."

"A face?" Walker asked.

"It was a man's face. He had black hair that floated around his face and—" She grimaced. "His face was badly scarred." She turned her own face away for a moment, jarred by the memory of the man's monsterlike appearance. She was reminded of her own scar, her own shame that went with it.

"Scarred how?" Walker asked, his voice sounding oddly strained.

Her fingers trembling, Anna touched her face, starting at just below her left eye and swinging over the bridge of her nose and down under her right eye across her cheek to her jawline.

"And his eyes," she added quickly. "I'd almost forgotten about them. They were a pale smoky gray reminding me of a wolf's." She saw the doctor exchange a look with Walker.

"You know someone with a scar like that?" she said. "It's a small town. If he's from here—"

"You're telling me that you saw all of this on the bottom of the lake in the dark," Walker demanded, now clearly angry.

"There was a light coming from somewhere," she said, uncertain, though. "Maybe he had a flashlight or I saw him somehow in the glow of my car's headlights. But I saw him." She had, hadn't she? She couldn't make something like that up.

Obviously the cop thought her capable of making up just about anything—including being in the car at the bottom of the lake.

Her fingers went to her scar again. She traced its path nervously as she caught another exchanged look between the two men.

"I saw a badly scarred man under the water. He saved my life," she said as she looked from the cop to Dr. Brubaker and back, confused by their reactions. "Don't you see? The seat belt was jammed. He must have gotten me out and brought me here. I can't imagine how else I survived. If you find him, he'll tell you—"

Walker let out a curse. His face was crimson, his brown eyes wild with anger and something she'd hadn't seen in them before—pain.

The doctor clasped a hand on the cop's arm. "Walker, I need a word with you in the hall, now, please."

"What aren't you telling me?" Anna demanded, her voice rising as high as her emotions again. "You keep looking at each other. Do you know this man I described? Is that it? If you just find him, he'll tell you—"

"Please, Mrs. Collins," Dr. Brubaker said as he forcibly

ushered the cop out the door. "Let me speak to Officer Walker a moment and I will be back."

Before the door closed, Anna saw the brief heated exchange before the cop said something that silenced Dr. Brubaker. The doctor glanced back at her. She saw his expression as the door swung shut.

Fear made her fingers tremble as she reached for the phone and tried her friend Gillian's number again. She needed more than a friend now. She had a bad feeling she needed a lawyer.

And she had no idea why.

Or why Marc would tell the police she'd been threatening to kill someone last night.

Gillian didn't answer her cell phone this time, either. Anna left a message to call the Shadow Lake Hospital in Shadow Lake. "It's urgent."

When she tried Gillian's office, she was told that her friend had taken a few days off. She'd left no forwarding number. Odd. Gillian hadn't mentioned anything about it when they'd had lunch. Nor was it like Gillian to take any time off. Anna couldn't remember the last time her friend had gone on vacation.

Something was terribly wrong.

WALKER ONLY MADE IT AS far as his patrol car. He sat in the darkness, his head swimming, anger eating him up inside. All he wanted to do was storm back into the hospital and make that woman tell him the truth.

She'd lied.

But for the life of him, he couldn't think of any reason she would do that.

He ran a hand over his face.

"You need to get control of yourself," Dr. Brubaker had told him as he'd led him down the hallway away from Anna Collins's hospital room.

"You heard her in there. She's *lying*."

"You don't really believe that woman in there killed anyone last night, do you?" Doc had demanded.

"Her husband seems to think she might have."

"Go home. Get some rest. You aren't thinking clearly. Give her some time to get her memory back. I'm sure all of this can be sorted out."

Walker had seen the way Doc was with the young woman. Protective, as if she were his own daughter. Who wasn't thinking clearly? he'd wanted to demand, but he'd had the good sense to keep his mouth shut and get out of the hospital before he did something he'd regret.

He didn't need Doc to tell him that he was running on emotion right now. A lot of loss of his own.

Maybe he'd pick up a six-pack and drop by Billy's. He went off shift over an hour ago.

Walker dialed the police chief's cell. It rang four times before Rob finally picked up.

"Yeah?"

Nash sounded funny.

"Sorry to bother you, but I thought I should give you a heads-up on this case I got last night around midnight," Walker said.

"The car that went into the lake," Chief Nash said.

"Yeah." He wondered how the chief had heard about it. "Anyway, I suspect it was an attempted suicide. The woman's over at the hospital. Doc seems to think she's going to be fine. But she swears she can't remember a thing including an argument with her husband when she threatened to kill someone."

"People make threats all the time, you know that," Nash said.

"Yeah. I just have a gut feeling about this one," Walker said, a little thrown by the chief's response. Nash always had questions, convinced the answers were always in the details. "How are things over in Pilot's Cove?"

"Fine. I got through sooner than I thought. I'm on my way back to town now."

"Anything you need help on?" Walker asked, still wondering why Nash had let him believe it had something to do with the Pilot's Cove Police Department.

"No."

"We tried to get the car out, but Mac had to find a larger, newer tow truck," Walker said, just for something to say since clearly the chief wasn't interested. "Once we get the car out, maybe we'll know more."

"Sounds like you have everything under control. So if there's no problem…"

He bristled at the chief's irritation. No problem except for who she said saved her life last night. The chief was probably just tired and trying to get home to his young new wife. "I got it covered."

"Good."

Walker hung up, wondering what the hell was going on with the chief. Something, that was for damned sure. Nash had sounded like he had more important things on his mind. Like what? Walker wondered.

The chief's job had been all that Rob Nash had had for so many years Walker couldn't imagine the old man giving it up. But maybe the position would be coming open. And sooner than Walker had even hoped.

ANNA HAD NEVER FELT SO alone. Everyone in her life had abandoned her. Even Gillian, the one person she'd depended on the most since Tyler's death. She'd finally reached rock bottom. What did it matter if the cop didn't believe her story? Nothing mattered. It hadn't from the moment she'd awakened to find that her son was dead.

But Anna found herself getting angry. She was tired of just lying down and taking it. Then she picked up the phone and called Marc's number, planning to demand to know why he had told Officer Walker all those awful things about her—and find out what she'd done last night to make him say them.

But when Marc's voice mail came up, she hung up and dialed Mary Ellen back.

"Anna." Mary Ellen sounded relieved to hear her voice. "Where are you? I tried to call you back—"

"Tell me why Marc didn't go through with the divorce." Anna felt anger bubble up inside her. "He's the one who wanted it so badly."

"You don't know how hard it's been on him," Mary Ellen said. "For six long months he didn't know whether or not you'd ever wake up. He'd already lost his son—"

"I lost my son, too," she interrupted.

"Yes, but Marc had months of not knowing if he was going to lose you, too. Then when you came out of the coma and didn't even know what had happened…"

Anna couldn't help but bristle at the words. She'd tried so hard to remember the hit-and-run accident that had taken Tyler and nearly killed her as well. The driver of the car that had hit her and her son was never apprehended because Anna couldn't provide a description. With what little the police had to go on, they hadn't been able to find out who had hit her car, killing her son and putting her in a coma. She'd never known if she had been somehow partly responsible.

"Marc had to relive it all again with you," Mary Ellen was saying. "He was dealing with all of it and then…"

Yes, Anna had come back from the darkness to make Marc's life even harder. She'd often gotten the impression he'd wished she'd died along with Tyler at the scene.

"I think Marc thought divorce would put an end to the pain by distancing himself from you and the memories," Mary Ellen said.

Anna sniffed and wiped her eyes. She wasn't insensitive

to Marc's pain. But she had also overheard him question the doctor about whether or not it was possible she'd stayed in the coma because she couldn't face the truth. "I know it was harder on him than it was on me."

"But you can put things back together again," Mary Ellen said brightly. "That's really what Marc wants. To start over, no more secrets between the two of you."

Anna had wanted that, too. She just hadn't expected Marc wanting to come back to her to be so bittersweet.

"He said he told me all of this last night?" Anna asked.

Silence, then Mary Ellen said hesitantly, "Yes. Are you saying he didn't?"

Had Marc told her? Then why had she taken off to Shadow Lake alone?

Anna had a flash of memory. A nasty argument. Had it been last night? She couldn't be sure.

Maybe it was last night, because she had a strong feeling that something had happened. Last night. And while she was in a coma. Something that Marc and her friends were keeping from her.

Marc's change of heart made her suspicious, given what he'd told the Shadow Lake police. Not that she was about to share that with Mary Ellen.

She'd learned that Marc was very deliberate in his decisions. Maybe that was why the outcome always benefited him the most.

If Marc had told her last night that he hadn't gone through with the divorce, he would have been expecting her to fall to her knees in gratitude. So maybe the argument she vaguely recalled *had* been last night, because she doubted she'd indulged him in that fantasy.

In fact, she suspected she hadn't been even gracious. If anything she would have been angry.

You scare me, Anna.

His words came back to her so clearly that they could have been from last night.

Not as much as you're scaring me, Marc.

She frowned. Why had she said that to him? And had it been last night? Lately, it seemed all the days ran together.

"Anna, are you still there?"

"Yes." She recalled Mary Ellen's words from earlier. *That's what Marc really wants. To start over, no more secrets between the two of you.*

Secrets?

"Did something happen while I was in the coma?" Anna asked, a trembling in her voice she couldn't control.

"What do you mean?" Mary Ellen sounded wary now.

Anna wasn't sure exactly *what* she meant. "Marc is so *different.*"

"Anna, of course he's different. How could he not be different after everything that has happened?"

She looked toward the hospital-room window. She knew she should stop, but it was as if too long, pent-up emotions had burst loose inside her.

She knew she should be talking about this with Gillian, not Mary Ellen. Gillian would understand. She wasn't so sure Mary Ellen could, especially given her recent "friendship" with Marc. But Anna couldn't seem to hold it back any longer.

"He's like a stranger, Mary Ellen. I don't know him. He…" She choked, unable to say the words out loud, even though she'd been thinking them for a long while now. She'd woken up after six months in a coma to a complete stranger who frightened her.

"I know Marc's made mistakes, but he really is sorry and wants to make it up to you."

Anna said nothing. She'd spent the past two months crying on her friends' shoulders. No wonder she didn't hear any sympathy in her friend's tone—except for Marc. No wonder Gillian wasn't answering her cell phone.

Anna had awakened from a coma as if only moments had gone by instead of months. Her friends had been by her side the whole time. They'd been relieved and exhausted and wrung out from the ordeal, and then when Marc had wanted a divorce, they'd tried to comfort her. Or at least Gillian had.

Mary Ellen's alliances seemed to have shifted more to Marc's side. Why was that?

"I wanted to let you know that I'm all right," Anna said, feeling strangely desolate and far from all right.

"You'll call Marc and tell him where you are so he doesn't have to worry?"

She bridled at the reproach. "Would you mind calling him? Tell him I'm fine. I really can't talk to him right now."

"Anna, he's worried sick about you. He needs to know that you're going to forgive him and take him back."

"I have to go," Anna said, too despondent to talk any longer. She hung up before Mary Ellen could argue further.

Her hand shook as she put the phone down and lay back in the bed, her eyes hot with unshed tears.

POLICE CHIEF ROB NASH DROVE to his house and pulled up in front of his garage door, remembering Lucinda running out last night to get in that other man's car.

He shut off the engine and sat for a moment just staring at his house. Lucinda had been too young for him and he'd known it. What would a woman her age see in an old man like him anyway? Security? A father figure?

The first time he'd laid eyes on her he'd known that she'd been running from something, that she'd needed a safe place. She had been happy when they'd first gotten together—that hadn't been his imagination, had it?

He saw the curtain move, caught a glimpse of Lucinda's face as she looked out the window at him before she let the curtain fall back again.

He couldn't sit here all night. He opened the car door, feeling even older than his years. Disgusted with himself, he shuffled to the door. It wasn't locked and swung open. She was standing by the window wearing that yellow dress he liked.

"Hi," she said too cheerfully. "I was hoping that was you."

"Who else would it be?" he asked, noticing that she was also wearing the diamond earrings he'd splurged on, and he caught a whiff of the expensive perfume he'd surprised her with on her birthday, a light scent that he loved on her.

Desire cut through him painfully. He closed the door, wanting to forget last night and take her in his arms and have everything be as it was before. But just the way she was dressed told him things were about to change.

"Rob, there is something I need to tell you," she blurted out, and he saw how nervous she was.

"Lucinda, I've been up all night. Can't it wait?" He stepped into the room, smelled pot roast, his favorite. He had no appetite, but he said, "Something smells good. I haven't eaten since yesterday."

"I made your favorite," she said, though she seemed disappointed that she would have to wait to tell him whatever it was. She'd obviously gone to lot of trouble tonight to set this up. "Would you like to eat and watch the basketball game? That always relaxes you."

He nodded, annoyed at her attempt to take care of him. Yesterday he would have thought it sweet the way his wife looked after him. Now it felt as if she were treating him like a feeble old man who needed to be waited on hand and foot.

As she stepped past him, he grabbed her, not sure at first if he planned to strangle her or hold her. His kiss was punishing as he shoved her against the wall and pressed his body to hers.

"Rob," she gasped against his mouth.

He worked his hand between their bodies and ripped the front of the dress open, shoving the bra away to roughly cup her breast in his big hand.

"Rob?" she gasped as he ripped off her panties. He covered her mouth with his, silencing her more than kissing her. He fumbled to get his pants unzipped, shocked at how hard he was. And then he was inside her, slamming her against the wall.

She clung to him as he drove into her. He ignored her cries just as he ignored the frightened look in her eyes. Or the sadness as he came, his body shuddering with his release.

He let go of her and stepped back.

She looked down at her torn dress, then up at him, tears in her eyes.

The shock of what he'd done hit him with a force that threatened to drop him to his knees. Was this the kind of man he'd become?

He felt sick. His beeper went off. He swore and turned away from her, unable to look her in the eyes and see himself as she saw him at this moment.

He felt like crying. Hell, he couldn't remember the last time he'd cried. "I have to take this."

He stepped into the den and closed the door, nauseated from the smell of perfume, sex and roast beef.

"Nash here," he said when he reached the dispatcher, his voice breaking.

"A Mr. Marc Collins is down here. He insists on speaking to you *tonight*."

"Walker—"

"Mr. Collins insists on talking to the police *chief*. He says it's urgent. Something about his wife's missing gun."

CHAPTER EIGHT

A DIFFERENT NURSE CAME in to check Anna. The small gray-haired woman's name tag read Elle. She smoothed the bed covers, offered soothing words and checked the IV attached to Anna's arm.

"Doc wants you to get some sleep," Elle said.

Anna didn't want to sleep. All she'd done was sleep. For six long months. And now here she was in another hospital bed being told to sleep. She had to remember what she was doing in Shadow Lake.

She watched as Elle closed the blinds against the approaching night and Anna's view of the darkening waters of the lake. For that alone, Anna was thankful. She couldn't get out of her mind the image of the man she'd seen outside her car window at the bottom of the lake—or his horrible scar.

She shivered and closed her eyes, knowing she wouldn't sleep. Couldn't.

When she got out of here she'd go back to the psychiatrist. Obviously, she was a lot sicker than she'd thought.

Elle left, turning out the lights and closing the hall door. Anna lay in the dark, her thoughts racing. She prayed that Gillian would call. Gillian could make sense of all this.

As she lay there in the dark, she knew in her heart that as much as she might have wanted to take the easy way out, she hadn't tried to kill herself last night. Which meant there was a logical explanation for all of this, including why she'd been headed for this town.

Remembering the items she'd found in her coat pocket, Anna suddenly sat up in the bed even though it made her head swim. Reaching over, she turned on the lamp on the nightstand and opened the drawer where she'd stuffed what she'd found in her coat pocket earlier.

The balled-up money had dried. She smoothed it out and put it and the credit card back in the drawer. There was no salvaging the credit-card receipt. She threw it away since the paper had disintegrated and the printing on it wasn't legible anyway.

She picked up the scrap of folded paper, surprised to see that it was half of an envelope. The heavy paper had dried, the writing nearly legible.

What surprised her was that the writing wasn't hers. The words and numbers were in Gillian's handwriting.

A shudder moved through Anna. How had she gotten this? And why did just the sight of it fill her with anxiety?

She turned the envelope over in her fingers and saw Gillian's return address. It appeared to be half of an envelope from Gillian's office.

Turning the paper back over, she tried to read what Gillian had written. Was this just some note Gillian had written to herself? Then how had it ended up in Anna's coat pocket?

On closer inspection, it appeared whatever Gillian had put down had been written in a hurry. A phone number? She tried to read what was written under the series of numbers. Her eyes blurred for a moment with the exhaustion.

Slowly, two words came into focus.

She felt her chest constrict.

Shadow Lake.

Anna stared at the paper, feeling light-headed.

She'd had this in her coat pocket. It had to be the reason she'd driven to Shadow Lake last night.

But where had she gotten it? Had she gone to Gillian's? Marc had told Officer Walker that she'd seen him last night. If that were true, had she seen him before or after she'd seen Gillian?

She didn't remember seeing either of them; nor could she explain why she'd been dressed as she had. But she'd obviously left for Shadow Lake in a hurry or she would have changed into something else. Walker had said there was a suitcase in the backseat of her car. She had a flash again of angrily throwing clothing into a suitcase.

Clearly there had been an urgency in her decision to drive to Shadow Lake. She was breathing hard now, fear growing inside her as she realized she'd been furious last night. According to Officer Walker, Marc had said she'd threatened to kill someone.

She made out two more of the words on the paper. Hwy 20 East. Anna's fingers went to her scar. She traced its path as she tried to decipher the rest of the words Gillian had written on the scrap of paper. Wherever she'd gotten this note, it appeared to be directions Gillian had written down for her. Or for herself?

Whatever this was, it meant something. Something important. Important enough that Anna had raced up here. Important enough that she'd asked where to find the Shadow Lake Police Department.

She concentrated harder on trying to read the words. A name. Fair—something. Fairview? Fairchild? No, Fairbanks, she thought turning it in the light. Why did that sound familiar? James Fairbanks, of course. The former senator. He'd died recently. Hadn't she read that he'd been buried in some small mountain town where his family had a summer home?

Underneath were two more words. Unfortunately the words, even if they hadn't been hard to read, made no sense. If there had been an address, it certainly didn't look like one now. In fact, it looked like it said "stop." Stop what?

Preceding the word *stop* was what looked like "must."
Must stop? The thought made her heart race. Must stop
someone? Gillian? If that were the case, then why hadn't she
just called the police department?

She looked in the drawer of the nightstand, found a Bible
and a phone book. There was no Fairbanks listed.

Studying the writing on the scrap of envelope again, she
saw that the first letter looked more like an *R* than an *M*. Rust
Stop? *Rest Stop*.

Her breath caught. Rest Stop. Fairbanks. Hwy 20. Shadow
Lake. And a phone number?

Was it possible she had planned to meet someone named
Fairbanks and that's why she'd driven to Shadow Lake? To
meet a total stranger at a rest stop? Never. It just wasn't something she would do.

Unless Gillian was meeting her there.

Or unless she was following Gillian there.

Neither made any sense except that she *had* driven to
Shadow Lake last night with an urgency that worried her.

All of it was so out of character, she couldn't even imagine
doing something so…impulsive.

She must have been out of her mind. Or…or, she realized
as her pulse spiked, it would have to have been a matter of
life or death.

She fingered the torn envelope, trying to make sense of
why it would have sent her racing to Shadow Lake like a bat
out of hell in the middle of the night.

A small corner of the envelope had been turned over. As
she flattened it out, Anna saw a tiny word printed in the far
right bottom corner almost like an afterthought.

Tyler.

Her heart took off like a missile.

While the rest of the words had been written in Gillian's
hurried scrawl, Tyler's name had been printed carefully.

Slowly. Small and perfect. Like Anna's son. The word as
rueful as a sigh. Like the prick of a knife to the heart.

Anna covered her mouth with her hand to hold back the
howl that she'd fought to keep at bay for the past two months.

Tyler.

She wanted to expel her anguish until her lungs burst. To
pound the walls with her fists until her hands bled.

Tyler.

Her heart swelled like the choked-back sobs in her throat.
The letters blurred, then came into sharp focus. Just the sight
of his name a physical pain.

Under it, even smaller was written "Luke 2:12."

Anna had seen the Bible in the drawer of the nightstand.
She took it out and, after hurriedly wiping her eyes, leafed
through it until she found the passage.

Luke 12:2: *"The time is coming when everything will be
revealed; all that is secret will be made public."*

ANNA HEARD THE DOOR TO her room open and quickly palmed
the note and shut the night-table drawer. She hid the scrap of
paper away like a cherished secret. If it meant what she
thought it did...

Her heart pounded at even the thought of what Officer D.C.
Walker would say if he knew about the note she'd found in
her coat pocket.

But why should she fear that? She hadn't done anything
except had a car accident and almost drowned in the lake.

Or had she? She didn't know what she'd been planning to
do once she got to Shadow Lake. Or worse, what she *had*
done. If only she could reach Gillian. She must be in a place
where her cell phone couldn't pick up.

The thought made Anna feel a little better. Still, it wasn't
like her to take off for a few days without letting either Anna
or Mary Ellen know where she'd gone.

The nurse bustled into the room. "I thought you would be out like a light by now."

Anna yawned. "Close."

Elle checked Anna's IV then picked up her water pitcher to refill it. "You want me to call the doctor and get you something to help you sleep?"

Anna shook her head and yawned again. "Is there a rest stop near Shadow Lake?"

The petite elderly nurse raised an eyebrow.

"I think I'm starting to remember more about last night."

Elle gave her a sympathetic smile. "The rest stop is at the top of the mountain." She pointed in the direction of the cliffs where Anna had gone into the lake.

"It must be close to where my car went off," Anna said in surprise.

"I'm not good with distances, but I would imagine you could have seen the rest stop in your rearview mirror from where you went off the highway." She parted the drapes. "You can almost see it from here."

It was too dark to see anything but some faint car lights through the trees. "Is it the only rest stop near here?"

"Only one for seventy miles," the nurse said, letting the drapes fall back into place as she continued to the bathroom to refill the water pitcher. "Is there anything else you need besides to quit trying to force your memory? What did Doc tell you to do?"

"Get some rest," Anna said.

Elle turned to smile back at her. "So you *were* listening. Take his advice. The doc knows what's best."

Anna nodded. "Have you known Dr. Brubaker for long?" she asked.

"All his life," Elle said, raising her voice to be heard over the sound of the running water. "He grew up here and came back after he finished med school. It's hard to keep a doctor in a town this far from everything. We're fortunate to have one, especially someone as good as Dr. Brubaker. I don't know what the town will do when he retires and now that his wife, Gladys, is gone…."

Anna licked her dry lips, her heart pounding as she asked, "Do you know the Fairbankses?"

"Personally?" she asked as she came out of the bathroom with the pitcher of water. "No. They don't come into town much."

"The family summer home isn't in Shadow Lake?"

Elle shook her head. "Big Jim's widow, Ruth, I heard is staying out on the island most of the year now along with her daughter-in-law. Jonathan usually stays in Washington, D.C., but I think I heard he's back now. Probably needs to spend more time with his mother now that Big Jim is gone. Big Jim had Alzheimer's. That's always so much harder on the family than the patient." The nurse shook her head.

"Where is the island?" Anna asked.

Elle patted her arm. "You think you can keep me chattering and I won't notice that you're stalling on going to sleep?" She chuckled. "You'll be surprised what some sleep will do for you. You'll be feeling much better in the morning. You'll see." She turned off the lamp next to the bed and started to leave. "Doctor won't like it if I tell him you're still awake." The door closed.

Anna waited until she heard the nurse talking to someone down the hallway before she snapped on the lamp again, opened her palm and looked down at the note in her hand.

It had something to do Tyler's death. It had to. The cryptic quote from the Bible. Tyler's name. The urgent way Gillian had taken down the information and on a scrap of envelope? That wasn't like Gillian.

Anna knew that Gillian had been searching for the hit-and-run driver for eight long months. But Anna also knew that she'd come up empty. Marc had said it was useless and that

continuing the search was only self-indulgent, wallowing in
the pain of Tyler's death. Any evidence was long gone.

But Anna knew Gillian. Her friend would never have
stopped looking. What if Gillian had found out something?
It would explain why Anna had been on that road last night.
Why Anna had inquired about where to find the police station.

The only thing it didn't explain was where Gillian was.

Picking up the phone, Anna dialed her friend's cell phone
number again, praying Gillian would answer. She didn't,
making Anna more anxious. Even if Gillian didn't have service
wherever she was, she always checked her messages routinely.

Anna had left a message on both Gillian's home phone and
her cell. Regardless of where she was, Gillian would have
checked her messages by now and called. Especially since
Anna had left a message saying it was urgent.

Her worry growing further, Anna stared at the scrap of
envelope and the words written on it. Impulsively, she tried
the numbers across the top.

A phone rang. It *had* been a phone number. The line continued to ring and ring. No answer. No voice mail.

After about fifteen rings, Anna hung up and dialed the
operator. "I've been trying to reach this number. I was hoping
you could help me." She read it off to the operator. "Does that
sound like a valid number?"

"Hold on." The operator came back a few seconds later.
"That's a pay phone and probably why you're not getting
an answer."

"Can you tell me where that pay phone is located?"

"Just a moment. That one is at a rest stop outside Shadow
Lake," the operator said.

"Thank you." A pay phone at the rest stop.

Anna hung up and lay back against the pillows. It appeared
either she or Gillian or both of them had been meeting someone
named Fairbanks at the rest stop last night. Her head ached.

She picked up the phone again, dialed the operator and asked for a listing for Jim Fairbanks. Even though the senator was deceased, Anna doubted the family had thought to change the listing.

"I'm sorry, that number is unlisted."

"Is there any other Fairbanks in the Shadow Lake area?"

"Yes, but they are also unlisted."

Anna hung up, then on impulse picked up the phone and dialed Mary Ellen's number. Gillian wouldn't have left town without telling someone where she'd gone.

Anna frowned as she waited for her friend to pick up. Maybe that's what her friends had been arguing about yesterday at lunch.

"Hello?" Mary Ellen said, picking up on the second ring.

"It's Anna. I'm sorry it's so late."

"Anna. I'm so glad you called back. I feel so badly about earlier. I hope you don't think I'm taking Marc's side."

Anna ignored that. "Have you heard from Gillian?"

"Why?" Suddenly her friend sounded wary again.

"I need to talk to her."

"Did you try her office?"

"They said she was going to be out of town for a few days."

"Well, then I guess that's why you haven't been able to reach her."

Anna heard something in Mary Ellen's voice. "Why are you angry with Gillian? Don't deny it. I sensed something wrong at lunch yesterday."

She realized now why she'd imagined that her friends were keeping things from her. They were.

She closed her eyes, rubbed her temple and blurted out, "I know something's going on. I've felt it since I came out of the coma. I can't shake this feeling that you know something, that you all are in on it, but you won't tell me what it is. You're supposed to be my friend." She was close to tears. "Why aren't you being honest with me?"

"I *am* your friend, honey."

"Then be honest with me."

Silence.

"What?" Anna demanded.

"I don't know what you want me to say?" Mary Ellen sounded as upset as Anna.

"Where has Gillian gone?"

"I don't know, Anna."

"I don't believe you. What are you two arguing about?"

"Marc," Mary Ellen said.

Marc. Of course. "Tell me why he *really* changed his mind about the divorce." The tears were flowing now and she choked on the words, her throat closing.

"I already told you. He wants to start over."

"It doesn't make any sense. Just a few days ago…" She couldn't continue. She fought to stem the tears, regain control. "Marc had to have told you more than that."

Silence on Mary Ellen's end, then finally she answered, "He said he couldn't abandon you now. That he was afraid of what you might do. That sometimes you get so angry, you become…violent. He was afraid you might hurt yourself."

She sniffed and made an angry swipe at the tears. "Marc *said* that? But it isn't true. Why would he even say something like that?"

Mary Ellen said nothing, and in the silence Anna realized her friend didn't believe her.

"Have you ever seen me violent, Mary Ellen?" Anna demanded. "Suicidal?"

"No, but—"

"Marc told the police that I threatened to kill someone."

"The police?"

"Yes, Mary Ellen, why would Marc do that?"

"Because he's afraid for you."

Anna shook her head, regretting this call. "You've never liked Marc and frankly, the feeling was always mutual. Why are you defending him now?"

There was an icy edge to Mary Ellen's voice that Anna had never heard before. "It's true, I've never been wild about Marc. I always thought he felt he was better than me. But I got to know him when you were in the coma. He was alone with his grief all those months after Tyler's death. He thought you were gone too, Anna."

Still, that didn't explain why Marc would go to Mary Ellen, and Anna said as much.

"Marc just needed someone to talk to. He was worried because he didn't know where you went last night after he told you the news. I was worried, too. I still am."

Anna sighed. "I'm sorry. I guess I just don't understand why, if you knew he was so worried about me, you didn't tell him I was on the line when I called."

"Anna, honey, you're my friend. I knew you were angry with Marc and needed to calm down before you talked to him again. I wasn't going to rat you out. So I pretended it wasn't you on the phone. I didn't tell him *anything*."

"What was there to tell him?"

"Are you sure you're all right?"

"I'm fine. I'm just upset."

"I'm upset, too. But you know why I didn't tell him you were on the phone. After he told me how you reacted…"

Reacted to the news he hadn't divorced her? Why would she need time to calm down before she talked to Marc again?

"I knew you wouldn't want to talk to him," Mary Ellen continued. "I'm sure that's one reason Gillian left for a few days. They both wanted to give you some time to calm down before they tried to talk to you about it."

Talk to her about *what?*

Mary Ellen was crying now. "You've lost so much. I don't want you to lose Marc, too. He said you told him that you hate him. I don't believe that, although I couldn't blame you if you did right now. And I don't blame you for threatening to kill them both. All I said was for you to let him know you're okay."

Anna felt panic rise inside her. "Mary Ellen, *what* are you talking about?"

"What Marc told you last night. About the affair he had with Gillian. Anna? Are you sure you're all right?"

IN THE VERY BACK OF THE freezer, Dr. Brubaker found a casserole his wife had made before her death.

He took off the lid, pleased that it was only a little freezer burned. He put it in the microwave to thaw, not even sure what the dish was. Not that he cared.

He had ended up eating little of the burrito he'd nuked earlier at the hospital and now he felt weak. He had to remind himself to eat something, he thought, thinking of Anna Collins back at the hospital. She would need an ally, especially since Walker was determined she was hiding something.

The microwave dinged. He hit Reheat and waited, standing by the counter in the quiet kitchen, thinking about Gladys and the hours they used to spend in here, visiting while they cooked or did the dishes. God, how he missed her.

He'd only taken a couple of bites of the casserole when his beeper went off.

"Doctor, there's a patient down here to see you." Elle sounded a little strange. Her voice dropped to a whisper. "It's Mrs. Nash."

"Lucinda?" A stupid question. There was no other Mrs. Nash in Shadow Lake. At least not living. Rob's mother was over at the graveyard.

What had thrown him was that Rob's wife had never been his patient. Probably because she'd never needed a doctor before.

"She seems upset," Elle said, whispering now. "Could you hurry?"

"I'll be right there."

Brubaker had been as shocked as anyone when Police Chief Rob Nash had run off to Vegas with the new waitress at the Lakeside Café. Because the town was so small, Brubaker had seen the young woman around.

Lucinda had seemed shy. Or scared. Maybe both. Was that what Rob had seen in her, what had made him start drinking coffee every morning at the Lakeside instead of the Coffee Cup where he'd been a regular for years?

It had raised a lot of eyebrows when Rob and Lucinda announced that they'd eloped to Vegas. The age difference aside, some said it was too quick. Rob hadn't known the girl more than a few weeks.

There'd been bets going around that the marriage wouldn't last a month. A lot of people had lost that bet since it had been almost three months now.

As Brubaker stepped into the examining room, he saw Lucinda standing by the window. She had a balled-up tissue in her hand and was biting down hard on her lower lip, as if she thought that would stem the tide of tears streaming down her face.

She quickly brushed at the tears, turning away to blow her nose.

"I'm Dr. Brubaker," he said, closing the examining room door. He noticed there was nothing about what was bothering her on the patient file he'd picked up from Elle, so he had no clue what this was about. Apparently Lucinda hadn't wanted to tell Elle.

"Why don't we sit down." He pulled out a chair and sat. After a moment she turned to face him, looking embarrassed and scared.

"I can't sit. I'm too worried." She studied him as if

making up her mind about something. "I shouldn't have come here."

"I'd like to help, Lucinda," he said quietly. "Your visit, as you know, is confidential. Whatever is said in this room stays here."

She took a ragged breath and bit her lower lip again.

He said nothing, waiting, knowing better than to push. She was scared. He could see that. And obviously in some kind of trouble.

She burst into tears. "I'm afraid I'm going to lose the baby."

He tried not to look shocked. "How far along are you?"

She shook her head and wiped again at her eyes. "I'm not sure. I'm sorry. It's just that I'm so scared."

"What makes you think you're losing the baby?"

"I'm bleeding a little."

"Okay," he said, getting up from the chair. "First off, let's not panic, okay? I want you to put on this gown and I'll take a look and see how things are going, all right?"

She nodded.

"Have you seen a doctor about the pregnancy yet?"

She shook her head and gave him a wan smile. "I didn't want to jinx it."

He wanted to ask if she would be more comfortable with her husband here, but decided to wait until he knew her condition. "I'm going to step out of the room for a moment." He handed her a gown and explained how to put it on. "You change and I'll be back in a few minutes."

He stepped out into the hall. He could see Elle down at the nurses' station looking in this direction. Normally when he did a pelvic he had a nurse in the room. But it was clear that, for whatever reason, Lucinda Nash didn't want the nurse to know about her pregnancy.

He waved to Elle that everything was fine. She smiled

and mouthed, *Sorry.* Sorry for calling him down if everything was fine.

He hoped that was the case.

He tapped at the door.

From the other side of the door, Lucinda said, "Come in." She was sitting on the exam table, nervously shredding several tissues in her fingers.

"Try to relax," he said as he approached her.

ANNA FELT AS IF SHE'D BEEN hit by a bolt of lightning. A direct hit to her heart, the pain so intense it was blinding.

She slumped against the pillows, her arm holding the phone dropping to the bed. She could hear Mary Ellen's voice, but it was unintelligible with the phone so far from her ear.

Marc and Gillian. *No.* Anna hadn't noticed if Marc and Gillian had gotten any closer from the months she'd been in the coma. In fact, they seemed more antagonistic. Had that just been an act?

She thought for a moment that she was going to throw up, but the nausea passed and, with it, the initial shock.

She put the phone to her ear again as she was filled with a tidal wave of anger. "Gillian wouldn't do that. She wouldn't. Not to me." For a moment Anna thought that Mary Ellen had hung up.

"Marc said she begged him not to tell you. I'm sure it only happened because they both believed they'd lost you when you didn't come out of the coma for so long and were comforting each other."

Anna squeezed her eyes shut. "Is that what Gillian told you?"

"She didn't tell me anything," Mary Ellen said, sounding mad. "But remember how she was acting yesterday at lunch?"

Anna remembered. Gillian had been distracted and had begged off early saying she had work to do.

"How long have you known?" Anna had to ask.

"Not long."

Anna had trouble believing that. Her best friend was screwing her husband. Her second-best friend hadn't told her. With friends like that…

"Marc said it's been over for a couple of months now," Mary Ellen said.

A couple of months. The same amount of time Anna had been out of the coma. She stared up at the ceiling, finally understanding the strange undercurrents she'd felt when she was around the three people closest to her.

"Are you sure you don't know where Gillian is? I really need to talk to her."

Mary Ellen let out a cry. "I can't believe you want to talk to her. She can't even face you, now that she's heard you know. She isn't answering her cell phone, right? Maybe you can forgive her, but I never will."

"When did Gillian find out that I knew?" Anna asked.

"Marc said he went by her office yesterday afternoon to warn her before he went over to your place to tell you."

Anna thought of the piece of envelope she'd found in her best coat pocket. She'd just gotten that coat back from the cleaner's yesterday morning before lunch. That meant the note would have gone into her pocket sometime after that. Gillian had been at her house for lunch but hadn't said anything. So it followed that it would have happened after that.

She'd heard that a shock rather than the bump on the head could cause memory loss. News of an affair between her husband and best friend definitely could be why she had no memory of last night before the deer appeared in her headlights.

"It's not like Gillian to go away and hide," Anna said, realizing it was true. If what Mary Ellen was saying was true, then Gillian would have wanted to tell her herself—not let Marc do it.

Either way, Anna knew she must have crossed paths with Gillian later in the day. What bothered her was that she didn't remember it. That and the fact that Gillian seemed to have disappeared.

"Mary Ellen, there's something else I have to know," Anna said. "Was Gillian looking for the hit-and-run driver who killed Tyler?"

A long sigh. "You know Gillian. She was determined to find the driver and bring him to justice, but as far as I know she hadn't learned anything. Why?"

"I have to go," Anna said.

"Wait, there's something you should know," Mary Ellen said. "Marc called earlier. He told me that you'd had another accident and were in the hospital in some town in the Cascades. He's driving up there, Anna."

"Why?" The word came out as a cry. Marc was the very last person on earth she wanted to see.

"He said that when he went by the house to see if you had returned, he realized that your gun, the one he made you buy when he moved out, is missing."

Anna hung up and squeezed her eyes closed, trying to shut out the pain. Her gun was missing? At least according to Marc. That was the least of her worries right now, though. All she could think about was Gillian and Marc. An affair. It couldn't be true. Not Gillian. Not her best friend in the world.

And now Marc was on his way to Shadow Lake? Might already be in town? She tried to imagine how things could get worse. Maybe they already had, since she had no idea where that stupid gun was. She'd put it in the drawer beside her bed as Marc had insisted and hadn't seen it since.

She looked again at Tyler's name printed so neatly next to Luke 2:12. She had to be right about this. Gillian had learned something about Tyler's death.

One thing was clear: Anna could no longer lie here and

wait for the other shoe to drop. Throwing back the covers, she swung her legs over the side of the bed. The movement sent a wave of nausea over her. She gripped the bed for a moment until it passed, then tore the IV from her arm, stood and padded over to the closet.

She'd been doped up and drifting too long, unable to accept what had happened to her son, to her friendships, to her marriage. She couldn't keep hiding in a daze of drugs and regret. Her son was gone. Her husband had been in the process of divorcing her. And now this.

She had nothing more to lose.

Except her sanity.

And if she was right, she might find the person who'd killed her son and destroyed her life and finally learn whether she'd somehow been at fault.

At the closet, she gripped the door frame as a wave of dizziness washed over her. She felt weak and knew she would have to move fast. If she could just get out of here…

She opened the closet door.

Her clothes were gone.

CHAPTER NINE

POLICE CHIEF ROB NASH DIDN'T go straight to the police station, although Marc Collins was waiting for him. He needed time to pull himself together so he drove to the edge of town, pulled over to the side of the road where he'd heard the woman had gone off the road. He could understand better why Walker thought it had been a suicide attempt. It was nothing short of amazing that the woman had survived.

As the night grew darker he watched a breeze feather the water's silvery surface and rubbed his eyes, his body and mind beat, heartsick. He couldn't believe what he'd done. The first drops of rain pinged on the roof of the patrol car, startling him.

Even thinking about Lucinda and her betrayal couldn't kick up anything more than a dull ache now. But what he'd done to her was fresh in his mind. He'd turned into a monster and couldn't stand himself. He could still smell her scent on him. Had he really wanted to kill her?

What the hell was wrong with him? He loved her, no matter what she'd done, and now he'd hurt her in ways he didn't want to think about.

Rain drummed on the car roof as the storm picked up. The windows began to steam up. He kicked up the heat, chilled. He felt lost. He needed to go to the station. He couldn't keep running.

As he looked out at the lake, he remembered that Anna

Collins's car was still down there in the rain-dimpled lake. And now her husband was in town, waiting for him at the police station, saying it was urgent.

Nash swore as he started the patrol car. Best to get it over with. He called Walker. "This is your case," he said after he told him about Marc Collins's demand to see him tonight. "I want you there. I'm on my way now. Can you meet me at the station?"

"I'll be there."

Nash hung up. He was a cop, had been a cop most of his life. And as tired, physically, mentally and emotionally wrung out and disgusted with himself as he was, Nash was still the chief of police of Shadow Lake.

But as he turned the patrol car around, then drove down the mountain to park in front of police station, he had a bad feeling tonight he was going to wish he'd retired a long time ago.

The moment he shut off the patrol car, he saw a thirty-something man in an expensive suit pacing impatiently in the reception area. So this was Marc Collins.

He watched Marc Collins pace for a few moments more, wondering what was so urgent it couldn't wait until morning. Walker pulled in next to him as Nash shoved open his door and stepped out into the pouring rain.

Neither spoke as they entered the building.

Marc Collins stopped pacing and stepped to Nash, giving him a firm handshake and a smile that reminded him of a car salesman who hadn't met his monthly quota yet. What was Marc Collins selling? he wondered.

"I thought I'd better see what's happening with my wife before I go by the hospital," Collins said as he shook hands with Walker.

Nash nodded, thinking that a husband who was worried about his wife's welfare would have stopped by the hospital first—not the police station.

B.J. DANIELS 95

"This is my officer second-in-command D.C. Walker. He's handling the investigation of your wife's accident. Why don't the three of us step into my office."

Nash shook the rain from his coat and hat, then hung both up before lowering himself into the chair behind his desk. He motioned to the straight-backed chairs. Walker spun one around to straddle it. Marc Collins took the other one.

Nash glanced toward his office window. Rain ran down the glass, blurring the lights of the neighborhood outside. He couldn't remember the last time he'd seen such a dark night. He thought about Lucinda, but quickly pushed her from his mind.

"What can I do for you, Mr. Collins?"

Marc Collins pulled his chair closer to the desk and leaned forward, crossing his arms on the worn desktop. Then he seemed to change his mind and leaned back in his chair. He was nervous and Nash couldn't help but wonder why.

"I'm going to need a place to stay tonight. Could you recommend one?" Collins asked.

Was this what was so important that Collins had gotten him down here tonight? "You might try the Pinecrest Cabin Court. It's not open yet, but Herb will probably rent you a cabin if you stop by the place. Herb lives in the largest cabin to the east."

Collins nodded. He looked as if he wanted to make a crack about what a Podunk town Shadow Lake was, but changed his mind.

"Would you feel more comfortable if you had a lawyer present?" Walker asked, his impatience showing.

Collins looked shocked by the question. "Why would *I* need a lawyer?"

"Some people aren't comfortable talking to the police without one and the dispatcher said you'd mentioned a *gun?*" Walker said, cutting to the chase.

"Has my wife been charged with something?"

Another strange question, Nash thought. "Charged? Is there some reason she should be?"

Collins let out an embarrassed laugh. "Not that I know of. It's just that last night she was so upset, making threats, and then she ends up in the lake in a town I've never heard of. And when I check, I find that her gun is missing. Like I need this right now. I'm a Realtor and with house sales down—"

"What gun?" Walker asked.

"It's a Thirty-eight Special registered to my wife."

Nash made a note on the pad in front of him. "Why did your wife have a gun?"

"For protection. We've been separated, actually considering divorce. She's been a little…" Collins paused. "Paranoid."

"Why is that?" Walker asked.

"Your guess is as good as mine."

"Maybe she was afraid of living alone," Nash suggested.

"So did my wife tell you what's going on, why she's up here?" Collins asked.

"Didn't she tell you?" Walker asked.

"I haven't talked to her. But I thought you said on the phone that she's suffering from some memory loss. *Again.*" Collins snorted.

Nash was having trouble hiding his dislike for the man and he could see that Walker was even less enamored with the man. Marc Collins was an ass and the past twenty-four hours had been a bitch. He needed to get the man out of his office before either he or Walker said or did something they might regret.

He glanced at his watch, then at Collins. "Was there anything else you wanted to tell us?"

Collins shook his head, seeming surprised that Nash was cutting this short. "So…I'm free to take my wife home?"

"That would be up to her doctor."

"What about her car?" Collins asked.

"Still in the lake," Walker said. "We had trouble getting it out today. A larger tow truck is coming up in the morning."

Collins nodded and rose from his chair. "Well, then I guess I'll go by the hospital—"

"It's late, Mr. Collins, perhaps it would be better if you saw your wife tomorrow," Walker said.

Collins's look said he didn't like being told what to do.

"The doctor said she needed her rest. She's been through quite a lot recently," Walker said.

"Okay, I suppose it would be best then if I waited and saw her tomorrow. I guess I'll go talk to this Herb guy about a cabin then."

Nash didn't get up. "Good night, Mr. Collins."

Collins rose from his chair slowly, as if he wasn't satisfied. He left, pulling on his coat with jerky, angry movements as he pushed out the front door of the station and darted through the rain to his silver SUV parked out front.

Nash watched him, frowning. Why had Collins got him down here tonight? To tell him about a gun? It seemed odd given that no crime had been committed. Same with Collins asking if his wife had been charged with a crime.

"Lousy son of a bitch," Walker said. "He knows something."

Pushing back his chair, Nash scrubbed his hands over his face. His head hurt and his stomach was giving him hell. Nash knew he should go home. Just as he knew he wasn't going to.

He felt like a coward and a cad, but he couldn't face Lucinda right now. He needed to get some things right in his head before he saw her again.

"Sorry you got called down for this," Walker said.

Nash nodded and got to his feet. "It's late. We can talk tomorrow."

Walker had the good sense to leave. Nash waited until he saw him drive away before he closed the door, then turned to survey his office and the pile of paperwork on his desk. There was always paperwork, even in a low-crime town like Shadow Lake.

"Should have retired years ago," he muttered to himself as he moved past the desk to drop down on the old couch at the back. He couldn't remember ever being this drained. It was as if his life's blood had seeped out of him and he was nothing but a walking shell.

Flopping over, he stretched out on the couch and closed his eyes, praying for oblivion.

Instead, his mind refused to rest. The past forty-eight hours ran like a tape, making him hate himself more than he thought possible.

When he finally dozed off, it wasn't Lucinda he dreamed about. It was that trail of broken small trees that ended in the dark, deep lake and the feeling that something was very wrong. It didn't help that the woman's own husband suspected her. But of what? Maybe once the car was brought up out of the lake…

THE HOSPITAL WAS QUIET. Anna knew she couldn't wait any longer. She'd been afraid the doctor would come back to the hospital to check on her. Or the nurse.

She listened to make sure she couldn't hear anyone coming down the hall as she unhooked the IV and retrieved the money, credit card and scrap of envelope from where she'd hidden them earlier in her nightstand. She felt a little guilty for her deception, especially when she thought about Dr. Brubaker. He'd taken up for her, protecting her as best he could from the cop.

But Anna feared not even the doctor could protect her much longer. Officer Walker seemed determined to lock her up for something. And given time, she feared he would find just what he was searching for.

She had to get answers and there was only one place she knew to go for them—the Fairbankses'.

The problem, of course, was clothing other than her hospital gown. Maybe even a larger concern was the fact that she was still weak and light-headed. First the coma, then she hadn't taken care of herself for the past two months—even before she'd gone into the lake and nearly drowned.

But she wasn't about to let any of that stop her. For months, she'd done nothing but cry and take pills that left her in a fog but still in pain. Now she had hope that Gillian had found out something about the hit-and-run driver and that had led her to the Fairbanks family.

Anna tried not to think about what Mary Ellen had told her about Marc and Gillian. She didn't want to believe it. And yet she feared it was true. If so, then it had been a moment of weakness for Gillian, who Anna knew would do everything in her power to make amends. And what better way than coming up with news about Tyler's killer?

Earlier Anna had noticed that not only was she on the ground floor, but also that the window opened out. She hurried to it now, opened it quietly, then took out the screen and set it aside.

After that light exertion she had to lean on the wall for a moment before she hoisted herself up on the windowsill, then swung her legs over to drop to the ground. She hit with a thud, losing her balance and pitching forward into the wet grass.

The air felt damp and the wet grass was cold beneath her bare skin. She glanced toward the lake fringed in black pines, then hurriedly turned away from it and the memory as she crept along the side of the building.

From what she'd gathered, there were no other patients in the hospital, but there was a rest home attached to it on the other side. She ducked under windows although none of the rooms in this section appeared to be occupied. She could hear the occasional sound of traffic.

She passed an open door and caught a scent she recognized. Stopping, she backtracked a few feet to the door she'd just hurried past moments before and took a whiff, filling her lungs with the warm familiar smell of fresh laundry. Warm clothes straight from the dryer sounded heavenly and the room appeared to be empty.

She stepped in, angling toward the welcoming drone of a large clothes dryer. From the looks of the clothes circling in the dryer, they appeared to have come from the attached nursing home.

She checked the hall through the window in the laundry-room door, then hurried over to the dryer again, opened it and waited as the drum rolled to a stop.

Quickly she dug through the assortment of clothing, looking for anything that would fit and be warm. She was freezing.

She found a teal velour sweat suit that was colorful enough it was easy to find both the top and bottoms, then plucked two socks from the dryer, not taking the time to find a pair that matched, and closed the dryer door to get it going again, afraid the quiet would bring an attendant.

She pulled on the sweatpants, tucked the hospital gown in and slipped her arms into the long-sleeved matching jacket, zipping it up to her neck.

On a bench in a corner, she tugged the socks over her cold feet and eyed a set of metal lockers. One door was partially open and she could see a pair of cross-trainers inside, along with a nurse's uniform.

The shoes were a little too large. Back at the dryer she found another couple of socks, put those on, then the sneakers.

The whole process had taken only a few minutes, but she was shaking with fatigue and fear of being caught as she slipped back out into the night. She told herself what she was doing just proved she was crazy. Why not wait until morning, check herself out of the hospital and go then?

Every instinct in her told her that by morning it would be too late. Even if Dr. Brubaker released her, she wasn't so sure Officer Walker was going to let her go anywhere.

Lights glittered in the distance. She could make out buildings through the trees. She stayed to the shadows, working her way toward the center of what she quickly saw was a small tourist-oriented town with ice cream, candy, fishing and antique shops—now all boarded up.

The cop was right about one thing. Not much was open. Most businesses had Closed For The Season signs in their windows.

As she skirted the main street, she saw few cars and even fewer businesses with lights on.

She was thankful for that. She could make her way to the marina without attracting any unwanted attention. She angled along the waterfront, knowing she would eventually find the marina—and a boat.

A car drove past. She put the hood of the sweatshirt up and kept her head down. The marina wasn't far from the hospital, but by the time she reached it, her legs were shaking from fatigue and her head ached.

As she expected, the marina was closed, if not because of it being off-season then the hour. She walked along the side of the building, a little shocked at what she planned to do.

She knew something about boats from growing up on a lake in Seattle. She could start an outboard and had no doubt she could drive most boats. But stealing a boat? Then again, at this point, she feared theft was the least of her problems.

As she looked out in the lake, she could see a faint light. Was that the island where the Fairbankses lived? She could only hope, because now that she was here she was beginning to see how foolish her impulsiveness had been.

But she couldn't turn back. Whatever fears had motivated

her to leave the hospital tonight were still driving her. That and hope. If this had anything to do with Tyler…

Several boats were moored at the dock next to the floating small marina building. A couple of smaller fishing boats and one ski boat sat under a large overhead light that cast the entire area in a circle of gold.

She moved down the dock and knelt to peer in at the ski boat. Just as she'd figured, from the size of the town and the fact that it was off-season, the key was in the ignition. It would be faster than the smaller fishing boats.

"Can I help you?"

She jumped at the sound of a voice behind her.

"Didn't mean to scare you." He was young, just a kid she saw when she turned around. He smiled at her as he wiped his hands on a rag and came farther down the deck toward her.

Behind him, the door to the marina office was open. She could see an outboard motor, the cover off and an assortment of tools spread around it.

"Hi," she said, straightening, doing her best to hide her earlier intention of stealing one of the boats. "I need to rent a boat. I know it's late."

He chuckled as if agreeing with the obvious. "Pretty dark to be going out." He glanced past her. "Especially alone. You know the lake?"

She managed a smile and avoided his question as best she could. "I'm trying to get out to the Fairbankses'. I understand the only way is by boat."

"Or helicopter." He eyed her more closely. "If you call them, I'm sure they'll send one or the other for you."

She wasn't so sure about that and not willing to take the chance. She had to do this in person and the best way was to just show up on their doorstep and wing it from there.

"I wasn't sure what time I'd be getting here so I told them

I'd just rent a boat and come out. I didn't realize it would be so late. I feel just awful. I promised I'd be there by dinner-time and now I'm going to have to call and interrupt their meal to have someone come get me."

He blinked. "They eat this late at night?"

She shrugged. "I guess they were trying to accommodate me. You see why I don't want to inconvenience them further."

He nodded, still eyeing her. "You ever run a boat?"

"I grew up on the water."

"You know how to get out to the island in the dark?"

She didn't even know how to get there in the daylight. "Is there more than one island?"

He grinned, then slowly stuffed the greasy rag into the hip pocket of his jeans. "I can run you out." He glanced back at the boat motor he'd been working on. "Let me close up."

"I'll pay you, of course."

"You can settle up with Harry tomorrow." He pointed toward the ski boat tied up to the dock. "Hop in that one. I'll just be a minute."

As she climbed into the boat, she glanced back toward the highway, half-afraid Officer Walker would catch her and demand to know what she was doing before she could get away. She reminded herself that she wasn't under arrest. Yet. But why did she fear she would be soon?

To her relief she saw no one pulling into the marina as she slumped into a seat, her legs like water. She couldn't re-member ever being this exhausted. Her whole body trembled as if plagued with some kind of nerve disease.

"Cold?" the young man asked as he climbed behind the wheel. "Sit up here. It's a little warmer out on the water." He pointed to the seat across from him and directly behind the boat's windshield.

She moved, stumbling a little. "Thank you," she said, smil-ing at him. "I really do appreciate this."

He looked embarrassed as he started the motor and pulled away from the dock.

She hoped she didn't get him into trouble. Just as she hoped someone would be home at the Fairbankses' house. If they weren't, she would wait for them to return. She refused to believe this was a wild-goose chase or that her actions were anything but rational and necessary.

Her greatest fear as the boat took off across the water and the lights of Shadow Lake, Washington, dimmed behind them was that the Fairbankses would have never heard of Gillian or have any idea what Anna was talking about.

"YOU CAN SIT UP NOW, Mrs. Nash," Dr. Brubaker said as he finished his examination.

"The baby?" Lucinda asked, sounding close to tears again.

"Everything looks fine." He gave her a reassuring smile. "Why don't you put your clothes on and then we can talk."

She looked startled and suddenly afraid again.

"Talk about prenatal vitamins, checkups, nutrition, exercise," he said quickly.

She seemed to relax a little, nodded and tucked the gown around her.

He smiled again, hoping to reassure her, and stepped from the room, his smile instantly fading the moment he closed the door behind him.

"Is everything all right?" Elle asked.

He hadn't even noticed the nurse come down the hall toward him with a box of unopened supplies. He instantly changed his expression. "Fine. No problem."

Elle didn't look convinced but nodded, glanced toward the closed door, then headed on down the hallway to the supply closet.

Doc waited then tapped softly on the door.

"Okay," Lucinda said from inside the room.

He opened the door, checking his expression before stepping in and motioning for her to have a seat. He drew up a chair and sat across from her.

She looked at him wide-eyed, her hands clasped in her lap, white-knuckled. "You're sure my baby's all right?"

He nodded, studying her. She was slim and blond, her eyes a clear blue fringed with dark lashes. Not a natural blonde. But that was no secret. He could see in her face and in those eyes that she'd had a hard life before ending up in Shadow Lake married to the chief of police, a man a good twenty-five years her senior.

"Is everything all right at home?" Doc asked.

"Yes," she said nervously.

"I would suggest you stay off your feet as much as you can over the next few days," he said. "The spotting has stopped. The baby's heartbeat sounds fine. But you need to take care of yourself, for your baby's sake."

Her eyes widened in alarm. "You said the baby was all right."

"We want the baby to stay that way. You need to eat properly. It is better to put on more weight than not enough. From what I can tell, you are about *three* months along. Let's make sure the baby's getting enough to eat, okay?"

She nodded and ducked her head, but not before he'd seen the tears.

"Also for the baby's health, you need to provide a healthy environment. That means a healthy environment for the mother-to-be." He reached over and covered her hands with one of his own. She looked up. "While there is nothing wrong with having intercourse, you do need to be careful. Your husband has to understand that he has to be more…gentle, okay?"

Her face flamed. She looked away. "He didn't mean to hurt me." Tears blurred the blue.

Brubaker took a guess. "Does he know about the baby?"

She blinked and pulled her hands free to wipe at her tears. "I haven't told him yet."

Doc leaned back, took a breath and asked, "Is there a reason you haven't told your husband about the baby?"

She bit her lower lip and shook her head. "I just haven't."

He sighed. "Lucinda—"

"I'm going to tell him," she blurted out. "I was just waiting for the right time."

"Are you worried he won't be happy about the baby?"

She nodded and rose as if to leave. "I know what you're thinking, but it *is* his baby. It was before we were married. We didn't use protection the first time when we…" She ducked her head, her hair falling around her face.

"I'm only asking these questions because I'm worried about you and your baby," he said. "Lucinda, whatever is wrong needs to be resolved if you hope to carry this baby to term."

She looked stricken. "I want this baby. More than anything in the world."

"Then I suggest you tell your husband." He began to write out a prescription for vitamins. "I want to see you again in a few days. In the meantime, stay off your feet and if spotting starts again, call me immediately." He stood, handed her the prescription and moved aside so she could leave. "One more thing." She stopped, her hand on the doorknob. "I'm here if you need to talk. Whatever is said will never leave this room."

She gave a nod and was gone.

He stood in the examining room looking after her, worried. It still surprised him the secrets people kept from those they loved. He thought of Anna Collins. Another woman with secrets.

Sighing, he decided there was nothing more he could do for Lucinda tonight. But while he was at the hospital he might as well check on Anna.

He walked down the hall and quietly pushed open her door. Her bed was empty. His gaze went from the disconnected IV to the window. Even before he looked out and saw her tracks in the soft, wet earth, he knew Anna Collins was gone.

ANNA LOOKED BACK AS THE lights of the small tourist town disappeared. The boat rounded a rocky bar of shoreline leaving a wide wake and she saw a few isolated lights blinking in the distance. The night was dark, a crisp chill in the air as the boat sped across the water. She wished she had a coat and wondered how much farther it was.

She'd had no idea that the lake was this large and quickly realized she would never have found the island on her own. As she watched the lake ahead, she tried not to consider the possibility that no one would be home, that this was for nothing.

After a few more turns, the boat slowed, and in the distance Anna could see faint lights flickering in and out. As the boat approached the island, the lights grew brighter, the pines along the shore melting back into the darkness to expose a monstrous house set against a backdrop of granite cliffs.

Her boat captain cut the engine. She heard the lap of water as the boat's waves overtook the dock, then the shoreline. Anna winced as the boat connected with a jolt and loud thud against the edge of the dock. She'd been staring at the house, at the dark stone thick with moss illuminated by a row of exterior lights. Only a little light bled from the edges of the thickly draped windows.

The young man caught the dock, steadying the boat as she stood and feebly climbed out, feeling drained from the cold and the trip across the lake.

"Are you all right?" he asked.

"I'm sorry, I didn't even ask your name," she said.

"Eric."

She smiled at him. "Thank you, Eric." She tried to give him

one of the twenties she'd found in her coat pocket, but he waved it away.

"I can wait if you want," he said. "I don't see anyone around."

He'd expected someone to meet her at the dock. She wondered if anyone in the house had heard the boat approach? She'd thought she saw someone watching them from a crack in the drapes upstairs, but she didn't trust her eyes any more than she did her judgment at this point.

"I'll be fine. Thanks for the ride out." If she had no way to return and someone was home, the Fairbankses would have to talk to her, wouldn't they?

"If you're sure." The dock light shone on his young innocent face. She couldn't help but think about Tyler and what he would have looked like at this age. The thought nearly leveled her.

"I'm sure." Weak and feeling more vulnerable than she'd ever remembered, she pushed off the boat with what little strength she had left. The motor roared to life and the young man turned the boat and headed back toward town.

She waited until the boat's lights disappeared behind a rocky outcropping, the sound of the motor dying off in the night. For a moment, she considered sitting down on the dock and resting for a few minutes before walking up to the house. But she was too cold and what she had to do couldn't wait. That sense of urgency still burned inside her. Madness? Or intuition?

She turned slowly, her body aching, and headed up what felt like a long walk to the house.

By the time she reached the Fairbankses' front door, Anna was sweating and having a hard time catching her breath. She leaned against the wall next to the door for support, dizzy and feeling faint. The air had gotten colder. She was shaking, burning up and chilled at the same time.

She rang the bell beside the door and waited. She had decided that if no one was home she would wait until they returned. What she hadn't considered was the cold night or her weakened condition. Letting Eric leave with the boat had been a mistake.

She rang the bell again, aware that she desperately needed to get in out of the damp cold and sit down. Someone had to be home. She didn't have a cell phone or any way to call for help. Too late she realized she had jumped from the frying pan into the fire.

When the door opened, Anna almost wept with relief.

"Yes?" asked a woman in a uniform. She was blocking the doorway, looking half afraid.

"I'm here to see…" Who? "Mrs. Fairbanks." Anna heard her voice break. She leaned a hand against the doorjamb. "Please, I need to sit down. Would you tell Mrs. Fairbanks I'm here."

"I'm sorry, Mrs. Fairbanks has retired for the night."

Anna hated the pleading she heard in her voice. "It's urgent that I speak with her."

She must have sounded like a lunatic—not to mention what she must have looked like after what she'd been through—because the maid was shaking her head and closing the door.

Anna put her hand against the door, but she didn't have the strength to force her way in. Past the maid, she caught a glimpse of a huge oil painting of a man.

She let out a startled cry. "Oh, my God. That's him. That's the man from the lake." She felt her legs give way under her, felt herself falling toward the darkness even before her body hit the porch floor.

CHAPTER TEN

ANNA WOKE WITH A START. She was lying on a strange couch in an ornate sitting room, a fire burning in a fireplace next to her. And for a moment, she had no idea where she was.

A stern-looking gray-haired woman sat in a chair across from her, her pale smoky-gray eyes fixed on Anna's face.

The eyes. Anna recognized the eyes and sat up. For a moment, she thought she would pass out again. Her skin was burning up and yet she felt chilled even with the fire next to her.

"Who are you?" The woman's voice was fierce.

Anna leaned back into the soft cushions of the couch although it took every ounce of her strength not to lie back down again and close her eyes. She felt sick and confused. And afraid. Not of the woman, but of the fear that this woman was going to tell her she'd made a terrible mistake. Not just in coming here, but in thinking the Fairbankses knew anything about Tyler's death.

She remembered the painting. It was the man she's seen last night in the lake. The man she believed saved her life. She hadn't been wrong to come here.

"Are you Mrs. Fairbanks?"

"I'm Ruth Fairbanks. This is my home. I asked who *you* are."

"Anna Collins." She thought the woman reacted to her name, that it had meant something to her. "Do you know me?"

The woman's lips pursed in anger. "If I knew you, I wouldn't have had to ask who you were."

Maybe she'd been wrong. "But you've heard my name before?"

The older woman shook her head in obvious frustration. "My maid said that, before you fainted on my doorstep, you said something about seeing someone in the lake?"

"The painting on the wall. That's the man I saw last night. I could never forget his eyes. They were the same color as yours. I saw him in the lake."

The woman blanched. *"What?"*

"He saved my life when my car went into the lake," Anna said quickly.

The woman looked frightened. "What kind of foolishness is this?"

In her fevered state, Anna felt even more confused. Something about the painting nagged at her, but her head ached too badly to recall what it was right now. Just holding up her head was taking all of her effort.

"Who is the man in the painting?" she asked, fearing it depicted a younger version of the woman's dead husband, which would explain Ruth Fairbanks's reaction.

"My son." Her face flushed. "But he most certainly did not save your life last night in the lake. I demand to know what it is you want."

Anna reached into her pocket. The woman flinched and drew back. "It's just a note." She retrieved the scrap of envelope and held it out to the older woman. "I think I was supposed to meet your son last night at the rest stop on the edge of Shadow Lake."

"That's preposterous," Ruth said, not taking the note.

"He must have seen my car go into the lake," Anna continued, as if the woman hadn't spoken. "He saved my life."

"I've heard enough." Ruth Fairbanks struggled to her feet. She was trembling with apparent rage.

"Please. I recognized him from the painting. Please—can't

you just ask your son? He either knows me or my friend, Gillian Sanders. She's an attorney in Seattle."

The woman looked livid. "*Why* would you make up such a story?" She snatched the piece of envelope from Anna's fingers. "Why it's barely legible."

"It was in my coat pocket underwater. The ink has run, but you can make out the name *Fairbanks,* along with *Rest Stop, Hwy 20 EAST* and *Shadow Lake.* The numbers at the top are the rest-stop pay phone. I think either I or my friend was meeting your son at the rest stop last night close to midnight."

"My son wouldn't have met anyone at a rest stop in the middle of the night."

"But he must have, don't you see, because that is the only way he could have seen my car go into the lake. He has to be the same man Gillian planned to meet at the rest stop. So please, just let me talk to him. I know he can clear this up. He's definitely the man in the portrait over your fireplace except…"

Ruth's voice was a whisper. "Except what?"

Anna wasn't so sure for the first time. "Maybe it had been just an optical illusion in the water and the way the light caught his face in the water, but I thought he had a scar." She moved her hand diagonally across her face in the pattern of the scar.

The older woman's face drained of blood. She staggered as if she might fall. Anna reached for her, but Ruth Fairbanks was much stronger than she looked. She shook off Anna's aid and righted herself by resting a hand on the end table beside the couch. A framed photograph toppled over.

Anna caught it before the photo hit the floor and froze as she stared down into two sets of the unusual pale smoky-gray eyes. "You have *two* sons?"

Ruth lowered herself back into her chair.

"Who is this?" Anna asked, pointing at one of the teens in the photograph.

"Jack," Ruth Fairbanks said in a whisper.

"That's his portrait over the fireplace."

The older woman nodded.

"He's the one I saw last night in the lake. I would stake my life on it."

"Then that would be a terrible mistake on your part," Ruth said. "Give me that," she snapped, thrusting out her hand for the framed photograph.

Anna ignored her. "This is the man who saved my life."

Ruth Fairbanks held out her hand, her voice breaking with obvious emotion as she said, "Please give me the photograph."

Anna handed it over and watched the woman look down at her sons. She traced each boy's face. "Jonathan is the oldest. Jack…Jack was two years younger." Her hand trembled as she put the photograph on the end table next to her chair.

Anna caught her breath as the word registered. *"Was?"*

"My son Jack is dead."

Anna felt as if the floor had dropped out from under her.

"So, as I said, you couldn't possibly have seen Jack last night," Ruth said, an edge to her voice.

"Mrs. Fairbanks, I'm so sorry. I lost my own son, so I know—"

"You know nothing." The words were like thrown stones. "How dare you come here accusing my son—"

"One of your sons *saved* my life. If it wasn't Jack, then it must have been his brother."

"Stop it," the older woman snapped. "Neither Jack nor Jonathan saved your life last night in the lake." The scrap of envelope fluttered from her lap to land on the floor under her chair.

"What on earth is going on in here?" demanded a male voice.

Anna swung her head around as the door to the room banged open and she saw the man framed in the doorway.

In an instant, she realized that this man had to be Jonathan, and Ruth Fairbanks was right.

His dark hair was cut shorter than the man's last night. And while tall and broad shouldered with the same smoky-gray eyes, she saw, as he moved, that this man couldn't possibly have been the one who saved her life last night in the lake.

"Jonathan, I'm handling this," Ruth Fairbanks said, bringing herself up to her full height as she stood to face her son.

"You let a complete stranger into our home? You call that handling this?" he demanded.

Anna felt herself sink deeper into the couch as Jonathan Fairbanks came toward her. He moved in a shuffling gait, dragging the left side of his body and leaning heavily on a thick cane.

"I've called the police," he said, looking at Anna as if she were a bug that had gotten into the house.

"Please, if you could just hear me out," Anna said. "I came here to talk to you about a hit-and-run accident that one of you might have witnessed." She rushed on. "A Gillian Sanders—I believe contacted you about—"

"What is she talking about?" Ruth Fairbanks demanded of her son.

"I have no idea, Mother. Clearly, the woman is delusional."

Delusional. The same word Marc had used to describe her.

Anna felt the last of her hope slip through her fingers. "I was so sure Gillian had contacted you." She recalled that the nurse had said that Senator Fairbanks had a daughter-in-law. "Perhaps your wife," she said to Jonathan.

She saw him blanch and then redden.

His face twisted into a sneer. "Another example of just how ill informed you are. Patricia is my brother's widow."

"I'm sorry." Anna knew the police would be here soon. "If you could just ask her—"

"Ask me what?"

They all turned toward the door. A striking woman with long red hair stood in the doorway. She had the look of a woman who'd become quite comfortable with wealth. She cocked her head at Anna, curiosity in her blue eyes, as she stepped into the room.

"Having a party without me?" she asked.

Ruth Fairbanks made a disgruntled sound. "Really, Pet."

"I was asking if you had been contacted by Gillian Sanders about a hit-and-run accident—"

"Gillian Sanders." Patricia "Pet" Fairbanks seemed to savor the name for a few minutes as if it sounded familiar.

Anna saw her gaze go to her brother-in-law's as she repeated the name.

"Clearly, we have never heard of you or your friend," Jonathan snapped, glaring down at Anna. "I don't know what you think you're doing coming here upsetting my household, but it was a mistake."

Anna could see that, but still she waited for Pet's answer.

"Sorry," Pet said with a shrug after a few moments. "Doesn't ring any bells."

Jonathan let out an exasperated sigh. "The police should be here at any minute. Pet, if you would please take Mother up to her room."

Plainly that was the last thing Pet wanted to do.

"Now—before the police arrive," Jonathan Fairbanks said through gritted teeth.

Pet did not look happy about it but, with a sigh and shake of her head, walked over to Ruth's chair and took the older woman's arm.

Ruth Fairbanks, to Anna's surprise, shook it off. "I want to know why you said you saw Jack in the lake. That he saved your life. That he had a scar…" Ruth began to cry.

"You saw Jack?" Pet asked. She'd gone deathly pale.

Jonathan Fairbanks swore under his breath. "Mother, go with Pet and let me handle this." He gave his sister-in-law a hard look. "Make sure she takes one of her pills."

"I didn't mean to upset your mother or your sister-in-law," Anna said, her voice small and weak as she watched Pet steer the elderly Mrs. Fairbanks from the room.

"The hell you didn't," Jonathan said, the moment the two women were gone. His face filled with rage as he shuffled closer, towering over her again. "You didn't realize that coming here and telling my mother that you saw her dead son in the lake was going to upset her?"

"I didn't know—"

"How could you not know? He was the son of a senator. Don't you read the papers, watch the news?"

She bit down on the reply that came to her lips. She'd either still been in a coma or just out of it when Jack Fairbanks had died. Not that she had paid any attention to the news in the weeks after she'd awakened to find out that Tyler, her precious son, was dead.

Anna knew he thought her delusional. That, at least, she couldn't argue, because she would still have sworn that the man she'd seen at the bottom of the lake was Jack Fairbanks. Or at least someone who looked enough like him to be his brother.

As if reading her thoughts, Jonathan Fairbanks said, "My brother didn't save your life last night and I certainly didn't, either." In a swift, angry movement, he drew up his pant leg to expose an artificial leg. "Are you quite through now?" he demanded.

Anna heard the doorbell. She coughed, her body aching. "I'm sorry. You're right. I shouldn't have come here."

"Damn right," Jonathan Fairbanks muttered.

Anna only wanted to close her eyes and sleep. She'd accomplished nothing by coming here. Instead, she'd managed to make things worse for herself.

There were no answers here, only more questions.

She looked toward the chair where the piece of envelope had fallen. It was gone. Ruth Fairbanks must have taken it with her.

"If you ever come back here, I'll have you arrested for trespassing, do you understand?"

She understood, but there was nothing else to say even if she'd had the energy to form the words. She heard footfalls headed in her direction and wasn't surprised when Officer D.C. Walker appeared in the open doorway.

CHAPTER ELEVEN

J‌ONATHAN F‌AIRBANKS L‌EANED on his cane as the cop entered the room, followed by Dr. Brubaker. "Get her out of here."

"No problem," Walker said. He shot Anna a look, fury in his expression. "Let's go, Mrs. Collins."

Dr. Brubaker hurried to her side as she tried to get to her feet, his brows quickly furrowing in concern as he touched her forehead. "Help me lift her to her feet," he said to Walker. "She's burning up. We need to get her back to the hospital."

"You know this woman?" Jonathan Fairbanks demanded, stepping between the police officer and Anna.

"Step aside," Walker ordered, his voice low and hard as the marble floor in the entryway.

For a moment, Fairbanks didn't move. Anna saw the police officer's hand go to the butt end of his weapon. Just a brief flutter of a touch, before Jonathan Fairbanks slowly limped to one side, both men glaring at each other.

"This woman almost drowned last night after her car crashed into the lake," the doctor said, stepping between the two men. "She needs to be in the hospital."

"Did you send her out here, Walker?" Jonathan demanded. "If I find out you're behind this—"

"I don't know what the hell you're talking about," Walker snapped as he swept Anna up into his arms. "Now get out of the way and let us get her back to the hospital."

Jonathan Fairbanks backed off and Walker carried her out

of the room. He didn't look at her and she could feel waves of anger coming off him. She'd seen the animosity between him and Jonathan Fairbanks, although she couldn't understand it. Nor did she have the energy to try.

As they passed through the house, Anna saw another photograph of the Fairbanks brothers. It had been taken when the boys were very young. They were smiling at the camera. They could have been twins, they looked that much alike.

"I don't want to see that woman again!" Jonathan shouted after them.

Walker had reached the front entry. Dr. Brubaker caught up to them and opened the door. As they hustled out, Anna caught a glimpse of Jonathan Fairbanks. She was certain it was fear she saw in his eyes that instant before the door closed behind them.

"You're damned lucky he isn't pressing charges," Walker said as he carried her toward the dock where a boat was waiting.

Anna closed her eyes, her teeth chattering.

"In fact, I'm surprised he isn't," Walker said. They had reached the boat and he glanced back at the house.

"Here, wrap her in the blankets I brought," Dr. Brubaker said, and Anna felt herself lowered into the boat.

She snuggled into the warmth of the blanket as she felt the soft rock of the boat.

RUTH FAIRBANKS STOOD AT her window watching the boat leave until the lights disappeared into the fog.

She hadn't taken her pill as Jonathan had suggested. Suggested? Ordered. He'd been doing a lot of ordering since his father died.

"How are you feeling?"

She turned to find her daughter-in-law standing in the doorway. Ruth thought she'd locked her door. Was it possible Pet had a key? The thought chilled her.

"I'm fine," she said. What had Jack been thinking marrying

such a woman? A moment of weakness, isn't that what he'd
called it? The divorce would have gone through by now if
Jack had lived and Ruth would have been shed of "Pet."

"Jonathan asked me to check on you," she said, making it
perfectly clear no love was lost between them. As if Ruth had
ever doubted it. "I didn't mean to *disturb* you."

Ruth heard the alcohol-laced sarcasm in her daughter-in-
law's voice. If she'd had her way, Pet would have been thrown
out of the house right after Jack's funeral. It was Jonathan
who'd said they couldn't put her out on the street.

What Jonathan meant was that getting rid of Pet was more
expensive than letting her stay. Pet liked being the daughter-
in-law of a senator, even a dead one, and living in big houses.
With Jack dead and the divorce in legal limbo, Pet was in a
position, according to Jonathan, to go after even more of the
Fairbankses' assets. Not to mention, Jonathan also pointed
out, what she might say about her marriage to Jack, no doubt
something the press would have a field day with.

Ruth had still wanted to cut the bitch a check and send
her packing.

"Let's at least wait until Dad's estate is settled," Jonathan
had said. "I fear you aren't thinking clearly, Mother. Not surprising since you've just lost the two most important men in
your life this year."

He was referring to her husband Big Jim and her favorite
son, Jack.

Jack *had* been her favorite of the two boys. Jonathan had
always been so hard to love. Was still so hard to love. If
anyone was to blame for the way things had turned out
though, she knew it was her.

"Jonathan wanted me to make sure you took your pill," Pet
said from behind her.

Ruth had completely forgotten the tramp was still in the
room. It angered her that Jonathan now had Pet keeping tabs

on her. Worse, that Jonathan had called her doctor and gotten her a little something for her "nerves." As if she didn't know what the sedatives were for. "Mother" was a lot less trouble when she was knocked out or too drugged to think.

It was bad enough having Pet wandering around the house on alcohol and whatever she could get her hands on. As if Ruth hadn't noticed the difference in her after one of her little shopping trips to Seattle.

"What should I tell him?" Pet persisted.

As Ruth turned, she picked up a small vase from a table by the window. "Tell him this." She hurled the vase at the bane of her existence.

She'd give Pet credit—the woman was fast on her feet, even half-sloshed and overdrugged. The vase whizzed past to shatter on the far wall of the room.

Pet turned slowly to look at the mess, then back at Ruth. She smiled. "I guess that's a no." She quirked a brow. "Shall I send one of the maids to clean it up? Or maybe you aren't through yet."

Ruth snatched up the figurine that had been next to the vase but, by the time she turned around, Pet was gone.

Her anger and strength left just as quickly. She staggered to the door, closing and locking it. Tomorrow, she would get a new lock on her bedroom door and make sure no one else had a key. She would throw away those damned pills. She would…

Her face suddenly crumpled with grief. She stumbled over to the window and looked out. The lake was dark, cloaked in thick fog. She could barely make out the light down at the dock now. Sometimes the fog was suffocating. As if she was drowning.

Ruth closed her eyes, squeezing them shut. Anna Collins. Had the name sounded familiar? She couldn't be sure. Had Big Jim mentioned the woman on one of his good days before he died? She shook her head, looking again out at the lake.

Jonathan was right about one thing—she seemed to be losing her memory. Not like Big Jim had. In the end, he wouldn't have been able to remember how to sit or lie down. Fortunately, a stroke had taken him before the Alzheimer's had.

Ruth shuddered, hugging herself. Still, she had no problem remembering how her husband had often not made any sense when he talked.

She didn't want to think about Big Jim, but how could she not think about Jack after that woman's visit?

A sob escaped Ruth's lips. She clamped them shut, covering her mouth with her hand. She shouldn't have stayed here at the lake house. She should have gone back to Virginia to the house there. But Jonathan spent most of his time there when he wasn't in Washington, D.C., following in his father's footsteps. She was better off here.

She touched the window glass. Here, she felt closer to Jack. Both he and Big Jim were buried here. Jim had bought the island, built her this huge, beautiful house and brought her back here as his young bride. She'd lived the life of a princess, blessed with two sons and a powerful political husband who'd provided her with luxuries as well as influence. She was envied and reviled and she'd loved it that way, she thought with a rueful smile.

But now Big Jim was gone and Jonathan had aspirations that far exceeded his father's. If Jonathan had his way, he'd be more than a senator from the state of Washington: he'd live one day in the White House.

Jack couldn't have cared less about any of that. He found politics boring and acquiring wealth just as dull. But Jonathan… She'd seen the way he'd picked up where Big Jim had left off, cultivating the contacts he would need. Ruth wondered how much of it was to show Big Jim, even in his grave, that Jonathan was the better son. All she knew was that she pitied anyone who got in Jonathan's way.

Reaching into her pocket, Ruth took out the scrap of paper the Collins woman had shown her. The writing on it was nearly illegible. She turned it over in her fingers and saw the return address. Gillian Sanders, attorney-at-law, Seattle.

Anna Collins had been disappointed when no one here at the house had heard from this Gillian Sanders or about a hit-and-run accident.

Ruth shook her head. The woman obviously was misinformed along with being—what had Jonathan called her? *Delusional.*

If Ruth strained she could almost make out the words. Would Jonathan have any reason to meet with the attorney? But even if it were true, he certainly wouldn't meet her at a rest stop on the edge of town at night. Unless... She stared down at the note. Unless he hadn't wanted anyone to know.

She heard the elevator. Jonathan. Hurriedly she shoved the note back into her pocket. "Yes?" she said to the light tap at her door.

"If you have a moment, Mother."

Jonathan was the last person she wished to talk to right now, but she walked to the door, unlocked it and said, "Come in, Jonathan."

He frowned. "Locking your door, Mother? Really."

He stepped in, looking around as if he hadn't expected to find her alone.

"If you're looking for Pet, I sent her away."

He frowned at the broken vase on the floor. "Can't you show her just a little kindness, Mother?" He sounded weary.

"It's late, Jonathan. You wanted something?" She regretted her words, as well as her impatience with her elder son, worse her inability to love him the way she had Jack.

His expression hardened. "I want to know about that woman. What did she say to you?"

"The same thing she said to you and Pet. She thought her

friend had contacted us about a hit-and-run accident. As you said, she was mistaken."

"You said she told you she'd seen Jack at the bottom of the lake," he reminded her.

Ruth waved a hand. "Dr. Brubaker told you. She was sick, burning up with a fever. Anyone could see that she was delirious."

He eyed her suspiciously. "Then you aren't upset?"

She raised her chin, her gaze locking with her son's. Lying came so easily. Especially to Jonathan. "I haven't given it another thought since clearly her claim was ridiculous. We all know that Jack is dead."

Jonathan seemed to relax. "Well, if you hear from her or she tries to come back out here, I insist you call the police and have nothing more to do with her. I have to go back to Washington on business. I don't like leaving you and Pet here alone."

Ruth laughed. "We have live-in staff. We've never been alone here."

"You know what I mean," he pressed.

"We'll be fine."

"And please, try to be a little nicer to Pet. After all, she was Jack's wife."

"He would have been divorced from her if he'd lived another week."

"Well, he didn't, Mother." He limped more when he was upset. Or irritated.

She watched him move toward the door, irritated herself. Jonathan seemed to have forgotten that this was her house, that he was the guest, not her.

"I heard the boat go out late last night," she said, unable to just let him turn his back and leave yet.

Jonathan stopped, his back to her. "You're mistaken, Mother." He seemed to wait for her to argue the point, then continued toward the door, his injured gait even more pronounced. At the doorway, he hesitated. "What was that woman's name? I seem to have forgotten it."

"I'm sorry, I don't recall, either," she said, lying right along with him. She'd heard the boat go out last night and now she was positive her son had been on it. Was it possible Anna Collins had been telling the truth? At least the part about an appointment with a Fairbanks.

"Good night, Mother." He closed the door and she listened to him retreat down the hallway.

She waited until she was sure he was gone before she dug her cell phone from her pocket. She wasn't foolish enough to use the house phone, since she knew he would be expecting that.

While she waited for the line to ring, she picked up one of the many framed photographs she kept throughout the house. This one was of Jack and Jonathan when they were five and seven. They *did* look like twins, but were as different as night and day. Jonathan sullen and serious. Jack— Tears blurred her vision. She could remember Jack's laugh and how it used to fill this huge house like summer sunshine. The pain of loss was nothing like the pain of missing that laugh.

When the other end answered on the fourth ring, she said, "It's Ruth Fairbanks." Her hand shook as she put the photograph back on the stand beside her bed. "I need to know everything you can find out about a woman named Anna Collins and a lawyer named Gillian Sanders of Seattle. I need it right away and I don't want anyone else to know about this. *Especially* Jonathan. Oh, don't sound so shocked. I'm more than aware of the kind of services you provided my husband." Her smile was cold enough to chill the room. "That's what I thought."

Ruth gave him her cell-phone number, disconnected and dialed the police department, insisting that she needed to speak with Chief Robert Nash at once.

When he came on the line, he sounded half asleep.

"I need to talk to you. Not tonight," she added quickly before he could make an objection. "In the morning."

"What is this about?"

"Make it seven o'clock at the Lakeside Café."

"The Lakeside isn't open for the season yet."

She smiled. "It will be in the morning." She disconnected and called the café owner.

"WHY WOULD YOU DO SOMETHING like this?" Dr. Brubaker asked Anna, once he had her back in her hospital bed. He looked down at her, worry in his tired, old face. "You have pneumonia. I've put you on antibiotics, but I want you to understand, you are very sick and the only way you're going to get better is if you stay in this bed and try to get well."

"I had to find some answers. I was coming *back*." She had dropped off into a deep sleep on the boat ride, wrapped in the blankets he'd brought for her. She'd barely awakened for the short patrol-car ride back to the hospital.

But since being hooked up again to the IV, her fever had dropped a little and she felt better already.

"It's too much of a coincidence that I find a note with the name Fairbanks on it and what appeared to be an appointment with one of them and then I find out that the man I saw at the bottom of the lake was Jack Fairbanks," she said. "Or at least his ghost."

Doc nodded sadly.

"That's why Officer Walker was so upset. He knew the man I had described was Jack Fairbanks."

"Jack was Walker's best friend. The three of them grew up together—Jack, Walker and their friend Billy Blake. They were inseparable."

"I'm wondering now if his face is really scarred. Tonight I realized it could have been an optical illusion because of the water and light."

"You really need to quit worrying about this and take care of yourself. I suspect you haven't been eating or sleeping well since you came out of the coma."

"Not really," she admitted.

"Well, you will be able to get the rest you need now," he said.

She had expected Walker to grill her endlessly about why she'd taken off the way she had to the Fairbankses' island. To her surprise he'd completely backed off. She was pretty sure Dr. Brubaker was responsible for that. She reached for his large weathered hand and squeezed it.

"Thank you." She felt a surge of emotion toward him as he started to leave.

"Don't go yet," she said impulsively. "Would you stay just a little longer?"

He smiled. "If you promise to stay in this bed until you're well."

"I promise."

He took a chair next to her bed. "If you'd just have told me you wanted to go out to the island…"

"You would have taken me?" She saw the answer in his face. "Why is everyone so afraid of the Fairbankses?"

He laughed uncomfortably. "Big Jim was an icon. He's barely cold in the ground, the family is still in mourning and you go out there and upset the grand duchess Ruth Fairbanks? Not to mention her son, who some say has his eye on the presidency. He's probably on the phone right now with the governor asking for your head on a platter for upsetting his mother."

"He's really that well connected?"

Dr. Brubaker laughed. "More connected than the Pope. But don't tell anyone I said that." He smiled his grandfatherly smile. "You mentioned something about a note?"

She quickly explained about finding the scrap of paper in her coat pocket and how that had led her to the Fairbankses.

He frowned. "Can I see this note?"

"I don't have it anymore. I showed it to Ruth Fairbanks and she kept it." She saw his surprise. "I think she knows something. Or at least suspects what I told her might be true. I noticed that Jonathan and Walker don't seem to get along."

The elderly doctor smiled ruefully. "Jack and Jonathan, although they looked alike, were very different. Are you sure I can't call your husband for you?"

Anna could feel herself fading quickly, but she needed to explain about Marc. She didn't want Dr. Brubaker thinking badly of her. "I was driving the car the night my son was killed. That's why Marc is so angry. He was divorcing me to punish me. I knew that. I know he thinks I must have been at fault."

"How is that possible if it was a hit-and-run?"

"I might have somehow caused it."

Dr. Brubaker covered her hand with his own.

Her voice broke. "I woke after six months of nothing to find out that my son was gone, dead, buried. I never even got to say goodbye to him. Maybe Marc is right. I can't even remember what happened to me *last* night. Maybe I *am* crazy."

"You're not crazy," Doc said quietly. "I'm sure the first memory loss was a direct result of your head injury. There is another possibility for your most recent inability to remember." He seemed to hesitate.

"I thought you said it was from hitting my head again?" Hadn't she heard him tell Walker that's what she had? Or had she imagined that, too?

"It could be a disassociative or psychogenic fugue state. Memory loss can be caused by a horrific event the mind can't accept. You have been under a tremendous amount of emotional stress, not to mention what's happened to your body."

"You think that would explain why I have no memory of why I drove to Shadow Lake? I wondered if it couldn't have been something like that."

"DF often involves sudden, unexpected travel from home with an inability to recall the past. Sometimes a person experiencing it will assume a new identity that will contrast sharply with his or her original identity."

"Like a split personality? But I know who I am."

"No, more like a form of amnesia, only there are no medical or neurological factors that account for the symptoms." He lifted his hand from hers and she felt bereft for a moment. "The good news is that half of all fugues last less than twenty-four hours."

"And the other half?" she asked.

He smiled ruefully. "Let's give it a little time and see what happens." He looked as if he wanted to ask her something, but then changed his mind. "I'm going to let you get some sleep."

She smiled her thanks, her eyelids drooping with fatigue.

He patted her hand and rose again from his chair. "If you need anything, have the nurse call me."

"Thank you. For everything," she said as her eyes closed.

"YOU LOOK LIKE SOMETHING the cat dragged in," Billy Blake said as Walker joined him on the deck overlooking the lake.

Billy had coals going in the barbecue and what smelled like pork ribs on the grill.

"Kind of cold to be barbecuing, isn't it?" Walker asked, popping the top on a beer from the six-pack he'd brought and handing it to his friend.

Billy took the beer, eyeing him suspiciously. "Bad day at work?"

Walker swore under this breath. "I just got back from a boat ride out to the Fairbankses'."

"Little chilly on the water, wasn't it?" Billy asked as if ignoring the part about the Fairbankses.

"You don't know how close I came to shooting Jonathan tonight."

Billy laughed. "You wouldn't waste a bullet on him and you know it."

"I'm serious," Walker said, even though he wasn't. His anger had been simmering since Jack's death, but hopefully he was too smart to shoot Jonathan Fairbanks and spend the rest of his life behind bars—if Ruth Fairbanks didn't talk the state into executing him.

"You aren't going to start with that conspiracy theory of yours again, are you?" Billy groaned as he got up to check the meat on the grill.

Walker saw that he'd been right. Pork ribs, his favorite. "Smells good. Kinda late for dinner though, isn't it?"

"Funny, I had a feeling you'd be stopping over after you got back from the island, so I made extra."

"You knew I went out there?" Walker asked in surprise.

"You forget. I've got a police scanner. Heard the call and since I saw the chief heading home earlier, I figured you'd have to make the run out," Billy said. "So what's the story?"

Walker wished to hell he knew. He popped the top on one of the beers and took the other chair near the grill. "That woman who went into the lake?" Walker asked.

Billy nodded, confirming that everyone in town had heard by now.

"She went AWOL at the hospital, stole some clothing from the nursing-home laundry and took a boat ride out to see the Fairbankses, who weren't glad to see her."

"No kidding." Billy sounded interested as he put the lid on the grill and sat back down.

"She's crazy. Seriously. First she tells Doc that her kid was with her when she crashed into the lake. Then she's like 'oh, sorry, no he wasn't.' Like it skipped her mind that the kid was dead and has been for eight months. Killed in a hit-and-run, mother driving."

Billy let out a low whistle. "Rough."

"Doc says it was because of her head injury from eight months ago, the hit-and-run, so she was all fouled up thinking she was in the hospital for the first accident and could rewrite history or some fool thing. That's why she thought her son was still alive."

Billy shook his head and stared out into the darkness.

"She says she doesn't remember anything before or after she went into the lake, but she takes off to see the Fairbankses'," Walker continued, glad to get it off his chest. "Doc, hell, he's buying into everything she says. He's acting like she's the daughter he never had." Walker shook his head and took a drink of his beer.

Feeling Billy's intent gaze on him, he turned and said, "What's that look for?"

"Just wondering why this woman has you so worked up?"

Walker snorted. "She's crazy as a loon and the chief is…hell, I don't know what he is doing. He's washed his hands of it."

"So she's attractive?"

"Are you listening to me? Sure, she's attractive, pretty, I guess. That's not the problem. She's *crazy*. A nutcase. And you should meet her husband." He swore and took another drink of his beer.

"Married, huh? So why'd she go out to the island?"

Walker shook his head. What the hell had Anna Collins been thinking? He'd wanted to question her tonight, but even he could see that she was sick. Doc told him she had pneumonia when he'd called a few minutes ago to check on her.

"She friends with the Fairbankses?" Billy persisted.

Walker had thought he wanted to talk about this but realized he didn't want to anymore. He put down his half-full beer and got up. "I really should go."

"Your shift's over, right? So what's the hurry? The ribs are almost ready. You had anything to eat today?"

Walker sighed. Even if he left now, he'd have to tell Billy sooner or later anyway. "She swears Jack Fairbanks saved her life the other night on the bottom of the lake."

"No shit," Billy said.

Walker rubbed the back of his neck. "Really, I should go. I'm lousy company tonight."

"Stay. We'll finish that six-pack you brought, eat some ribs and freeze our butts off out here on the deck."

"That's all you have to say about her claiming she saw Jack?"

Billy laughed. "Hey, you already said she was crazy. Kind of blows the hell out of your theory that Jonathan killed him, unless Jack has come back for vengeance."

"Not funny. And yeah, I still think Jonathan had something to do with Jack's death. He's been jealous of him since they were kids."

Billy raised a brow. "Then he must have been pretty freaked out when your woman nutcase told him she'd seen his brother alive on the bottom of the lake."

Walker hadn't thought of that. "Yeah," he said as he lowered himself back into the chair and picked up his beer again. Now that he thought about it, Jonathan *had* been rattled. It gave him no small amount of satisfaction to realize that.

The smell of the ribs made his stomach rumble.

"You know, he did seem…scared." Walker glanced over at Billy. "I've said from the beginning that son of a bitch is hiding something."

"Wonder what Jonathan will do if she keeps insisting Jack is alive," Billy said, giving him pause.

Did Anna Collins have any idea just who she was messing with? Jonathan would crush her like a slug under his boot heel.

"I can't figure out what her game is," he said.

"Blackmail? If you're right about Jonathan's guilt…"

He looked over at Billy. "What if she knows something about Jack's death?" Walker said, thinking out loud. "Something that could bring down Jonathan Fairbanks?"

"I'll drink to that," Billy said, lifting his beer can. Somewhere in the distance, an owl hooted. Closer, a car engine revved, the sound dying away into the darkness.

AFTER RUTH FAIRBANKS'S CALL, followed by a call from Doc about his patient, Chief Nash didn't even try to sleep.

What had been a slow winter with nothing going on other than the usual nuisance calls about barking dogs, snowed-in side streets or a vehicle off the road, Nash hadn't expected all hell to break out come spring.

He wondered if there had been a full moon the night Anna Collins went off the road and into the lake. The same night he'd caught his young wife cheating on him.

He rubbed his hands over his face. And now Ruth Fairbanks had demanded a meeting with him first thing in the morning. Just what he needed. Anna Collins had certainly stirred up a hornet's nest.

He thought of Lucinda. He felt like shit. He couldn't keep hiding from her or what he'd done or what he'd seen. He shoved himself up from the couch.

It was late enough that he didn't see a soul on the drive the few blocks to his house. When he pulled up in front of the garage, the house was dark and he was hit with a horrible thought. What if Lucinda had left him?

As he got out, he checked the garage, terrified he wouldn't find her car in it. With more relief than he deserved, he saw that her car was still there. She hadn't left him. At least not in her own car.

He reminded himself that she could have left with her lover. The thought made him break out in a cold sweat.

Clumsily, he got out of the car, fear making him weak as he headed for the front door. As he entered the house, he held his breath, desolate at the thought that he would find it empty.

For the first time, he admitted that he'd made mistakes when it came to his wife. He should have dealt with a lot of issues before they'd run off to Vegas to get married. He'd known she had secrets, but he hadn't wanted to open that can of worms. He'd hoped that once they were married they could just put the past behind them.

The dishes were still on the table untouched from earlier. He could smell the fading scent of pot roast. His stomach growled. He hadn't eaten in almost forty-eight hours. No wonder he felt so weak.

He stumbled past the kitchen and peered into the darkness of the bedroom, his chest heaving painfully. For a moment, he didn't see her. She was so small, curled on her side in their bed. Relief swept over him and he slumped against the doorjamb, fighting tears.

He loved her. Damn it. He loved her. He could forgive her almost anything.

He moved to the chair beside the bed like a sleepwalker, his heart pounding so hard he feared she would hear it. Lucinda's blouse was lying over the back of the chair by the bed. With trembling fingers, he drew it up, clutching the fabric to his face, gulping in his wife's scent on a sob as he sat down.

He didn't know how long he sat there, crying quietly, clutching her blouse. After a while he put it down, went into the bathroom, closed the door and washed his face with cold water. He hardly recognized the face in the mirror.

As quietly as possible, he took off his uniform and, after opening the bedroom door, slipped into bed. He lay motionless for a few long minutes just listening to Lucinda breathe. She hadn't stirred, but he had a feeling she wasn't asleep.

Slowly, he rolled over and gingerly put an arm around her. Her body felt stiff, but within seconds, she softened and leaned back into him, spooning into the curve of his big body. He could hear her crying softly.

He pulled her closer, snuggling against her, his heart threatening to burst as he fell asleep holding his wife.

CHAPTER TWELVE

RUTH FAIRBANKS WAS ALREADY sitting at a table by the window when Police Chief Nash arrived the next morning. It was one of those dark and gloomy rainy spring days that perfectly matched his own mood.

Seeing her expression, he glanced at his watch. Five minutes early and she still gave him a look of impatience, as if she'd been made to wait and didn't like it.

What was so important that they had to meet here in secret this time of the morning anyway?

"Coffee?" she asked as he grumbled "Mornin'" and pulled up a chair across from her.

He nodded yes to the coffee and removed his hat. The place was empty, of course, since it wouldn't open for weeks.

She poured him a cup from a carafe. The table was set with cloth tablecloth and napkins, china dishes and real silverware along with a bowl of fresh fruit and an assortment of pastries that looked homemade.

Amazing what a call from Ruth Fairbanks accomplished. But then the Fairbankses were royalty in this town and everyone knew it. Especially Ruth, who wielded more power here than the president.

Nash reminded himself that he was no exception to that control, either. The matriarch had got him here at this hour of the morning without even telling him why. He'd had to leave Lucinda, who'd still been sleeping, when it was the last thing he wanted to do.

The thought did nothing to improve his bad mood.

"What is all this about?" he asked with a wave of his hand at the table. He hadn't touched the cup of coffee she placed in front of him and didn't plan to until he knew what she wanted.

She sighed, picked up her china cup, took a slow sip of her coffee, all the time watching him over the rim with the clearest steel-gray eyes he'd ever seen. Both her sons had gotten her eyes, but neither could freeze a man with only one look the way their mother could.

He reminded himself, though, that he was one of the few people left around who had known Ruth before she became *Mrs.* Fairbanks. Looking at her now, he could barely recall the scrawny little girl who'd shown up on the first day of school so many years ago in a threadbare dress.

Her name had been Ruth Ashworth back then. The dress was a hand-me-down that swallowed her skinny frame. Her face was freckled, the gray eyes huge and scared. He remembered feeling sorry for her because everyone knew she was the only daughter of Pete and Mabel Ashworth, a couple of early hippie types who lived a hand-to-mouth existence out on one of the islands in the lake.

That was back when land like that wasn't worth much. A person could squat on the land for a while and take over ownership.

So it was no wonder that on the first day he'd laid eyes on her, Nash couldn't even imagine that one day Ruth Ashworth would grow into a true beauty, who would marry a rich older man who would buy that island and build her a mansion on it. What Nash could never understand was why Fairbanks left intact the shack that Ruth used to live in on the other end of the island.

Maybe, like Nash, Big Jim Fairbanks wanted to remind Ruth of her past.

"Ruth," Nash said, using her first name to remind them both where she came from even though, in this town, anyone else who remembered Ruth's humble beginnings wisely kept it to himself. "You didn't ask me to meet you here to have coffee and fancy pastries."

His plate was too full for bullshit this morning and if she was going to give him hell about Anna Collins coming to her house, he just wanted her to get it over with so he could go home and have that talk with his wife.

"You and I used to be friends, Robert Nash. I need to know something. From you, I expect complete honesty. You saw the body they found in the lake. Was it my son's? Was it Jack's?"

He couldn't have been more surprised if she'd asked him about flying saucers. He picked up his coffee cup and took a swallow, burning his tongue.

"I'm asking you as a friend." Her voice broke. "Are you one-hundred-percent positive it was Jack?"

He hadn't expected this and wasn't sure how to answer kindly. "Ruth, whose body would it have been if not Jack's?"

"It's a simple question, Rob," she snapped. "Are you one-hundred-percent positive it was my son's?"

Nash sighed. The body had been badly decomposed from being in the water for so long, but he didn't want to tell her that. "Ruth, Jonathan made the identification. Why aren't you asking him?"

"So you aren't sure." She leaned back, nodded and picked up her coffee cup.

"I didn't say that."

"I'm no fool, Rob. I know the body was in bad shape. So if I want to know positively, without any doubt that Jack is in that grave, then I have to open the casket, compare his dental records and maybe even run DNA tests, right?"

Nash swore. "Ruth, you don't want to—"

"I already called Judge Gandy this morning."

"I'll bet he loved that, given the hour," Nash quipped.

"You'll be getting the required documents needed to oversee the exhumation. I want it done as quickly as possible and as quietly. How long will it take to get the results of DNA tests?"

He shook his head. "Weeks. In your case, days." He could well imagine the headlines if the press got wind of this. "Ruth, does Jonathan know what you're doing?" He knew even before he asked that Jonathan would never have gone along with this. "Are you sure you want to proceed?"

She gave him a look that left no doubt. "Now that we have that taken care of, tell me what you know about this woman, Anna Collins."

He sighed. "You're talking to the wrong person. Officer Walker is handling the incident."

She lifted a brow. "Why aren't you handling it?"

"I was out of town when the call came in and it's just a traffic accident."

She kept looking at him.

"Truthfully, you probably know more about Anna Collins than I do," he said.

"Don't be ridiculous. I'd never seen the woman before she ended up on my doorstep. Although—" she frowned "—her name sounded familiar. Why is that?"

As if he had a clue. "I wouldn't know."

"Don't be obtuse. It's all over town that her car went into the lake and she almost drowned. Is there something else to know about her?"

He drained his cup and poured himself another, eyeing the pastries. The way this conversation was going he would need all the caffeine and fortification he could get.

"She told me that she thinks Jack saved her life," Ruth said, making him nearly spill his coffee.

"What?" Walker hadn't told him this. But then again, he hadn't given Walker a chance to tell him much of anything since he hadn't been interested. He'd had other things on his mind.

"So you really *don't* know anything," she said impatiently. "Where did her car enter the lake?"

"On the edge of town. She came out to your house to tell you Jack saved her?"

"Actually, no. Apparently she didn't know who the man was until she saw a painting of Jack in our living room. She seemed to think that some friend of hers, an attorney, had contacted us about witnessing a hit-and-run accident."

Nash didn't know what to say.

"Apparently, it was why she came to Shadow Lake and ended up in the lake," Ruth continued. "She said that either she or this friend, a Gillian Sanders, was supposed to meet someone named Fairbanks at the rest stop outside of town that night. Do you know *anything* about this?"

It was news to him. "No."

Ruth pursed her lips, making it clear she didn't think he was doing his job. He really needed to retire.

"What I want to know, Rob, is why she thought she saw Jack."

"Obviously she's mistaken. I guess she has some kind of head injury and nearly drowned. Now she has pneumonia." He was glad Walker had filled him in on that much at least. "I hope you aren't having the exhumation based on what this woman claims, given her mental state. She lost her son in a car accident and was in a coma for six months. She's clearly not stable."

Ruth said nothing for a moment, just fixed him with that unwavering icy stare. "Anna Collins said Jack had a scar across his face." Her voice broke and Nash swore silently, cursing Anna Collins for putting Ruth through this.

"Ruth, I really think you should reconsider the exhumation."

"Don't even bother to try to talk me out of it," she said stiffly.

"Ruth, there is no evidence that—"

She reached into her purse and handed him a scrap of paper. He wiped his hands on his napkin and reluctantly took what appeared to be half of an envelope. There was something written on it, although he could barely decipher the words.

"What is this?" he asked.

"Anna Collins said she found it in her coat pocket."

"It's just some scribbles."

Ruth reached over and took it back. "Why are you being so difficult?"

He looked down at his coffee cup and bit his tongue. He wanted to state the obvious: Jack was dead. And because of that Anna Collins couldn't have seen him on the bottom of the lake. And digging up his body was only going to cause a lot of pain for nothing, plus bad publicity if it got out.

"What aren't you telling me, Robert?"

"Ruth—"

"Don't use that tone with me, Robert Nash. I've known you my whole life. The woman saw a painting of Jack and fainted on my doorstep. I saw her expression when she looked at a photograph of Jack. She *saw* Jack. She believes he saved her life."

Nash groaned, knowing there was nothing he could say to convince Ruth otherwise.

"Are you going to investigate her claim or not?"

He stared at her. "We're getting Anna Collins's car out this morning. I should know more then." But even if Walker could prove the woman hadn't seen Jack Fairbanks on the bottom of the lake, he doubted it would change Ruth's mind about the exhumation.

"Thank you." She put down her coffee cup. It clattered on the plate and, for the first time in a long time, he saw her lose her composure. Her gaze met his and he saw the raw pain in those frosty gray eyes.

His cell phone rang. "That's probably Walker calling me now to say the wrecker's here."

THE WRECKER OPERATOR WAS waiting with a larger, newer tow truck when Walker arrived.

The beer and spareribs he'd had last night weighed heavy on his stomach as he got out of his patrol car and walked to the edge of the mountain to watch as the cable was lowered to the lake where the divers were waiting.

The air felt damp, the threat of rain and low-hanging clouds over the lake giving him only fleeting glimpses of the water. He felt anxious as the blue Cadillac finally broke the surface.

This time he stood back as the behemoth was winched from the water.

He called the chief when the wrecker arrived only to find him upset. Ruth Fairbanks apparently now wanted an exhumation of Jack's body, proof that there was no way Anna Collins could have seen him under that water. He hoped there would be answers to a lot of questions as he watched the car surface.

The Cadillac had been on its top when the divers had found it. Anna Collins had said that she was trapped upside down under the water. Had she been?

Walker rubbed his forehead, thinking about a note the chief said Ruth Fairbanks had shown him. Apparently, Anna Collins, or a friend of hers who was a lawyer, had been meeting someone named Fairbanks at the rest stop. At least that's what Anna Collins had gleaned from the note that Walker had yet to see.

In fact, he wondered why Anna Collins had failed to mention it to him? He'd known she'd used her in-car emergency service to map out the route to Shadow Lake—and the police station. She hadn't come to town by accident.

Maybe later he'd drive up to the rest stop and take a look around just in case she had met someone there before going in the lake.

The big blue Cadillac inched up the mountainside to crest the top. Walker watched as the wrecker operator and his crew hurried to release the steel cable and flip the car over onto its wheels for transport.

Water streamed from every crack in the car. He could see the large suitcase. When the car was flipped back over, it landed in the backseat. Strange she hadn't put the suitcase in the trunk.

"Just a minute," he said to the wrecker operator. "There's something I need to check before you take it in to the garage."

The guy looked at him as if he was nuts. They'd been holding up traffic, even if it wasn't much traffic. The sooner they got the car off the highway the better. "It can't wait five minutes?"

"No," Walker said. The front side windows had both been broken out to run the strap through to hook up the tow cable. He reached a gloved hand through the window opening and popped the lever on the trunk. "There's something I want to check."

"Trunk seems to be stuck," the wrecker operator said. "I've got a crowbar you can use."

Walker took the tool and walked to the back of the car. He forced the crowbar under the lid and pried until he heard the lock break.

Curiosity getting the better of him, he lifted the lid.

"Shit," Walker said as he saw what was inside.

CHAPTER THIRTEEN

ANNA WOKE WITH a start. Disoriented in the dim room, she jerked back as she felt a hand touch her arm and turned to find Officer D.C. Walker sitting again on the chair beside her bed.

Anna had expected to see Marc. Hadn't Mary Ellen said he was on his way? So why hadn't he stopped by the hospital yet? Maybe he'd changed his mind about coming up to Shadow Lake. She could only hope.

"Nightmare?" Officer Walker asked, studying her.

The expression on his face made her sit up, pulling the covers to her chin. The clock beside her bed read 1:32 p.m. She vaguely remembered dozing off after both breakfast and an early lunch.

The good news was that she felt a lot better. Her skin was cool to the touch and for the first time in almost two days, her head didn't ache.

She braced herself for what she knew had to be about last night and her trip out to the island. From what Dr. Brubaker had said, upsetting the Fairbankses was going to have repercussions.

"I don't recall."

His smile could have cut glass. "That must be hell, not remembering when you're asleep *or* when you're awake."

She felt dread settle into her bones.

"We pulled your car from the lake," he said as he reached into his pocket and pulled out a small tape recorder. He placed it on the nightstand.

Her pulse began to pound in her ears.

"I need to ask you a few questions," he said as he punched Record. "I'd like to tape our conversation, Mrs. Collins. Would that be all right with you?"

She heard the hospital room door open and was relieved to see Dr. Brubaker step in.

"I asked Dr. Brubaker to join us," he said. "I'm filling in for Chief Nash in his absence."

She saw the doctor's somber expression as he went over to the window and opened the curtains. Outside, the sky was overcast and gray as if about to rain if it hadn't already. Dr. Brubaker leaned against the wall and didn't meet her eyes, seeming to tell her that he could no longer protect her.

But protect her from what? Were the Fairbankses going to press trespassing charges? Could they? Heart racing, she turned to see the police deputy take the pencil from behind his ear and open his small notebook.

She needed a lawyer. Every instinct told her to stop this right here and demand a lawyer.

The truth was she had no one to call. She'd always depended on Gillian.

"What is this about?" she asked, needing to know just how much trouble she was in.

"If you have no objections with me taping this, Mrs. Collins…"

"No, no objections," she said and felt fear burrow under her skin like a painful splinter as the cop began with, "Your name is Anna Collins, isn't that right?"

"Yes."

"You're married to Marc Collins of Seattle?"

"Separated."

He looked up at her. "But still legally married."

"That's what I've been told. I don't know that for a fact."

"Mrs. Collins, I've spoken with your husband on several occasions and again this morning before I came here. He has told me that he called you two nights ago and informed you that he hadn't gone through with the divorce. He says the two of you planned to have dinner out to celebrate a reconciliation."

Had she really agreed to that? It would explain the clothing she'd found in her hospital-room closet. His favorite black dress on her, high-heeled sandals, her dress coat. Exactly what Marc would have wanted her to wear for a night at some too-expensive restaurant.

She recalled the first time she had ever laid eyes on Marc Collins. She'd been in the process of getting her mother's home ready to sell and had some real estate questions. She'd seen his sign next to a small, nondescript office.

Something about it had appealed to her. Apparently his office manager had just quit. He'd been bent over a desk full of papers, his dark hair standing up at all angles from running his hands through it, his tie loosened, his office in complete chaos. He'd looked up and appeared so lost and desperate…. Her heart had gone out to him.

It was the vulnerability in him that would have made her go back to him.

She saw that Walker was waiting for an answer. "I have no memory of talking to my hus—to Marc."

He raised an eyebrow at her obvious resistance to call Marc her husband. "Tell me what you do remember."

She told him again, starting with her last memory of that evening, from the deer that bounded onto the highway to letting out her breath in the submerged car at the bottom of the lake at the sight of the horribly scarred man at the side window. At least, his face had *appeared* scarred. She explained that she now wondered if the scar had been an optical illusion.

Walker's jaw tightened, obviously convinced she was lying. He stared down at his notebook for a moment before he asked, "Where were you headed?"

A rest stop on the edge of Shadow Lake, if she'd read Gillian's handwriting correctly on the scrap of envelope. "I don't know, but I did find a note in the pocket of my coat that leads me to believe I was meeting someone at the rest stop."

He didn't seem surprised to hear this. "What was on the note?"

She told him. "According to the operator, the number is that of the pay phone at the rest stop."

"Did you meet one of the Fairbankses at the rest stop?"

Her trembling fingers went to her scar. She traced the familiar pattern without realizing at first that she was doing it. "I don't know. I can't…remember seeing anyone before I saw the deer on the highway." She could hear the tears behind her words and willed herself not to break down.

"You're telling me you believe you were meeting *Jack* Fairbanks at the rest stop?"

"I can only assume that was what the note meant, given that I saw him right after my car went into the lake." She looked over at her doctor. He had his head down. She willed him to look up, but he didn't, and she felt bereft without even him on her side.

"You are aware that Jack Fairbanks is dead?" Walker asked, an edge to his tone.

"I have been told that."

"Who gave you the note?" he asked.

"I'm not sure how I got it, but I recognized the handwriting. It's my friend Gillian Sanders's."

"Your friend. Did she give it to you?"

"I can only assume she did. I can't remember seeing her that night. Or maybe I was meeting her there as well." Anna shook her head. "I wish I knew."

He nodded, studying her. "Wasn't it out of character for you to drive to Shadow Lake late that night?"

She knew the moment he said it that this was coming from Marc. "Not if I thought Gillian had found out something about the hit-and-run accident that killed my son. I would do anything, anytime, to get to the truth about that night."

He raised a brow.

"Even go out to the Fairbankses' island without being invited."

She assumed that's what this was about. "Once I found the note, I knew it had to be the reason I'd come to Shadow Lake. I was sure one of the Fairbankses must have witnessed the hit-and-run—or had some information about it, given what Gillian had written on the note."

"Yes, the note. And where is this note?"

"I assume Ruth Fairbanks still has it."

"You don't think it's strange that she would keep it?" he asked.

"Very."

"You told Mrs. Fairbanks that you saw her dead son?"

"I told her what I saw. Just as I told you," she said simply.

He shook his head, anger sparking in his eyes. "Why would the Fairbankses lie about this appointment you supposedly had at the rest stop?"

She hesitated, knowing she was treading on thin ice, given the family she was about to impugn. "I think they might be covering for Jack."

He stared at her incredulously. Even Dr. Brubaker was finally looking at her, as well, as if she'd lost her mind.

The cop eyed her for a long, unnerving moment, then cleared his throat. She could tell he was trying to rein in his temper. "If your friend Gillian Sanders wrote this note, why didn't she give you more information?"

It was a question she'd asked herself. "Maybe she did and I just don't remember. Look, I didn't mean to upset Mrs. Fairbanks, but the note with the name of this town and Fairbanks on it was all I had to go on and I needed answers, because apparently you think I've done something."

His brown eyes focused on her. She saw something almost tender in them. Sympathy. "Why did you feel the need to sneak out of the hospital last night? Why not wait until morning or after you were released before you went all the way out to the island to talk to the Fairbankses?"

"I felt it was something that couldn't wait," she said, believing she was digging the hole she was in even deeper. "Please, if I need to apologize to the Fairbankses, I would be happy to."

He looked down at his notepad, took a breath and let it out slowly. When he looked up, the fury was back in his eyes.

"I'd like to know what's going on now." It was almost impossible to keep the tremor out of her voice.

Walker seemed to get himself under control. "Why was there a suitcase in the backseat of your car and not the trunk, Mrs. Collins?"

She stared at him. "Why would that mat—"

"Just answer the question please."

She felt her pulse jump. Had she put the suitcase in the backseat? If she'd really seen Marc that night, then he could have put it there. If only she could remember what had happened before she saw the deer in the road and crashed into the lake.

She shook her head. "I don't know."

"Don't you?" Walker asked, his tone mocking.

She glanced at the doctor. He was propped against the windowsill, his head down again.

"Either you tell me what's going on right now or I'm not answering any more of your questions," she said, trying to keep her voice steady. Her head ached, her stomach was queasy. But mostly she was terrified.

The cop looked down at his notes and then up at her. "Tell me about the passenger in the car with you."

She blinked. "There wasn't *anyone* with me. I know I thought my son was in the car when I first woke up. I've already explained that to you." Her voice broke.

"Mrs. Collins, there was a body found in the lake."

She let out a startled cry. "No." She stared at him in confusion. "The man who saved my life?"

"The body we found wasn't a *man's*," Walker said impatiently. "And it sure as hell wasn't Jack Fairbanks, since he's already dead and buried."

Her head swam. "Are you telling me that I hit someone with my car?" It had been a deer she'd swerved to miss, hadn't it? "Oh God, please tell me." This couldn't be happening. History repeating itself. Only this time, *she* was the hit-and-run driver.

"Mrs. Collins, you didn't run over *anyone*," Walker snapped as if his patience had finally run out. "The body we found in the trunk of your car was a *woman's*."

CHAPTER FOURTEEN

"THAT'S NOT POSSIBLE," Anna heard herself say in a voice she didn't recognize. She gripped her hands in her lap as if she could keep her entire body from shaking.

Officer D.C. Walker's eyes were on her. "Don't you want to know whose body we found in your trunk, Mrs. Collins?"

"I want to call a lawyer," she said, suddenly horrified.

"There's the phone right there. Call one."

She picked up the phone and dialed Gillian's cell phone, knowing it was a waste of time. She didn't leave a message when she reached voice mail again. She hung up the phone.

"What? No luck?" he asked. "You want to wait until you can find another lawyer or do you want to know who we found in your trunk?"

She looked up at him and waited, too frightened to speak.

"Along with the woman's body was her purse. We were able to identify her from her photo ID. Her name is Gillian Sanders."

All breath rushed from Anna. Blood surged in a deafening roar in her ears. The room began to spin. Everything in her wanted to lash out. He was lying. Gillian wasn't dead, couldn't be dead. This wasn't happening.

"It can't be Gillian," she whispered. "There has to be a mistake."

"We have a positive identification. There's no mistake."

Anna buried her face in her hands. Not Gillian. Not dead. No.

"How did Ms. Sanders end up in the trunk of your car, Mrs. Collins?"

She could only shake her head. Gillian. Dead. In the trunk of the Cadillac. Anna shuddered at the horrifying thought.

"This can't be happening," Anna said.

"What was your relationship with Gillian Sanders?"

"I told you. She's my friend."

"Was she friends with your husband as well?"

She met his gaze. He knew. Marc must have told him. The reminder of the affair between Marc and Gillian pierced her heart like a poison dart.

"Your husband and Gillian Sanders were more than friends, weren't they, Mrs. Collins?"

She lifted her chin and said nothing.

"I have spoken to your husband. Along with identifying the victim, he also told us he'd had an affair with Gillian Sanders while you were in a coma. He said he told you about the affair and you threatened to kill Gillian."

She could feel his attention on her, waiting for her reaction. "I don't believe that."

He raised a brow. "Why would your husband lie?"

She shook her head. She had no idea. None of this made any sense. Anna's eyes burned, her throat closing as her chest filled to overflowing. "Gillian was my best friend. I never would have hurt her. If I threatened to kill anyone it would have been Marc."

The cop raised a brow. "Where is your gun?"

She glanced at the phone again, then at Walker. She tried to tamp down the panic. "I'm not saying any more until I have a lawyer," she said, her voice cracking. "Please. I need to be alone. Gillian was my friend. My *best* friend."

"Don't make this harder on yourself," Walker said. "Your husband told you about the affair. You confronted your friend. Things got out of control. You didn't mean to kill her."

"I told you—"

"I can understand. You felt betrayed by those closest to you. You threatened her. Maybe the gun just went off. You panicked. You had to get rid of the body. You got her into the trunk of your car, programmed in Shadow Lake and the police station. You wanted to make sure it wasn't near the spot where you were going to dump the body."

"Please, I want—"

"Come on, Mrs. Collins, she was your *best* friend."

Out of the corner of her eye, she saw Dr. Brubaker step away from where he'd been at the window. "She said she wanted a lawyer."

A loud commotion in the hallway outside her room made them all turn in surprise. An instant later, Anna's husband stormed into the room, a nurse Anna hadn't seen before trying to stop him.

"I'm sorry. I told Mr. Collins you didn't want to be disturbed," the nurse said.

"What the hell is going on here?" Marc demanded.

Anna stared at her husband, thinking about all the things he'd told the police and the fact that he hadn't bothered to come see her before this. Just the sight of Marc made her sick to her stomach.

Walker let out a low curse. "Let me know when you get a lawyer, Mrs. Collins. In the meantime, don't leave town." He turned off the tape recorder and pocketed it, meeting her gaze in a questioning look as he left.

Anna closed her eyes, squeezing them shut, praying that this all was one huge mistake.

"I asked what's going on here," Marc demanded loudly.

"I was just questioning your wife, Mr. Collins. I have your statements from earlier, but I'd like to get your sworn statement after you visit your wife. You know where my office is."

"And who's this?" Marc asked.

Anna opened her eyes and saw her husband glaring at Dr. Brubaker.

The doctor ignored him. "Anna, ring your call bell if you need me."

"Anna?" Marc mimicked and Anna realized her husband had been drinking. "Got real cozy here I see." He turned his attention to the doctor. "I want to talk to my wife. *Alone.*"

"Five minutes," Dr. Brubaker said. "She has pneumonia and needs her rest."

Marc said nothing as the doctor and cop left the room, leaving the door open. Marc stepped to the door and slammed it, then turned to glare at her. "Anna, what the hell have you done now?"

WALKER STALKED DOWN THE HALL, too angry to speak. He'd almost had her. Just a few more minutes…

"What has gotten into you?" Doc demanded, grabbing his arm and swinging him around to face him.

Walker couldn't have been more surprised if the doctor had slugged him. *"What?"*

He glanced back at the nurses' station. Cindy was watching them. "Let's take this into my office.

"What is wrong with you? I've never seen you like this," Doc said, the moment his office door closed behind them.

"I almost got her to confess," Walker snapped.

"She said she wanted a lawyer. You're too good a cop not to know that even if she had confessed, it would have been inadmissible since you hadn't read her her rights and you ignored her plea for a lawyer."

"She *killed* her lawyer," Walker said angrily.

Doc shook his head. .

"She's lying through her teeth. About the murder, about Jack—"

"That's really what this is about, isn't it," Doc said, not unkindly. "Jack Fairbanks."

Walker looked away. "Why did she have to say she saw Jack down there?"

"What's eating at you, son? I've seen it ever since Jack died."

"I knew something was bothering him." The words were finally out. Walker took off his hat and raked a hand through his hair. "Damn it, Doc. I saw what kind of state he was in and I thought whatever it was, it would blow over."

"Do you really think that if Jack was set on killing himself that you could have stopped him? If he hadn't done it that night, he would have some other time."

Walker shook his head. "I don't believe for a minute that he killed himself."

Doc stared at him. "Walker, what are you saying?"

"He and Jonathan. There was something going on between them."

Doc sighed and sat down behind his desk. "I've known Jack and Jonathan since they were born."

"Then you know that Jonathan blamed Jack for the loss of his leg. He never forgave him. There was bad blood between them."

Doc nodded. "But to even suggest—"

"Jonathan may not have pushed him overboard that night, but you will never convince me he didn't leave him out there to drown." It felt good to finally voice the suspicions to someone other than Billy.

Doc shook his head. "You can't take all this out on that woman down the hall."

"Maybe I was a little rough on her, but Doc, she's got a dead body in the trunk of her car—a body belonging to the woman she threatened to kill."

"According to her husband," Doc said.

"She's guilty of something."

"Anna Collins is not your ex-wife," Doc said quietly.

"She's enough like her to be her twin." Walker wished he could take back the words the moment they were out of his mouth. "Okay, maybe I do see Jessica in her. But that still doesn't change the fact that she has a dead body in her trunk."

"She didn't kill anyone."

Walker shook his head.

He'd seen the way Doc had taken to the woman like the daughter he'd never had.

"You have to admit she looks guilty as hell."

Doc nodded. "That alone makes me suspicious. How about you? Haven't you wondered? For instance, why her husband is so forthcoming with such incriminating details about a woman you say he hoped to reconcile with. Or how someone who weighs maybe one twenty-five could get the dead weight of another woman…" He looked to Walker for a weight.

"Five-nine, a hundred-and-fifty pounds give or take," he said, aware of what the doctor was getting at.

"A woman larger and heavier into the trunk of her car." Doc shrugged.

"She could have had an accomplice," Walker said knowing he was grasping at straws.

"Well, once you have a look at the car I'm sure you'll be able to confirm her story about the seat belt jamming," Doc said. "Or maybe you already have."

Walker chewed at his cheek. Once he'd found the body, he'd come straight to the hospital to talk to Anna Collins.

"I'll be curious to hear what you find."

"She's going to disappoint you, Doc." Walker would bet the farm on that.

"Maybe," he said congenially.

Walker shook his head, smiling ruefully, as he left. There was no fool like an old one. Anna Collins might have fooled the doc, but she hadn't fooled him. And he was going to prove it.

ANNA STARED AT THE MAN standing in her hospital room as if he was a stranger. Marc was, in so many ways. He had the kind of good looks that made women stare. It was ironic that she'd fallen for what she'd thought was vulnerability the first time she'd seen him. Now she knew what she'd seen was a glimpse of the pettiness of a cruel unforgiving man.

He wore a new suit, obviously expensive, and she knew he'd purchased it because he'd wanted to make an impression on the small-town cops. Marc liked to present himself as a man with everything going for him. Part of what had attracted Marc to her, she realized now, was her money. She came from wealth and had never had to work for a living. That too, she saw now, had made Marc jealous and bitter since he had come from the opposite background.

"I need to be alone," she said. "They just told me about Gillian." She began to cry, the shock of it still too much for her.

Her mind was reeling. She was scared and angry and mourning the loss of her friend. And certainly not up to dealing with Marc right now.

"Please."

He ignored her.

She watched him walk over to the window.

"Nice view."

She tried to pull herself together. If it was true that she'd seen Marc before she'd come to Shadow Lake that night, then he might be able to fill in the blanks. She had to try to understand what was going on and why Gillian was dead.

"Tell me you didn't have an affair with Gillian," she said to his back.

"Sorry," he said with a shrug. "I can't do that." He glanced back at her, his look full of blame. "You had taken everything away from me. Gillian…well, she was there."

"You would have had to catch her at her weakest moment

or knocked-out drunk," Anna said. "She must have hated your guts after that."

He laughed. "I came up here thinking you needed my help, but you seem to be doing just fine. Couldn't you find an older doctor?" He laughed.

She bristled at his comment but didn't take the bait. She was reminded of waking up in the other hospital in pain and confusion only to have Marc tell her that she'd killed their son.

"You didn't even call me to let me know you were in the hospital," he said now, in that same accusing tone. "Your own husband."

"Why would I call *you?* The last I heard, you were divorcing me. I'm fine, but thanks for asking. Your concern for my welfare is touching."

She watched him tamp down his temper as she had so many times before. But she knew it was just below the surface, simmering, ready to explode without warning. He'd been in town since yesterday according to Mary Ellen. What had he been doing? Why *hadn't* he come to see her?

He'd always blamed her for his volatile behavior—she made him that way. But she no longer believed that. She no longer believed anything Marc Collins said.

"What are you really doing here?" she asked, her own anger also rising.

"I'm your *husband.* Whether you believe it or not I care about you. I feel…responsible. I would never have told you about Gillian and me if I thought—"

"Stop it, Marc. You know I didn't kill Gillian. I would never have hurt Gillian."

He gripped the end bed rails and leaned toward her. His smile was pitying. "Even knowing that she wanted me? That she was the one who came on to me?"

She laughed in his face. "What else are you lying about? I would never have agreed to a reconciliation with you."

He reared back, his face twisted in anger. "You need me. You've always needed me. You *jumped* at the chance to start over." He moved away from the bed, walking again to the window, his back to her. "I told you I wasn't going through with the divorce. I suggested we have dinner and make a fresh start." His expression softened as he moved back to the end of the bed. "You were happy, excited. I told you to dress for someplace nice."

She must have been stunned and put on the black dress, his favorite, and the high-heeled sandals without giving any thought to what she was agreeing to.

"But we never went out, did we?" she guessed.

"No, Gillian called, said she had to see you." He frowned. "You really don't remember?"

"Why did she want to see me?"

He shrugged, but she got the impression he knew and for some reason, was glad she couldn't remember. "Gillian calls and you drop everything and you wonder what went wrong with our marriage?"

"You and I fought because you didn't want me talking to her."

His eyes narrowed. "I thought you didn't remember."

She was putting the pieces together, pretty much able to guess what must have happened, knowing Marc.

"You and I were discussing getting back together," he said, sounding peeved. "I thought that was a little more important than your stupid girl-talk with your friend."

She had a flash of memory. Marc trying to grab the phone, ordering her to hang up. But she hadn't, because there had been something in Gillian's voice… "Why didn't you want me to talk to her?"

"I didn't want her telling you about our affair. I wanted to be the one to do that," he said.

She shook her head. "There was no *affair*." It had been exactly what she'd thought it had been. Marc had taken advantage of Gillian when she was down. Just as Anna knew that Gillian would never have forgiven him. Gillian would have known that Marc would use it against her. No wonder she'd picked up even more animosity between them after her coma.

"For someone who can't remember anything, you certainly have all the answers," he said, eyeing her as if he suspected she was lying about her memory loss. Just as he had when she came out of the coma.

"Too bad you still don't know what happened the night our son died," he muttered.

Marc had been upset when she'd gotten pregnant. She'd thought it was because the pregnancy wasn't planned and Marc liked to orchestrate everything right down to how she spent her days.

After Tyler was born, she saw a side of her husband she didn't like, but she'd been so happy with her son that she'd told herself Marc would outgrow his jealousy.

She'd never been able to remember the night she'd taken Tyler and left the house. She'd always felt there was more to the story, something Marc hadn't told her—like why she'd left with Tyler that night.

Looking at Marc now, she finally admitted something she hadn't wanted to. Their marriage had been a disappointment to them both. And she hadn't loved Marc Collins for a very long time.

"Gillian was still looking for the hit-and-run driver, wasn't she?" Anna asked, thinking of the note. "That's why she called me that night. She'd discovered something."

"You tell me—you're the one who went to see her," Marc said, banking no doubt on Anna not being able to remember.

Had she gone to see Gillian? Anna felt a chill snake up her spine. What had happened once she got there? And why couldn't she remember seeing Gillian?

"You're kidding yourself if you think it had anything to do with the hit-and-run," Marc said. "She'd given up that quest months before. She only told you she was still looking to appease you."

"That's not true." Anna clung to the belief that Gillian would have never stopped searching for information about the hit-and-run, because she knew how much Anna needed to know.

"She just wanted to tell you about the affair between us before I did," Marc said smugly.

Anna shook her head. "Gillian had news about the hit-and-run. That's why I went over there."

"Oh, yeah? Then why did you take your gun?" He smiled at her surprise. "I checked. It's gone."

AFTER HIS EARLY MEETING WITH Ruth Fairbanks, Police Chief Rob Nash had been called down to the station to take care of the paperwork involved in Jack Fairbanks's exhumation.

When Walker called, Nash had been shocked to learn about the body found in the trunk of Anna Collins's car. It was time to call in the state criminal investigation division to take over. Shadow Lake didn't have the manpower, especially when all Nash wanted to do was get home to Lucinda.

He'd told Walker to handle the interview with Anna Collins. "Write up your report for CID. I'll call them and have them take over the investigation."

At half-past one, he'd driven home, afraid he'd find Lucinda long gone. Pulling into the driveway, he shut off the engine and just sat there. The lights were on in the garage for some reason. He could see the top of Lucinda's car through the window.

She was still here apparently, and that surprised him just as much as it had last night.

He couldn't believe the past few days. He tried to catch his breath as he thought about confronting his wife, his cheating wife. His chest constricted. He told himself he was having a heart attack, but he knew that would be the easy way out and not the way his life had ever gone.

He'd have to face her. He knew it was part shame and part fear that kept him now rooted in the car. He was afraid what she would tell him. Even more afraid of what he might do—especially after last time.

Why hadn't she been smart enough to leave him? Her lover would have given her money to leave. Nash would bet on that.

He had to resolve this. He couldn't concentrate on his job. Now that a body had been found in the trunk of Anna Collins's car, Shadow Lake had a murder on its hands. While the state boys would handle the case, Nash would still need to be available to assist—especially with the Fairbankses somehow involved in all this.

He'd known when he told Walker about Ruth Fairbanks's plan to have Jack's body exhumed that he'd hit the roof. He had. Walker was too personally involved with the Fairbanks to handle the Anna Collins investigation after today.

But it wasn't until Nash had parked in his driveway that he realized he'd forgotten to call the state boys. Tomorrow. Later, after he talked to Lucinda.

One mistake had already been made in the investigation—opening that damned trunk with a crowbar without reasonable cause.

It was going to be a pressure cooker the next few days. The state CID boys wouldn't be happy about the crowbar incident, since it would hurt a case against Anna Collins.

Nash knew he had to get his head back on straight. He didn't want to end his career on a sour note, not with as many years as he'd put in and the pride he'd once had in the job he'd done.

On top of the trunk incident, Walker had apparently tried

to get a confession out of Anna Collins and ignored her request for a lawyer. Nash rubbed his forehead. The only person he wanted to force a confession out of right now was his own wife.

Dropping his head in his hands, he told himself that Anna Collins wasn't going anywhere. Walker had followed procedure and had her car taken to Tiny's Garage. It was locked up tight and the body had been photographed and taken to the Eternal Rest Funeral Home to be refrigerated until an autopsy could be done. No real harm had been done since it appeared to be an open-and-shut case.

It was now time for Nash to take care of his personal life. Then get back to work.

Clumsily, he got out of the car, closed the door and headed for the house. He saw the curtain move. Lucinda had been watching him from the window. Hoping he wouldn't come home? Or hoping he would, so she could tell him whatever she'd planned to tell him last night. He figured he'd stopped her from confessing about the boyfriend and the fact that she was leaving him.

He opened the front door and stepped in, struck by a sense of déjà vu. The house still smelled like pot roast.

"I heated up leftovers for dinner," Lucinda called from the kitchen. He could hear her scurrying about the kitchen, trying to act as if everything was normal. "If you want to wash up…"

He stood just inside the doorway, glancing around as if he'd never seen his house before. As usual, the place was spotless. He frowned as he noticed that the dining room table was set with his mother's good china and candles flickered from the centerpiece Lucinda had made out of pinecones the first week they were married—just as it had been last night.

His throat was so dry it hurt to swallow.

"Rob?" She sounded tentative. Or was it fear he heard?

"I'll just wash up and change," he said, voice cracking.

Like her, he wanted to pretend that nothing had happened.
Nothing had changed. He moved toward the bedroom, afraid
of what he would find.

But when he stepped into the room, he didn't see anything
out of place. Moving to the closet, he opened it. Her clothes
were still hanging beside his. He slumped against the wall
with relief even though he knew he couldn't live the rest of
his life coming home every night expecting her to be gone.

He heard her behind him.

"Rob?"

Something seized up in his chest. He didn't turn to look at
her. "I saw you." He was crying, the words coming out in
chest-heaving sobs. "I saw you with Jonathan Fairbanks. I
know you've been having an affair with him."

"What?"

A note of shock instead of alarm in her voice made him
turn to look at her.

She appeared dumbfounded.

He took a step toward her. "Don't lie to me, Lucinda. I saw
you get into his car the night I went to Pilot's Cove."

"I'm not lying." She held her ground. "I would never have
an affair with that bastard."

The fierceness of her words was like being doused with
cold water. "Then why would you—"

Her face crumpled. "I've wanted to tell you, but I was
afraid of what you would do when you found out." She wrung
her hands. "I've changed since I met you. You have to believe
that. But I did things before I met you…."

"What does that have to do with Fairbanks?" he demanded.

"I came to Shadow Lake looking for him."

Nash shrank back, shaking his head. She reached for him, but
he withdrew even farther, unable to stand her touch right now.

"You don't understand. I came to Shadow Lake to *blackmail* him."

CHAPTER FIFTEEN

NOTHING LUCINDA COULD have said would have surprised the police chief more. Nash stumbled over to the bed and sat down heavily. "Blackmail?"

"Well, not really blackmail exactly."

He looked up at his wife and patted the bed next to him. "What *exactly*?" He watched her rub her arms, as if she was cold, as she gingerly sat down next to him.

"It had to do with his brother, Jack."

"Jack? Jack is dead."

"I know that now, but at the time… When you met me I wasn't passing through town like I told you. I wasn't on summer vacation. I was broke and…desperate."

He remembered the way she'd been then, a waitress at the local café. She'd so obviously needed help. And he'd been ready to step in.

"I didn't have any idea who the Fairbankses were," she said, and grimaced. "I've never really paid any attention to politics, you know. I was so shocked when I found out that they were rich and lived on an island. And that the father was a senator. I'd never even seen the guy."

"Jack Fairbanks?"

She nodded. "Or his brother Jonathan."

"Then how could you blackmail him?" Nash asked starting to lose patience.

"I just knew about Jack Fairbanks's *car*," she said.

"His car? Lucinda—"

"I'm sorry. I know I'm doing a terrible job of explaining this, but it's because I hate to tell you," she said, putting her head down and placing her hand over her stomach. "I didn't want you to know some things about me, about my past."

He didn't have the heart to tell her that he knew all about her past. Did she really think he would marry someone without doing at least a little checking on her? He was a police chief, for heaven's sake.

"I *was* going to tell you sometime though, really."

Sure she was. "I don't care about your past."

"I planned to tell you last night."

He felt his face flame. "I'm sorry if I hurt you—"

"I understand now why you were upset with me."

"I saw you get into Jonathan Fairbanks's car at midnight. What was I supposed to think? Lucinda, what is this about blackmail and Jack Fairbanks's car?"

"I used to know this guy who did stuff."

Nash groaned inwardly. "Leon Markowitz. He stole cars, stripped them down and sold the parts. He went to prison for it. I know, Lucinda. You got probation because you didn't know anything about the operation."

She ducked her head again. "That wasn't true."

"Honey," he said turning her to face him. "Tell me what any of this has to do with the Fairbankses."

"One of the cars that Leon stole belonged to Jack Fairbanks."

Jack had driven a fancy SUV, black with every gadget known to man. "Your boyfriend stole Jack's car?" Nash remembered. He'd filled out the police report. The car had been stolen in Shadow Lake and was never recovered. "You saw the car?" he asked, frowning. "You came to Shadow Lake?"

She shook her head. "The car was stolen in *Seattle*. Leon always dumped everything that was inside the stolen cars

into a plastic bag and then we would go through it together."
She bit her lip.

"I'm not going to arrest you, all right?"

Lucinda smiled and kissed him on the cheek excitedly, as
if glad to finally be telling him about this. "Guess what I found
in the stuff from the car? *Drugs.*"

He stared at her. "Drugs? This is the big secret?"

"Hey, drugs in the senator's son's car. What if a newspaper got hold of that information?"

"I thought you didn't know who Jack Fairbanks was?"
Nash challenged.

"I didn't. But Leon told me to keep the stuff, not the drugs,
but the other stuff in case I ever needed money because I could
shake down the Fairbankses. He would have probably done
it himself but he got busted."

Nash looked at his wife and felt such a tenderness for her.
He knew it was nuts, being relieved she was only a car thief's
accomplice and a blackmailer. "So you decided to blackmail
Fairbanks since Leon was locked up and, hey, why waste the
information."

She frowned at his sarcasm. "I'll admit I used to be an op-
portunist." Not that long ago. "I figured the Fairbankses
would blow me off, but I had nothing to lose. I was a different person back then, you have to believe that." Her eyes
were wide and bluer than he could ever remember seeing
them. "I've made a lot of mistakes." She rolled her eyes. "A
whole lot of mistakes, but don't you see, you changed me."

He wanted to believe that. "You didn't come into an inheri-
tance shortly after you got to town, did you? Your car and all
the new clothes?"

"Jonathan Fairbanks," she said, and nodded.

"How much did you blackmail him for?"

"Twenty-five thousand."

Nash let out a curse. *"What?"*

She stood. "I knew you'd be angry. See why I didn't tell you?"

"Lucinda, I just can't believe that Jonathan Fairbanks would pay you twenty-five thousand dollars to keep you quiet about some drugs found in his dead brother's car. First off, you could never prove it. Second, any evidence you have would only incriminate you. And third, no newspaper would print the story without proof."

"But with the stuff from Jack's car—"

"It only proves that you were involved in stealing the car." He shook his head, amazed Jonathan Fairbanks would let himself be blackmailed. Even to cover for his brother. Maybe especially to cover for his brother. "This doesn't make any sense."

"I'm telling you the truth."

Nash had been a cop for too long. There was no way Jonathan Fairbanks would fork over twenty-five grand to a blackmailer. Especially someone like Lucinda.

But Jonathan had. And that's what scared the hell out of Nash as he looked at his young wife.

IT WAS LATE BY THE TIME Walker drove to Tiny's Garage where Anna Collins's car had been taken.

The garage, one of two in Shadow Lake, was closed this time of year. That's why the police department used it to store vehicles involved in accidents that needed to be investigated by the state patrol.

Walker planned to get in and out as quickly as possible. The state boys would be down tomorrow and take over the case. He knew this would be his only chance to check out the Cadillac. His fear was doing anything more that could jeopardize the case against Anna Collins.

He parked next to the darkened garage and hesitated, telling himself he shouldn't be here. Nash had made it clear that he was to let him and the state boys take it from here.

Walker had already screwed it up by opening the trunk. He'd catch holy hell for that. A good lawyer would use that to try to get Anna acquitted. But when he'd had the trunk opened, he sure as hell hadn't expected to find a *body*. He'd just been curious about why she'd put that damned suitcase in the backseat of such a nice car instead of putting it in the huge trunk.

Swearing under his breath, he got out of the patrol car and used the police station's master key to open the garage.

It was pitch-black inside the shop. He felt around for the light switch, flipped the switch and blinked as the overhead lights came on.

Anna Collins's Cadillac sat in the middle of the largest bay, the one used for motor homes. The top was crushed, the pretty blue paint scraped off from being dragged up the steep mountain over the rocks and sheered-off trees. A piece of pine bough was caught in one door, and the interior was still soaking wet.

As he stepped closer, he drew the latex gloves from his pocket and tugged them on over his large hands.

The suitcase had fallen into the backseat again after the tow operator had righted the car for the trip into town.

He didn't dare look inside the suitcase, although he was curious about what he'd find there.

He'd been so sure there was something not quite right about Anna Collins's story. Being right gave him little satisfaction.

Now he wondered if he was also right about his suspicion that she'd purposely driven her car into the lake—and hadn't even been in the car when the Cadillac had gone into the water. At first he'd thought she'd done it for attention from her husband who was supposedly divorcing her.

He suspected now that she'd done it to get rid of the body, but that something had gone wrong and she'd ended up

getting caught in the car and going into the lake as well.
Hadn't she realized the car would be pulled from the lake and
the body discovered?

No doubt she hadn't been thinking straight. Still wasn't,
if she was to be believed. Like coming up with the story that
Jack Fairbanks had saved her life. Walker still couldn't believe
she'd gone out to the island.

But this was turning into a cop's dream case. It had it all:
the body—complete with bullet hole—in the wife's car trunk,
the husband's alleged affair with the victim and the wife's
threat to kill the victim. All that was missing was the gun.

It all wrapped up so nicely. Even with him blowing some
crucial evidence, Walker didn't doubt that the state boys
would be able to make a case for murder one.

He approached the driver's-side door of the Cadillac and,
clasping the door handle, carefully swung the door open.

Reaching for his flashlight, he clicked it on and shone the
beam into the front seat. Sure enough, the seat belt wasn't
connected. So it *hadn't* been jammed, after all.

He pulled on the belt and felt a start. The driver's side re-
straint had been cut. Holding the cut end under the beam of
the flashlight, he couldn't believe what he was seeing.

The end hadn't been cut clean. The edge was ragged, as if
sawed through in a manner that would suggest urgency.

He let out a breath. What the hell? Leaning in, he shone
the flashlight beam around the inside front of the Cadillac,
looking for what Anna Collins had used to cut the seat belt.
She must have had one of those tools…

There was nothing in the front of the car, but he told
himself it could have been lost when the car was retrieved
from the lake.

He looked at the seat belt again. On closer inspection, he
saw that whatever had been used to cut the seat belt had left
some kind of shiny residue. And that's when it came to him.

If he was trapped underwater drowning, with nothing to cut a jammed seat belt, what would he use? He'd heard of guys using fingernail clippers, dull pocketknives, a piece of glass. Automobiles now came with safety glass, which was worthless for cutting anything.

The only other thing you might find in a car, especially a fancy one, was a vanity mirror.

He flipped down Anna Collins's visor and saw the gaping jagged hole where the mirror had been ripped out. As he shone his flashlight over the front of the car again, he didn't see any pieces of broken mirror on the floor.

Then he remembered. The car had been *upside down* on the bottom of the lake, according to Anna Collins's story. He shone the beam on the headliner and spotted the tiny slivers of the mirrored glass embedded in the lush fabric.

The seat belt hadn't just been cut with a piece of broken mirror. It had been sawed, with the car upside down at the bottom of the lake.

Walker swore again. Cutting a seat belt with a piece of broken mirror would have been an extraordinary feat for a man trapped upside down underwater—let alone a woman.

And it would have been impossible for the person not to cut herself.

He recalled Anna Collins's hands during his interviews with her. There hadn't been any cuts. Had she worn gloves?

Suddenly he wasn't so sure. Anna wasn't a physically strong woman. Doc was right about Anna being weak after everything she'd been through. She'd lost a lot of weight during her time in a coma and clearly hadn't gained it back in the two months since. According to Doc, it was one reason she'd contracted pneumonia.

Did Walker really think Anna could have cut the seat belt? But if she hadn't, then who had?

With a curse, he closed the car door and went back to the

trunk. The lid had been secured with a bungee cord to keep it from opening, since Walker had broken the lock.

He removed the strap and lifted the lid. Shining his flashlight into the trunk, he considered how Anna could have lifted the dead weight of someone Gillian's size. It seemed impossible.

That's when he saw the bullet hole. He blinked. That's how she did it. She had Gillian climb into the trunk and then she shot her. The beam of the flashlight made a large gold circle on the pale blue carpeted bottom of the trunk. He stared at it, not realizing at first what he was seeing.

He hadn't questioned it before, since the car had been underwater and he'd just assumed the water would have washed away any evidence.

His heart began to pound. He hurried out to his patrol car, got his forensics kit from the back and entered the garage again.

He knew even before he sprayed the luminol onto the carpet he wasn't going to find the blood residue which should have been there. He swore and felt his head spin.

Gillian Sanders had been shot in the trunk of this car and yet there was no blood. Which could mean only one thing. She was already dead when she'd been put into the trunk— and the gunshot to her temple hadn't been what killed her. So given there was no blood at all in the trunk, how the hell *had* Gillian Sanders been killed?

ANNA COULDN'T BELIEVE SHE'D taken the gun when she went to see Gillian.

What *had* she been thinking when she'd been hit with the news about Marc and Gillian coming right after the roller-coaster ride of the divorce and Marc changing his mind? Gillian's betrayal could have been the last straw. How could Anna be sure what she'd done?

"Please, I need you to leave." She felt as if they'd been at this for hours. It had definitely been longer than five minutes.

She thought about ringing for Dr. Brubaker but feared Marc would get into it with him.

"Marc, please."

"I know. You'd never hurt Gillian," he said in a mocking tone. "Then what was she doing in the trunk of your car and the cops asking about your gun?"

She looked at him, eyes narrowing. "The police wouldn't have known about the gun unless you told them. You're the one who insisted I get that gun," she said, remembering how he'd forced it on her. "You know I hated having a gun in the house. I wouldn't even touch it."

"Well, apparently you did more than touch it." He shook his head at her. "I never dreamed you'd kill Gillian or I wouldn't have told you about the two of us."

She didn't bother to argue the point again. "What do you want, Marc?" She felt nothing but contempt for him. He'd hurt her so badly, blaming her for Tyler's death when she'd been too sick from the accident to fight back. When she'd blamed herself and was grieving. When she'd needed someone so desperately to give her comfort.

"Nothing," he said, looking at her.

Anna felt too tired to speak. Just looking at the man she had once loved drained life out of her. But she had to ask, "Why didn't you go through with the divorce, *really?*"

"Why can't you believe I wanted to salvage our marriage?"

"Did you ever love me?" she asked, her voice a whisper.

"I thought you would make me a good wife."

"I thought I had."

His gaze met hers, his a mixture of anger and alcohol and…fear. The fear surprised her. Gillian's call. What had Gillian said to her on the phone? Something that had sent her rushing to her friend's house. Not about an affair. Something else. Something that had made Anna furious enough to take the gun.

She frowned, realizing how little sense that made. She wouldn't have been furious by news of a possible witness to the hit-and-run. And she couldn't believe she would have felt more than hurt about what transpired between Gillian and Marc.

So why was Marc still afraid if all he was worried about was Gillian telling Anna about the two of them?

"The doctor says this time my memory will come back," she said, knowing it was the last thing Marc wanted to hear.

The look on his face confirmed her suspicions. Gillian had told her something that night that Marc didn't want Anna to remember.

"What else did you tell the police about me?" she asked.

He gave her a droll look. "I had to tell them the truth. That I wanted to reconcile, start over with a clean slate, no secrets. When I told you about me and Gillian, you went ballistic."

Didn't he realize she knew him so well she could tell when he was lying? Obviously not. "Why, if I was so upset and had the gun, why didn't I shoot *you?*"

"Because women always blame the other woman," he said. "Especially after I told you that Gillian begged me not to tell you."

That sounded nothing like Gillian. Anna felt an awful ache in her chest at the reminder that Gillian was gone.

"Why did I pack a suitcase?" she asked.

He shrugged. "You were leaving me."

"But it was my house." She'd bought the house with her own money.

"It was *our* house and, as your husband, I had every right to move back in," he growled.

That's why she'd been packing so furiously. Marc had planned to stay in the house. She must have been going to a motel until she could get her lawyer to have Marc evicted. That's why she hadn't taken the time to change her clothes. She'd left to get away from him.

Or had it been to get to Gillian's? Something about her friend's call?

"You broke my heart, Anna. I wanted this marriage to work. You know I've been having financial problems with house sales down..."

"Who took my suitcase downstairs?" she asked.

"What?" He looked like he might have heart failure. "I'm pouring my guts out here and you're worried about your damned suitcase?"

"Did you put it in the backseat or the trunk?"

"The trunk." He frowned. "You were struggling with it so I carried it down for you. Why do you care where..." He gave her a knowing smirk. "I guess you moved the suitcase to put Gillian's body in the trunk after you killed her."

She didn't bother to deny it. Instead, she tried to remember the drive out to Gillian's, ringing the doorbell...

She looked up to find Marc standing next to the bed and it suddenly hit her. If convicted of murder, she would be going to prison and Marc, as her husband, would have the house and everything else, including her money.

"YOU KNOW I ONLY *ASSIST* ON autopsies," Dr. Brubaker said as they entered the morgue at the funeral home. "I really don't think this is a good idea, Walker."

"We're just going to take a preliminary look at the body," he said as he pulled out Gillian Sanders's body and handing a pair of latex gloves to Doc, snapped on a fresh pair of his own before he unzipped the body bag.

Doc sighed and stepped closer to inspect the body. Walker watched him inspect the bullet hole in Gillian Sanders's temple.

The cold water of the lake had preserved the body well. Nothing like the lake water had done to Jack Fairbanks's body.

Walker had to look away for a moment at the thought of Jack's decomposed body. No one would have been able to get a positive identification from it. Jonathan had provided dental records. Walker frowned, remembering how the coroner had said they matched that of the dead man.

Doc cleared his voice.

Walker turned back to him. "Well?"

"I can only give you my opinion. Until there is an autopsy…"

"Yeah, yeah," Walker said impatiently. "Sorry," he said at Doc's chastising look.

"See this?" He pointed to a spot on the side of Gillian's head. "I believe she died of blunt force trauma to the head. She definitely did not die from the bullet wound. She was shot after she was dead."

"I'll be damned," Walker said as he watched Doc carefully rezip the bag and return the body to the cooler.

"I need to get back to my patient," Doc said. He seemed to hesitate. "What does this mean for Anna?"

Walker shook his head—he wished he knew. But there was somewhere he had to go, something he should have done sooner. Something he had to do tonight before the state boys got here.

As he drove out of town, he realized he was starting to believe at least some of what Anna Collins had told him.

Incredibly, she'd survived the crash off the mountain and escaped drowning after being trapped in the car at the bottom of the lake.

He couldn't ignore that more of her story might be true. Obviously not the part about who had saved her life. But what if she *had* been meeting someone at the rest stop? There was another Fairbanks brother and if anyone was capable of a clandestine meeting late at night in an isolated spot, it was Jonathan Fairbanks.

Walker passed no other cars as he drove up the mountain

road. His mind was reeling. Anna Collins couldn't have cut that seat belt with the mirror. Nor, he realized, could she have lifted Gillian Sanders into the trunk.

Just past the spot where Anna had gone off the highway, his headlights picked up the turnoff to the rest stop.

He recalled what Marc Collins had told him about putting Anna's suitcase in the trunk of the Cadillac.

So when had the suitcase ended up in the backseat of the car and Gillian Sanders's body in the trunk? At Gillian's house? Or at the Shadow Lake rest stop?

The rest stop was closed for the season, the road in barricaded with a gate. The buildings sat back off the highway, the gate a quarter of the way in, leaving room for a person to pull off, since past the rest stop was a scenic view of the lake that could be walked to.

As he swung his patrol car in to park, he could barely make out the rest-stop building through the pines. But closer, there were muddy tracks where more than one car had driven around the gate.

"Oh, hell," he muttered. He'd dismissed Anna Collins's story—especially after she'd told about the man who'd saved her life and the description matched that of Jack Fairbanks, a dead man.

But Walker knew he'd let that—and his biases about the woman—cloud his judgment, just as Doc had accused.

He parked, cut the engine and lights and sat for a moment, the darkness seeming to close in around him. Blackness had settled into the pines and along the shadowy sides of the isolated closed-for-the-season rest-stop buildings.

Behind the structures, Walker knew that a rusted fence marked the scenic view where the land dropped over a cliff to the lake far below. To the right of the closed buildings was a handicap-access trail to the overlook. To the left was another closed road. This one led to a small county gravel pit.

He picked up his flashlight, opened the car door and stepped out. Up here on the mountain the air was colder, damper, and the rain felt more imminent. Walker snapped on his flashlight, pointed the beam at the tracks in the mud.

There were two sets of distinguishable car tracks. Both had gone in, but only one had come back out.

Unsnapping the release on his holstered weapon, he followed the tracks back into the darkness of the pines. A few yards in, he stopped to listen. Something rustled in the brush off to his right. He felt himself tense until he heard it again, along with the chatter of a squirrel.

Careful not to disturb what could be a crime scene, he made a wide circle to the rest-stop building, shining the flashlight on the locks to make sure they were still intact. They were.

Two sets of the car tracks indicated where two drivers had turned around. Only one of them had left, though. The other car tracks trailed off to the left of the rest-stop buildings toward the old gravel pit.

He hadn't gone far on the old gravel pit road when his flashlight picked up the glint of chrome ahead. His heart began to beat harder.

A car was parked behind a small pile of gravel. Approaching the car, Walker tried the driver's-side door. It swung open. He shone the flashlight beam into the car. The registration was in a plastic sleeve on the back side of the driver's visor.

Walker read the name—Gillian Sanders—and let out an oath.

NASH TOOK HIS WIFE'S HANDS in his. "Lucinda, I need you to tell me everything. Why did Jonathan Fairbanks come to the house the other night when he thought I was gone?"

She sighed. "Well, the problem is I made this deal with him that I would take the money and leave town, but that was before you and I got involved. He's really upset that I stayed, let alone married the chief of police. When he heard you were going to Pilot's Cove, he insisted on seeing me."

Nash felt his blood boil. "Did Jonathan Fairbanks threaten you?"

"See, this is why I didn't want to tell you."

"Luci." He dragged her into his arms. "You should have come to me right away with this." He'd known something was wrong and he'd been right. It just hadn't been what he'd thought. Not in a million years.

He drew back to look into her eyes. He'd been taken with her the first time he saw her, even though she was years too young for him. But there was something about her. A sweetness along with a street-wise strength that had drawn him to her and made him convince himself that age didn't matter.

"I didn't want you to know. I didn't want to disappoint you. I'm telling you the truth."

"Honey, twenty-five thousand dollars is a lot of money and I know Jonathan Fairbanks. He's too smart to give money to a blackmailer, even if you had tangible incriminating evidence against *him* rather than his brother. What's to keep you from bleeding him dry?" He looked at his wife's expression. "Don't tell me you tried to blackmail him again the other night."

"No, no, no," she said quickly. "I told you I've changed. I handled it myself, but I knew I had to tell you the truth."

Her story didn't make sense and yet for some unknown reason, he *did* believe her. The question was: why had Jonathan paid the blackmail? And what the hell was he going to do about the man? He knew what he wanted to do.

"Rob, there's more I need to tell you," she said in a tentative whisper.

He looked at his wife, fear in his heart.

"I'm pregnant with your baby." She grinned through tears as she put both hands over her belly. Her grin faded when he only stared at her, too shocked to speak. "I was hoping you'd be happy about this."

A baby. He'd never dreamed he would have children, having never married until so late in life.

Lucinda started to cry. "If you aren't happy about the baby—"

"Happy?" He let out a whoop, grabbed her and swung her around. "Happy? Lucinda, are you kidding?" He couldn't quit laughing as he put her down quickly and dropped to his knees in front of her. "The baby's all right?"

She nodded, still crying.

"Our baby?" he asked.

She grinned. "Our baby."

He pressed his face to her belly and kissed the slight mound.

"I really want this baby with you, Rob." She brushed his hair back and bent to kiss his forehead.

He looked up at her. God help him. "All I care about now is you and our baby." He would protect her any way he had to.

"I love you, Rob, and I want this baby more than anything. You have to believe that."

He looked into her eyes and made himself a promise that if he were ever to believe anything, it would be that one thing.

"Yes," he said as he hugged her to him. "I believe you. But maybe you'd better tell me exactly how you *handled* things with Fairbanks?"

"I told him I had more evidence against his brother in a safety-deposit box and if anything happened to me, you had the key." She shrugged.

"So you lied?"

"About the safety deposit box and you having the key."

"Wait a minute. You are still in possession of items from Jack Fairbanks's stolen car?"

She nodded and went over to her top drawer, dug in the back and brought out a box filled with photos, letters, cards from past birthdays and Christmases. The woman saved everything. She sorted through it until she found a sealed plastic bag. She handed it to him.

"Leon suggested putting it in a plastic bag," she said.

"That Leon. Smart boy." Nash felt a start as he stared down at what appeared to be the deceased Jack Fairbanks's car registration. "I thought you gave this to Jonathan when he gave you the money?"

"I gave him the proof of insurance and some other papers," she said matter-of-factly. "So I'm thinking we should just throw away the car registration?"

Nash let out a curse as he looked closer at the registration. "Damn, Lucinda, this has got blood all over it."

She nodded and shrugged. "So did the other papers I gave him."

CHAPTER SIXTEEN

ANNA WAS MORE THAN relieved when she heard the door to her room open.

"Mr. Collins," Dr. Brubaker said from the doorway. "I'm going to have to ask you to leave now. My patient needs her rest."

Marc didn't look as if he was finished, but he stormed out, shoving past the doctor.

"Are you all right?" the doctor asked, coming to her bedside. "I'm sorry, I had to leave the hospital. I should have come back sooner."

His concern brought tears to her eyes.

She shook her head in answer.

He took her hand and sat down as she fought to control the pain. Tyler was gone. Now so was Gillian. Her chest heaved and her whole body began to rack with silent sobs.

She cried for the loss of her friend until she'd exhausted her tears. Dr. Brubaker handed her the box of tissues as she wiped her tears.

"I didn't kill Gillian," she said when she could finally speak.

He seemed surprised by her bluntness. "I never thought you did." He actually sounded as if he meant it.

"You might be the only person in town who believes me."

"She was a good friend?" he asked.

"My best since college." Anna smiled through her tears, warmed by her memories. "Gillian was the kind of person who, if you were her friend, would fight your battles for you. She wouldn't quit on you. Never. It wasn't in her nature. I always knew I could depend on her. Since I came out of the coma, Gillian has been the only sane, reliable constant in my life."

He nodded.

"I know what you're thinking. Marc claims he and Gillian had an affair. Well, I know them both. If it happened, it was only once and I can tell you that Marc caught Gillian at her lowest point. I wouldn't have blamed Gillian in any case."

Dr. Brubaker gave her hand a light squeeze before he withdrew. "I can't see you hurting anyone. Especially a good friend."

"Do you have any idea how much that means to me?" Tears stung her eyes again. "Do you have children?" She could see him with grandchildren on his lap. He was the kind of grandfather who would read with them and share the cinnamon candies he seemed to love so.

He shook his head. "Gladys couldn't conceive and by the time we tried to adopt, we were too old. But our house was always full of children. Gladys loved to bake. She kept the cookie jar stocked." His eyes filmed over with tears and Anna's heart broke at his loss. He would have made a wonderful grandfather.

"How long has Gladys been gone?"

He smiled. "Too long." He rose and changed the subject. "I'm glad to see that your fever had left and your lungs sound better. You do realize I can't keep you in the hospital much longer."

She knew what he was saying. Once she was released, there was a strong chance she would be arrested.

"Do you know a good lawyer?" she asked.

"Don't you have someone you can call in Seattle?"

She shook her head. "Isn't there one in Shadow Lake?"

"I would think you'd want the best criminal attorney money could buy."

"I'm hoping that won't be necessary. Anyway, the last thing I want is to look as if I need the best criminal attorney money can buy. I'd feel more comfortable just getting some advice from a local attorney."

He appeared skeptical. "Well, there is one lawyer in town. But I can tell you right now Billy Blake's never been involved in a case like this one and he's Officer Walker's good friend."

CHIEF ROB NASH SHUT OFF both the house phone and his cell. He needed this time with his wife to adjust to the fact that he was going to be a father.

He felt like a teenager. A man his age having a baby. One minute he thought himself the biggest fool ever. The next he was thanking God. A baby.

Other men his age had grandchildren.

He looked over at Lucinda. They'd spent the evening talking about baby names. If it was a boy, she wanted to name him Robert Nash, Jr. If it was a girl, Lucinda wanted to name her April.

"You know, like the month. This month," she'd said. "The happiest month of my life."

How could Nash argue with that?

Now Lucinda was napping, a half smile on her pretty face. He brushed a strand of blond hair back from her temple. He couldn't have loved her more than he did at this moment. People would talk. A man his age with a young wife and now a baby. No one would believe it was his baby.

He smiled. Let them talk. Let them speculate until the cows came home. He didn't care. He was happy. The thought surprised him. He'd pretty much known that Lucinda had married him for all the wrong reasons, but it hadn't worried him. At least that's what he'd told himself.

Obviously, he'd been suspicious or he wouldn't have set her up the other night. His heart pounded as he remembered

wanting to kill her and Fairbanks. Not that he didn't still want
to kill Fairbanks. But thank God he hadn't gone off half-
cocked and done something stupid and horribly tragic.

Getting up carefully from the bed not to wake her, he col-
lected his clothes, dressed and left a note for Lucinda in case
she stirred before he returned.

He had a lot on his mind. Jonathan Fairbanks, for one. Nash
wasn't sure what to do about him, but he took the clear plastic
with Lucinda's "blackmail" document with him as he left the
house.

He'd been shaken ever since he'd seen Jack Fairbanks's
bloody car registration. Just having it in his possession scared
him. It incriminated the hell out of his wife as part of a car-
theft ring—or worse. The blood on the registration definitely
had him thinking "or worse."

As he drove out of town, he knew what he had to do with
the plastic bag containing the evidence. He was a cop. But he
was also a husband with a wife who was having his baby.

When he'd checked his messages on his cell, he'd seen that
Walker had called four times, each time leaving a message
for Nash to call at once. He could only assume that Walker
was still working the Anna Collins case even though Nash had
told him to leave it be and let the state boys handle it.

Nash reminded himself that he still hadn't called the state
investigative unit. The problem was he feared what would
come up during the investigation if he called in the state
patrol. He'd handled a murder early on in his career. No
reason he couldn't handle this one. He could keep it low
profile. He would make sure the Fairbanks weren't involved.

He thought about his meeting just that morning with Ruth
Fairbanks, their discussion of Anna Collins and Ruth's request to have Jack's body exhumed.

Was it possible Jack was alive? Nash glanced over at the
plastic bag sitting on the seat. That would mean that Jack had

faked his death. If so, Nash had to wonder if it had something to do with what was in this plastic bag.

Nash couldn't let himself think too long about whose blood might be on the papers. Or how it had gotten there.

The bag and its contents represented a threat to Nash's wife and baby, to his future and his family's. That's all he let himself think about as he drove out of the town as the early evening light began to fade.

A few miles out of town, he pulled off onto one of the pine-tree-lined narrow roads that led to the lake. From the lack of tracks in the wet earth, he knew he would be alone.

Parking at the edge of the water in the dense pines, he cut the engine, picked up the plastic bag and got out. This was a favorite spot for summer keggers. Teens had been holding beer-drinking parties here since he was a teen himself.

The used fire pit was filled with ashes, charred beer cans and several logs that hadn't burned all the way through. Nash bent down and moved one of the logs aside to get to a dry spot. He placed the plastic bag and its bloody contents beside the log and took out the matches he'd borrowed from the kitchen.

For a moment he hesitated. Never in his life had he destroyed evidence. But then never in his life had he thought he'd be a father.

He struck a match, blocking the slight breeze coming off the lake to keep the flame alive as it touched the plastic bag.

The plastic shriveled back from the heat, wrinkling and blackening. The soiled dry paper of the registration caught fire in a heartbeat and burned to ashes almost as fast. Nash didn't have a chance to change his mind. He stayed crouched next to the fire pit until nothing lingered but his disappointment in himself.

One thing was clear. He wasn't going to be able to call in the state CID. Not as long as there was even a chance the Fairbankses were somehow involved and it might lead back to Lucinda.

BILLY BLAKE DIDN'T LOOK MUCH like a lawyer when he
showed up the next morning.

He came into Anna's hospital room wearing a fishing vest
and waders, grinning as he described to Dr. Brubaker a fish
that got away.

"I'm telling you it was a good two feet long," he said,
holding his hands at least three feet apart.

Anna watched the two, the thirty-something Billy Blake
grinning, his face sunburned around squint lines, and the
doctor laughing in that easy way of his. She suspected that
Billy was one of the boys that the doctor's wife, Gladys, had
plied with cookies.

Anna wanted to stay in this moment, listening to their
good-natured banter and Dr. Brubaker's laughter.

"Why is it that the big ones you catch, Billy, always
manage to get away?" the doc joked.

"I was planning to throw this one back anyway. You know
me, catch and release Blake."

"I've never known you to throw back a big fish without
showing it off at the Watering Hole first, Billy Blake," the
doctor said.

"See how he is?" Billy said to her as he dragged off his
fishing hat. Several large flies were pinned to the brim along
with a half-dozen lures that twinkled and jingled as he tossed
the hat aside and turned his grin on her.

"William Blake, attorney, at your service," he said holding
out his hand. "Call me Billy. Everybody does."

His hand was warm and dry, deeply tanned up to his wrist,
making her suspect he spent most of his time fishing.

"Anna," she said, adding, "Collins, I guess." His eyes were
a deep warm brown.

Doc excused himself, telling Anna she was in good hands.

Billy Blake instantly turned serious. "Doc told you I
haven't had much opportunity in Shadow Lake to defend

anyone in a murder trial, but I can recommend several good criminal lawyers from the Seattle area."

"I don't want to hire a high-profile lawyer. It will only make it appear I need one."

He laughed. "That's one way to look at it. Of course, the other is that those lawyers get the big bucks because they're good and I've got to tell you, I think you do need a lawyer."

"Then it's a good thing I called you."

Billy shook his head, eyeing her with a smile. "I'll be happy to give you legal advice, but I can't let you retain me. I'm close friends with the police officer who's investigating your case. It's too fine a line for me to walk. But I'm full of advice and anything you tell me, of course, would be confidential."

"Okay, I'll take any advice you can give me."

"Then I guess you'd better fill me in."

She told him everything she could remember, along with what Officer Walker, her friend Mary Ellen and finally Marc had told her.

He listened, nodding occasionally, taking no notes.

"I want to cooperate with the police," she said in conclusion. "I have nothing to hide." At least she prayed she didn't. "I want to help them find Gillian's killer."

"Yeah," Billy said. "Nice attitude. I commend you on it. But unless you want to spend the rest of your life behind bars, I'd suggest we consider some other options. Did you give Officer Walker permission to look in your car? Open the trunk?"

"No."

"Illegal search. Could maybe keep that evidence from being allowed during the trial, but believe me the prosecution will find a way around it."

"Trial?" Her voice sounded unusually high. "You don't really think I'll be arrested and stand trial? I didn't kill Gillian."

"Has Officer Walker told you how Gillian was killed?"

"No, but he was asking about my gun so I just assumed…"

Billy nodded. "If the victim was killed with your gun and your prints are on it, then yeah, you'll be arrested. So where is your gun?"

"I don't know."

"Last seen?"

She hesitated. "Marc said I took it with me when I left the house to go see Gillian."

Billy winced. "If you weren't angry with Gillian, why take your gun?"

She shook her head. "I get the feeling that I thought I might need the thirty-eight to protect myself. It doesn't look good, does it?"

"Motive, opportunity and a good possibly your gun was the murder weapon with your fingerprints on it? No, it doesn't look good."

"But we don't know that my gun is the murder weapon, right?"

"No, but you can bet if Walker was asking about it, then the murder weapon was a thirty-eight. And the way things are looking, it will be your gun," Billy said.

"I didn't kill her."

"She bonked your husband."

Anna flinched at his crudeness.

"Let me honest with you. You're sitting between a rock and a hard place. You say you can't remember—"

"I can't."

He nodded. "Doesn't make any difference. No judge or jury is going to believe it."

"But I'm innocent."

Billy laughed. "Like no judge or jury has ever heard that before."

She felt herself flush with frustration. "It's the truth. I wouldn't kill my best friend."

"If it comes to a trial, every juror is going to be sitting there thinking what he or she would do if their best friend had an affair with their spouse while they were in a coma. You'll never convince them that you didn't kill her."

"This is ridiculous," she snapped. "All we have is Marc's word that he slept with Gillian."

Billy raised a brow. "Denial, too? Why would your husband lie?"

"To hurt me." She looked away. "You have to understand. My husband has been through so much this past year. I was in a car accident that killed our son and left me in a coma for almost six months. Marc didn't know if I was even going to survive. And then, when I finally did come out of the coma, I didn't remember anything. I couldn't remember anything about the accident or even what I was doing out that night with our son."

"Had Marc been drinking when he came by to see you?"

She started, surprised he'd ask that.

"There are no secrets in Shadow Lake," Billy said. "So let's talk about your husband. You still in love with him?"

"No."

"Then why were you defending him a few minutes ago?"

"He was my son's father."

"Is that why you're still wearing your wedding ring?"

She stared down at her hand, surprised to see it still there. "No."

"Then take it off. It makes you look like you were trying to hang on to him and that you would kill to save your marriage."

"That's ridiculous." Anna looked down at the wedding ring on her left hand. The diamond was large and unfamiliar. When she and Marc had gotten married, he'd given her a small diamond ring. She'd loved that ring, but Marc had insisted he was going to buy her a decent diamond when his business took off. He'd put this ring on her finger when she'd been in the coma.

As she tugged off the ring, she wondered what he'd done with the other ring, the one that had meant something to her.

"This guy break your heart?" Billy asked as he watched her drop the ring onto the top of her nightstand.

"No. Yes. But a long time ago."

Billy nodded. "It still shows. You look like hell and are clearly hurting. Makes you look guilty."

"Marc isn't the reason I'm hurting. I lost my son, and now my best friend. That's what broke my heart and my spirit. I wasn't reconciling with Marc."

"He says you were. It isn't just his word against yours, either. It's the way you were dressed that night."

She traced the path of her scar, then caught herself and folded her hands in her lap. "All I can assume was that I was stunned by his change of heart. But then…"

"What?" he asked.

"When Gillian called, I just have this feeling that whatever she told me on the phone that night, it's not just the reason I came to Shadow Lake." She shook her head before meeting the lawyer's gaze. "It's the reason I can't stand the sight of Marc now, the reason I took the gun, the reason I can't shake the feeling that it has something to do with the Fairbankses and the hit-and-run and my son's death."

"That narrows it down." He studied her openly for a moment. "You're taking his affair with your best friend awfully well."

"That's because I know what the circumstances had to have been, if Marc is even telling the truth. Gillian didn't like Marc."

"He's a pretty good-looking guy, successful, sharp dresser," Billy said. "What's not to like? You're in a coma, she's always wondered what he would be like and she decides to try him out."

Anna actually laughed.

"What makes you so sure it didn't happen that way?"

"Because I told Gillian *everything*," she said. "Including what Marc was like in bed. If Gillian slept with him, she wasn't looking for sexual fulfillment."

Billy let out a howl of a laugh. "Now we're getting somewhere. You're going to have to be dead-on honest with yourself if you hope to sort out this mess. You had a body in your trunk, but what is hurting you most is your husband's statement that one—" he ticked off on his fingers "—he told you about the affair and you went berserk and two, you threatened to kill Gillian and left in a murderous rage with your gun to go over to her house—which you did. He gave you both motive and opportunity. The guy was divorcing you, but at the last minute didn't go through with it. Why'd he change his mind, anyway?"

She swallowed, tears burning her eyes at just the thought of the damage Marc had done. "I don't know. If I told you what I suspect, you'd think I was crazy."

Billy looked at her and chuckled. "You think Jack Fairbanks saved your life on the bottom of the lake. I already know you have to be crazy."

"Okay, then it probably won't hurt to tell you that I think Marc wanted to reconcile to keep me from learning whatever it was Gillian told me that night. And it had nothing to do with his sex life or lack there of. But it's the reason Gillian is dead."

Billy let out a low whistle. "You think Marc killed her to shut her up before she could tell you?"

Anna had to admit it had crossed her mind. "I don't know. Maybe."

"That could explain why he's trying so hard to get you arrested," Billy said.

"So what can I do?" she asked.

"Get yourself a high-profile, expensive lawyer." He glanced toward the diamond ring she'd left on the nightstand.

"If you don't have the money, hock your jewelry. If I were you, I wouldn't wait."

"What are my chances if I do that?"

"Well, you have jury sympathy going for you. Life has crapped all over you. You get hurt in a hit-and-run accident, your only child is killed. You're in a coma for months and when you wake up, your husband wants a divorce. You think it can't get any worse and *bam!* Your husband hits you with the ultimate betrayal. Your closest friend since college is bonking your husband. Any juror would feel for you. Hell, nobody should have to go through what you did. But bottom line, they're going to send you up. They've got to because they can't condone murder. Now if you'd killed your cheating no-account husband, a good lawyer would have had a much better chance of getting you off."

"Are you trying to comfort me, because if you are it isn't working."

"From me, you get honesty. You believe you're innocent, want to help the police find the real killer, don't want to look guilty. Well, I'm here to tell you, forget all that. You're in a hole. Your husband helped dig it. He'll bury you for whatever his reasons. The best thing you can do is keep your head down, because you look guilty as sin and no matter what you say you're only going to dig that hole deeper if you aren't careful."

She said nothing for a moment. "I don't understand why Marc would say the things he has."

"Sure you do. He blames you for his son's death."

Was Marc's motive that transparent that everyone saw it?

"He's shooting off his mouth to anyone who will listen, telling everyone that you need psychiatric help."

"But it's not true." At least she hoped not.

Billy raised a brow. "Excuse me? You think you saw a dead man at the bottom of the lake." She started to protest. "You think that's not going to be used against you? Like I said, best keep that one under your hat at least until this murder rap is behind you. That means staying clear of the Fairbankses. Mess with the Fairbankses and you'll get the death penalty."

"My only hope of finding out who killed Gillian is the Fairbankses," she said. "It's the only clue I have."

He groaned. "How did I know you were going to say that? This scrap of envelope that puts you at the victim's house," Blake said. "You say Ruth Fairbanks has it?"

"I showed it to her when I went out there and…she kept it. At least I think she did."

He raked a hand through his hair. "She said she didn't have any idea what you were talking about, but she kept the scrap of envelope?"

"I don't think she was telling me the truth."

"You think?"

"I've been accused of being too trusting."

He grinned at that. "There are worse faults." His grin broadened. "The good news is that if people are lying to you, then they have something to hide."

What did Ruth Fairbanks have to hide? she wondered.

Billy rubbed the back of his neck, studying her.

"I'm perfectly sane," she said, just in case he was wondering. "There is an explanation for everything that has happened."

He grinned again. "I'm sure there is. But what if that explanation is that you're a murderer? You might be better off crazy."

CHAPTER SEVENTEEN

ANNA FELT BETTER AFTER Billy Blake left, but when she saw the expression on Dr. Brubaker's face when she found him, she could see that he seemed worried.

He'd been standing by the window, the rain-streaked glass reflecting his face. He had appeared to be staring out at the lake, his face etched against the dull light of day. She'd been surprised by his expression. He'd looked as if he carried the weight of the world on his shoulders.

But he smiled as he turned to her, coming to her as if nothing was wrong.

"How are you feeling?" he asked with forced cheerfulness as he walked her back to her room.

"Much better."

After she'd climbed back into bed, he lifted his stethoscope and leaned toward her. "Take a deep breath for me. Let it out slowly."

She did as he said, staring up at the ceiling as he listened. When he finished, he nodded.

"I'm well enough to be released, aren't I?" she asked suspecting that was part of the concern she saw in his face.

"You know you won't be able to leave town," he said.

"She's *not* leaving town."

Startled, they both turned. Anna couldn't have been more surprised to see the woman standing in the open doorway.

Ruth Fairbanks wore an expensive gray pantsuit with black

trim and looked as if she was off for a day of shopping in the big city. "I'd like to speak with Mrs. Collins alone, please."

Dr. Brubaker looked to Anna. All she could do was nod.

"I came to invite you out to the island," Ruth Fairbanks said, the moment the doctor left the room.

Anna blinked. Not twenty-four hours ago Ruth Fairbanks was calling the police on her and Jonathan Fairbanks was threatening to have her arrested for trespassing. "I don't understand."

"It's simple enough. As the doctor said, you aren't going to be allowed to leave town. I'm inviting you to stay with me rather than in one of Shadow Lake's less than inviting motels. I think you'll be more comfortable in my home."

Anna wasn't so sure about that, based on the reception she'd gotten the last time. "Why would you do this?"

"We need to talk," Ruth Fairbanks said. "Let me be frank. Apparently it is only a matter of time before you'll be arrested for murder. I can be a powerful ally."

Anna stared at her. "Knowing that, you'd still invite me into your home? How can you be sure I'm *not* a murderer?"

Ruth Fairbanks waved a hand through the air as if that was of no concern to her.

"I'll need to speak with my lawyer first," Anna said.

"I've already spoken with Mr. Blake. Call him if you like, but I can tell you that he is strongly opposed to it. However, I suggest you take *my* advice, which is that you would be a fool not to take me up on my offer." She arched a brow. "From what I've seen of you, you are no fool."

Anna was only a little surprised that Ruth Fairbanks knew she'd talked to Billy Blake. Ruth didn't seem to know, though, that Anna hadn't actually hired the lawyer.

She had to wonder what Ruth wanted to talk to her about, but clearly Anna wouldn't be getting any more out of her here. Nor had Anna forgotten that Ruth had kept the scrap of

envelope with "Fairbanks" written on it in Gillian's distinct
scrawl. Also Ruth Fairbanks had seemed to recognize Anna's
name. All leading Anna to believe that she and the woman
definitely had something to discuss.

A man appeared at the door, carrying several large shopping bags from several expensive Seattle stores whose names
Anna recognized. Ruth Fairbanks turned and motioned him
in with an impatient flick of her wrist. He put the bags down
and left without a word.

"I took the liberty of purchasing a few items of clothing
for you," Ruth said. "I understand the clothing you were
wearing is being held as evidence. So, can I expect you then?"

Anna didn't know what to say. "Your offer is very kind. I *will*
take you up on it," she said, meeting the woman's steel-gray
gaze.

"Good. I've already cleared it with Judge Gandy since I
couldn't reach Chief Nash. As soon as Dr. Brubaker releases
you, a car will be waiting to drive you to the marina where
the boat will bring you out to the island. As you can see, I've
taken care of everything."

So it seemed.

Without another word, Ruth Fairbanks turned on her heel
and left. A moment later, Dr. Brubaker came into the hospital
room.

"She wants me to come out to the island," Anna said, answering his questioning look. "It seems there's something we
have to talk about."

"I take it you're considering it then?"

Something in his tone surprised her. "You knew about
this."

"Ruth Fairbanks and I have known each other for years,"
he said. "She is the most determined woman I think I have
ever known. Also, she wields a lot of power in this state. She
could prove a valuable asset—if she was on your side."

"And if not?" Anna asked, already suspecting the answer.

"She could be very dangerous," he said bluntly. "But nothing compared to her son Jonathan. Be careful out there."

Anna told herself that the invitation proved the Fairbankses were why she was in Shadow Lake. Maybe even why Gillian was dead. "You are going to release me, aren't you? I feel much better and it's not like a boat ride in the middle of the night."

He sighed. "You're well enough to go if you continue to take care of yourself." He reached into his white lab coat pocket and pulled out a small card and several cinnamon candies. He handed her a candy and the card. "My cell phone number is on the back." His meaning was clear.

AFTER HIS TRIP TO THE OLD fire pit south of town, Chief Nash had gone home, crawled into bed with his pregnant wife and held her to him to take away the chill that had settled into his old, tired body.

This morning he left Lucinda sleeping peacefully and wandered into the kitchen to make coffee. He decided to have some orange juice and a bowl of cereal instead of skipping breakfast as he usually did.

He had to take better care of himself now that he was going to be a father. It still hadn't really sunk in, but he loved the thought. Except for the fact that he would be over seventy when his son or daughter graduated from high school.

Mostly, he wanted to make his child proud of him. He wanted to be a good man, an honest man, a fair one. From this day on.

That was one reason he'd had so much trouble getting to sleep last night. He couldn't forget what he'd done. Before daylight this morning he'd decided to announce he would be retiring after this case. It was the only thing he could do. He was no longer the kind of cop he wanted to be.

He'd lain awake for hours, his mind circling from Jonathan

Fairbanks to that damned bloody car registration and back again. Nash wanted nothing better than to go out to the island and confront the man everyone believed would one day be the president of the United States.

But he'd been a cop long enough to know that the best thing he could do was forget it. If that were possible. He needed to put all his energy into Lucinda and being the best father he could be for their baby.

Unfortunately, this Anna Collins investigation weighed heavily on his mind. His fear, of course, was that exhuming Jack Fairbanks was going to bring everything crashing down not only on the Fairbanks family—but also Lucinda. Jonathan would have been smart enough to conceal that twenty-five thousand in blackmail money he'd given Lucinda. There would be no way to prove anything.

Nash needed insurance that Jonathan could never use Lucinda's blackmail as leverage against him or their child. Fairbanks had the ability to put Nash in a worse position than he was already in.

Nash wasn't stupid, though. He knew Jonathan wouldn't have paid the blackmail demand unless he had something to hide. The cop in him wanted to know why Jonathan had paid Lucinda to keep quiet. It couldn't have been to hide the fact that Jack had been involved with drugs, something Nash questioned to begin with.

He'd known Jack Fairbanks. He couldn't see Jack being an addict. His wife, Pet, was another story. Still not blackmail material, though.

No, what Jonathan had to fear was tied to that blood on the car registration.

Nash's every instinct was to retire as quickly as possible, leave Shadow Lake and go somewhere where no one knew him and Lucinda. The problem was that a man like Jonathan Fairbanks would be able to find them, no matter where they went.

His cell phone rang and he realized he'd forgotten to turn if off after checking his messages. He snatched it up. "Nash."

"Chief."

He heard the exasperation, the accusation, the frustration in that one word. "You didn't get my messages?" Walker asked.

"Sorry, I had my phone off and didn't realize it." Nash knew Walker wasn't going to buy that. "I've had some personal things to take care of the past few days. What's up?"

"Anna Collins. I know you said to let the state CID handle it, but I haven't heard from them and I had to check on a few things."

Nash swore.

"I drove up to the rest stop last night. I found Gillian Sanders's car hidden behind a gravel pile near the rest stop— just up the road from where the Collins car went into the lake. It appears that's where Gillian Sanders was murdered. I found two sets of car tracks. One matches the Sanders car; the other Collins's Cadillac. I also found a man's boot prints in the mud. The tracks lead to a cove on the lake below the rest stop where it appeared a boat had been tied up."

Walker rushed on as if fearing Nash might try to stop him. "I also checked out Collins's car. The seat belt that she'd said was jammed. I think she was telling the truth about being trapped in the car. I also found evidence that supports her story about someone rescuing her. Whoever cut the seat belt to get her out of there used the vanity mirror. There's no way she could have done that."

Nash had to sit down. He dropped into one of the kitchen chairs. "Who?"

"That's the part that has me thrown."

"You aren't going to tell me you think it was Jack Fairbanks."

"No, but I'm worried that the Fairbankses are involved based on the note Anna Collins said she found in her coat pocket. The one you said Ruth Fairbanks showed you. It looks as if Gillian Sanders really was meeting someone at the rest stop. Presumably one of the Fairbankses."

The connection to the Fairbankses. It just kept coming back to the Fairbankses. His heart pounded hard against his chest. Maybe Ruth was right to want Jack's exhumation.

"I secured the crime scene and typed up my report for CID," Walker was saying. "I know you want them to handle it. But there is one more thing I thought you'd want to know. I found a bullet hole in the trunk and when I checked the body—"

He'd checked the body. Nash swore again under his breath.

"Gillian Sanders was shot *after* she died. It looks as if someone is trying to frame Anna Collins for the murder."

Nash didn't know what to say.

"There's more," Walker said with a sigh. "Judge Gandy called. He gave Ruth Fairbanks permission to have Anna Collins stay at the island until this is resolved."

Nash felt his chest constrict. He glanced toward the bedroom. He could see Lucinda. She was lying on her side, her hands under her head, her blond hair framing her face.

"Thank you for letting me know," he managed to say.

"I left a copy of my report on your desk," Walker said. "I have the next few days off, but I'm not going anywhere, so if CID or you need—"

"Nice work, Walker." He hung up, his hand shaking.

What the hell was going on? He recalled the note Ruth had shown him, the one Anna Collins said she found in her coat pocket. It just kept coming back to the Fairbankses.

And that's what scared him. That and Walker. The cop reminded Nash of himself when he was that age. Young and idealistic. Walker wouldn't stop until he got to the bottom of this, even without the state criminal investigation division troopers.

Nash heard a sound in the bedroom. When he looked up he saw Lucinda watching him, a worried expression on her face, and he knew it was time to tell Walker he'd decided not to call in the state CID, that they could handle this within the local department.

Walker would be suspicious, but Nash had to get a handle on this investigation. It was the only way he could protect his wife, because, sure as hell, Jonathan Fairbanks was involved.

Which meant it wouldn't be any time before Fairbanks would use that leverage he had against Lucinda to get Nash to make this all go away.

AFTER WHAT HE'D DISCOVERED IN the garage last night, Walker hadn't been able to sleep. He'd gone fishing, then just before light, he'd stopped by the police station and requested phone records for the past eight months for Anna Collins, Marc Collins, Gillian Sanders and all of the Fairbankses, including Jack.

He wasn't surprised that within the hour he received a call from Judge Gandy telling him he would need a court order to get the phone records on Senator Big Jim Fairbanks.

"I'm investigating the murder of Gillian Sanders," Walker said. "I believe she was meeting one of the Fairbankses the night of her murder."

"Unless you have definitive proof regarding a specific Fairbanks, I wouldn't think of giving you a court order for their phones," the judge said emphatically.

Walker hadn't been surprised. He knew that Judge Gandy and Ruth Fairbanks were tight.

He'd known it wouldn't be easy to get anything on the Fairbanks family even though he was more convinced than ever that they were somehow involved. Of course he'd known *that* the moment he'd heard Ruth Fairbanks had been to the hospital to bust Anna Collins out. The question was Anna Collins's involvement with the Fairbanks.

She'd sworn she'd never met any of the Fairbankses before coming to Shadow Lake. Nor was she aware of any contact Gillian Sanders might have made with the family prior to that time.

Walker hoped the phone records, both landline and cell, would provide the answer.

Meanwhile, he wondered if Anna Collins had any idea what she was getting herself into by agreeing to stay with the Fairbankses. Ruth was a viper who protected her nest at all costs.

And Jonathan…

Walker hoped to hell bringing Anna Collins to the house wasn't his idea. Anna Collins could end up in the lake again, with more tragic results, if Jonathan had anything to do with it.

AS ANNA DRESSED IN THE clothing Ruth Fairbanks had purchased for her, and she was only a little surprised.

The clothes didn't just fit perfectly; they were in a style, cut and color that Anna might have chosen for herself. Ruth had a good eye and had thought of everything including lingerie, a robe, slippers and several types of shoes for both casual and dress.

Anna had said something to Dr. Brubaker about the almost formal attire Ruth had purchased for her.

"The Fairbankses dress for dinner," he said with the quirk of one bushy gray brow. "Apparently she intends for you to stay a while."

Apparently. The question was why she was treating Anna with such graciousness, especially after their first meeting had almost landed Anna in handcuffs and a jail cell.

Doc signed her release form and carried the spare clothing out to the waiting car Ruth had sent. Anna felt as if she was climbing into the lion's den as the driver opened the door for her and she slid into the backseat.

"Remember to call if you need anything," Doc said as the driver loaded her clothing.

"Thank you." She'd called Billy Blake. Ruth had been right.

Billy thought it a terrible idea. Anna was starting to think he might have been right as the driver pulled away from the hospital.

Not that she was about to change her mind. If she had any hope of getting out of this mess, she had to determine what had happened the night she went into the lake, the night Gillian was murdered. Ruth Fairbanks had to know something; otherwise, why invite Anna to stay on the island?

Anna had to question why Ruth Fairbanks would want an alleged murderer on her island—let alone in her house. Unless Ruth Fairbanks knew with certainty that Anna was innocent. But wouldn't that mean Ruth Fairbanks knew who had murdered Gillian? Or at the very least why Gillian thought the Fairbankses knew something about Tyler's death?

DR. BRUBAKER WATCHED THE car drive away with Anna Collins and tried not to worry.

As he started to go back into the hospital he heard a voice behind him. He turned to find Father Tom Bertonelli coming toward him.

"A moment of your time, Gene," the priest said as he stopped to catch his breath.

Gene had a bad feeling the good father hadn't stopped by to collect for a priests' old-age home. He greatly regretted that moment of weakness the other night when he'd gone down to the church and confessed. Confession might be good for the soul, but it had done nothing to make him feel better. Nor did he believe it had absolved him of anything.

"A miserable day to be out for walk, Tom."

The old priest nodded solemnly under the shadow of his large black umbrella.

"I was just heading home," Gene Brubaker said, hoping to cut short whatever this was. "I have to pick up some papers for a patient." He figured lying to a priest at this point was the least of his worries. Lying to an old friend was harder.

Tom met his gaze, held it, then nodded slowly as he said, "In that case, I'll walk with you."

With no other option now, he followed the priest up the street, forced to share the umbrella. Doc slowed his pace to match that of his old friend.

"I've been thinking about you, Gene," Tom said as they walked at a snail's pace along the main street.

He was thankful there was no traffic. Nor was there anyone else out for a stroll. He felt a headache coming on and realized he hadn't eaten anything this morning.

"Thinking about the talk we had the other night," Tom said.

"You mean my confession," he said.

Tom didn't look at him. Instead, the priest kept his eyes on the sidewalk, his gait awkward, as if walking was the last thing his legs wanted to do anymore.

"Hmm, yes," Tom said. "I've thought of little else. What you told me has left me troubled."

His pulse quickened. "I thought confessions were confidential."

"Indeed they are." The priest stopped under the dark still-bare limbs of a maple in sight of the church. He took a deep breath and let out a long sigh. He looked ancient, his face in deep shadow, his expression grave.

Brubaker felt a wave of sadness. When had they both gotten so old? Worse, he realized that the priest, like himself, wasn't long for this world.

"This burden you carry," Father Bertonelli said, his voice low and aggrieved. "It must be a very difficult one. You did the right thing confessing and turning it over to God. I have prayed that you will receive the guidance you need. I would hate to see you take such a burden with you to your grave."

Brubaker said nothing. This wasn't something that a few Hail Marys could make right. "I killed my wife, Tom."

His old friend nodded. "To end her suffering as she begged you to do in the last hours of her life."

Tears sprang to Brubaker's eyes. "Semantics."

"Gladys is at peace. It is you I'm concerned about. Your soul, Gene." The priest regarded him. "I know how much you miss Gladys and want to join her. I've seen you pull away from the church, the community, old friends."

Brubaker couldn't look at him.

"I would hate to see your life cut short, but more than that, I couldn't bear for you to do something that would keep you and Gladys from being together for eternity." Tom patted his shoulder. "You'd better get those papers for your patient." With that, his old friend shook the rain from his umbrella and hobbled off across the street to the church, never looking back.

Brubaker took a deep breath. Overhead, a flock of birds swept past, their dark bodies silhouetted against the pale blue sky, reminding him of when he was a boy and the nuns used to sweep down the school hall in a whisper of dark mysterious fabric.

The image sent a wave of dread through him as the elderly priest disappeared inside the church, the door closing without a sound behind him.

AS THE BOAT NEARED THE island, Anna spotted the huge stone mansion with a sense of apprehension. The afternoon sun slanted across the water, making the stones gleam with blinding intensity. Seeing it now in the daylight, Anna thought the place was even more intimidating. As was the family.

To her surprise, the island appeared to be larger than she'd first thought. The house stood on the south end, surrounded on three sides by both beach bluffs and rocky shoreline. Trees graced the large expanse of grass that separated the house from the shore.

But to the north beyond the house, the land became more rugged, with thick stands of pines and fleeting glimpses of sheer cliffs that disappeared in the low clouds.

As the boat pulled into the dock, Anna looked up and saw a man's face at the farthest window to the north on the second floor. Jonathan Fairbanks. He disappeared at once, leaving Anna with the impression that he hadn't wanted to be seen. A moment later another face appeared in the window. This one a woman with long red hair. Pet.

CHAPTER EIGHTEEN

"ANYBODY HOME?" BILLY BLAKE called as he came around the side of the house to Walker's back screened-in porch, as if knowing where to find his friend this time of day.

The sun was almost down, the air cooling quickly as dark shadows settled into the pines around the cabin Walker called home. The cabin had belonged to his grandfather. He'd spent many an evening sitting here, just as he was now, watching the sun sink into the lake.

Only this evening, Walker had been battling with himself and the ghosts in his life. It was one reason Billy was a sight for sore eyes.

"Beer?" Walker asked as Billy climbed the steps. He handed him a bottle of cold beer from the cooler beside his chair. "I ordered a pizza. Had a feeling you might be stopping by."

Billy grinned as he took the beer and slouched into the beach chair next to him. Neither said anything as Billy twisted the cap off the bottle and took a drink.

This was Walker's favorite spot. He loved the backyard with its huge trees and wide grassy slope that ended at the lake. In the far distance, he could make out the dock light glowing at the Fairbankses' island. He and Jack had a signal they used during the summers when they were kids. When Jack couldn't get a boat to sneak off the island, Walker would pick him up.

"So you heard," Billy said.

Walker grunted. "I can't believe Ruth Fairbanks is having Jack exhumed."

"I meant about Anna Collins staying out at the Fairbankses. I heard Ruth went through Judge Gandy."

"It's crazy. Why would Ruth Fairbanks offer Anna a place to stay after calling the cops and having Anna thrown off the property just hours before?"

"A change of heart?" Billy suggested.

Walker snorted.

"Well, Anna Collins is safer there than with her husband."

"That's not saying much."

Billy took another long draw on his beer. "Maybe Ruth Fairbanks got Anna out of the hospital to kill her," he joked. "Naw, that would be hell on Jonathan's political career and we all know that's the only thing the Fairbankses care about."

"Everyone seems to have forgotten that a woman has been murdered." Walker swore. "Especially Rob Nash."

"I guess everyone just assumes the killer is Anna Collins."

He shot his friend a look. "A damned good reason not to invite the woman to stay at your house if you ask me."

"Any idea what Ruth or Jonathan want from her?" Billy asked.

Walker didn't answer. He took a drink of his beer and stared out at the lake through the trees, not sure if he really wanted to open this Pandora's box. There was a chill in the air that had settled in him tonight.

"That's just it," he said finally. "None of this makes any sense."

"I agree. Why would Anna Collins shoot her best friend and put the body in her trunk?"

Walker shrugged.

"What?" Billy asked with interest. "You know something?"

"I found Gillian's car parked behind a pile of gravel near

the rest stop on the hill." He also told him about what he'd found at the garage.

"She didn't do it." Billy raised his beer bottle. "I knew she didn't do it."

"The evidence isn't enough to exonerate her," Walker pointed out. "But there are a lot of unanswered questions. Like who put the body in the trunk of the Cadillac."

"A man who wanted to frame Anna Collins for murder," Billy said simply. "No way Anna could have lifted Gillian Sanders's dead weight.

"People under stress have been known to lift automobiles," Walker argued, for the sake of argument more than anything else. He'd already had this same discussion with himself and decided she couldn't have put the body in the trunk.

"She loaded the body to go fifty yards and drive into the lake?" Billy laughed. "No one is *that* crazy."

Walker lifted a brow. "Let's not forget that she's still claiming that Jack saved her."

Billy eyed him, grinning. "But you don't think she purposely drove into the lake anymore?"

"I told you. I don't know what to think. If you buy into part of her story, you kinda have to buy into the rest, don't you think?"

"There is probably a logical explanation," Billy said. "Like she saw Jonathan Fairbanks at the rest stop."

"And that's how she thought she saw Jack under the water? It was *Jonathan?*" Walker snorted. "Even if Jonathan Fairbanks was physically able, he wouldn't have gone in the water to save anyone and you know it. But Jack would—"

"Wait a minute," Billy interrupted. "You saw the body when it was brought in. It was Jack Fairbanks, right?"

"After that long in the water…"

Billy was staring at him now, his beer forgotten. "Oh, hell. Are you telling me you're actually starting to believe that Jack is alive?"

THE MAN, WHO HAD TOLD Anna she could call him Gregory, parked the boat next to the dock and got out, steadying the craft to allow her to disembark.

She stood for a moment on the dock, hoping Gregory was planning on coming up with her.

"Mrs. Fairbanks is waiting for you," he said, making no move to accompany her to the house.

She nodded. "What about—"

"I have been instructed to take care of your belongings." Gregory slanted his head toward the house in an impatient gesture.

She glanced again at the second-floor window as she walked toward the front entrance. The waning sun broke free of the clouds to glint off glass like a mirror. She couldn't tell if someone was standing at the window peering out. But she had the feeling that she was being watched as she made her way up the slope to the house.

Gregory, she'd noticed, had tied up the boat and taken the clothing Ruth Fairbanks had purchased around to the back of the house.

Given that someone definitely knew she had arrived, she'd expected Mrs. Fairbanks to meet her at the door.

That assumption was wrong she realized when she had to ring the doorbell and wait and, not for the first time, she wondered what she was doing here.

Anna was about to ring the bell again, her apprehension growing, especially after seeing Jonathan and his sister-in-law in that second-floor window.

Suddenly the door flew open and she found herself face-to-face with Jonathan Fairbanks.

"What the hell?" he bellowed. "I thought I made it perfectly clear that you were never to set foot on this island again. Carol," he said to the maid nervously waiting behind him. "Call the police."

Anna looked past him and, with relief, saw Ruth Fairbanks coming down the stairs.

"Carol, you will do no such thing," Ruth said in a tone that could have turned the lake water from liquid to ice. "I invited Mrs. Collins here."

"*Mother?* Have you lost your mind?" Jonathan demanded. "What am I saying? Of course you have."

Ruth Fairbanks's lips curled up in a tight smile. "While that is what you would have people believe, Jonathan, I know exactly what I'm doing." She gave Anna a speculative look. "Carol, show my guest to her room."

Anna hesitated. "Maybe I should—"

"I will be up shortly," Ruth said, cutting her off. "I thought you might want to freshen up before dinner. Gregory has already taken your belongings up." With that, she dismissed Anna's objections and turned to her son. "Jonathan, I will speak with you in the den." Ruth Fairbanks had already turned her back and was heading down the hall, her slim body appearing as unyielding as a steel beam.

Jonathan glared at Anna before turning and limping down the hall after his mother.

Carol cleared her throat. "This way, madam." Her tone made it clear she agreed with Jonathan at least on this matter.

As Anna followed the starched-uniformed maid up the stairs, she could hear raised voices in the den and wondered how long before she was on a boat headed back to town. Hopefully long enough to have that talk with Ruth Fairbanks.

Carol led her up the wide staircase and down a long hallway to a guest bedroom at the back of the house.

The first thing Anna noticed was the view from the small terrace. She could see more of the island, the cliff she'd only glimpsed earlier, a stand of pines and a small sandy beach at the edge of a sheltered cove. Beyond it, at the far northern end of the island, she saw what looked like the roof of an old cabin.

"If you need anything, you may ring for it," Carol said, glancing around the room as if to memorize its contents. Anna figured she would also count the silverware after Anna left.

Half expecting Carol to lock the door behind her, Anna was surprised when she didn't even close it. Apparently, Ruth Fairbanks wasn't worried about her loose in the house.

At the window, Anna looked out at the lake again. The last of the day's sun painted the water gold, making the pines at the edge jet-black.

She couldn't hear the mother and son arguing, but she didn't doubt they were. She had little doubt also how it would end. Jonathan appeared to be a man who always got what he wanted—one way or the other. What would she do when she was sent back to town? She had a bad feeling she'd be forced to stay in Shadow Lake until everything was resolved. Hopefully, she wouldn't be spending that time in jail.

"Is the room satisfactory?"

Anna spun away from the window to find Ruth Fairbanks standing in the bedroom doorway. The room was beautiful. That wasn't the problem. "I'm sure your son would prefer I not stay."

The older woman stepped in, closing the door behind her. "My son doesn't run this house—he simply tries to." Ruth moved through the room as if making sure that everything was as it should be.

Anna realized she'd underestimated Ruth Fairbanks. "Not that I don't appreciate your hospitality, but why am I here?"

The older woman looked at her with a piercing gray-eyed gaze that was especially chilling given that Anna had seen that same look at the bottom of the lake only nights before.

"Are you aware that your...husband," Ruth said with obvious distaste, "has been petitioning the local judge to have you locked up in a mental institution?" She smiled at Anna's surprise. "He failed to tell you that, I see. I convinced Judge Gandy that what you needed was rest and that I would make sure you got it."

Anna abhorred the thought of being indebted to this woman. Worse, to be held captive here.

"What are you saying? That I'm a prisoner here?" Anna asked, shocked by this turn of events.

"Of course not," Ruth said and smiled. "You still have options. Of course, if you left, the judge would probably agree with your husband that you belong in a mental institution, since anyone who'd turn down my gracious hospitality would have to be crazy, don't you think?"

Anna took a breath and let it out slowly, reminding herself why she was here. The note with Gillian's handwriting. Someone in this house knew about the hit-and-run accident. Knew why Gillian was dead.

"When you put it that way," Anna said carefully, "then I should thank you for rescuing me. However, while I am appreciative, I do have to wonder about your motivations."

Ruth Fairbanks laughed and gave her a measured look. "I would think less of you if you didn't." She studied Anna openly. "I make up my own mind about people."

Anna frowned. "You mean whether or not I'm a murderer?"

Ruth gave that indignant wave of her hand again. "All I care about is your claim that you saw my son Jack. I could care less if you killed that woman they found in your car trunk." She smiled at Anna's shock. "You find me cold and calculating? Then there shouldn't be any surprises for you. We dress for dinner in this house. I hope the clothing I purchased for you is adequate."

"More than adequate, Mrs. Fairbanks, but I—"

"Call me Ruth. I'll call you Anna. It's much less bother that way. If you need anything before dinner, just ring for Carol."

"I really don't think having dinner with your family would be a good idea given the way your son feels about me being here."

Ruth's smile was brittle. "A word of advice, Anna. For the time that you're a guest in my home, you would be wise not to question my decisions. In case you're having second thoughts about being here, remember, you need my help." She turned to leave.

Not to look a gift horse in the mouth, Anna refused nonetheless to be bullied by this woman. "Apparently you need mine, as well. But I have to wonder if we aren't working at cross-purposes. Mine, to get proof of my innocence and yours, to keep the truth from coming out."

Ruth stopped and slowly turned back around. She narrowed her gaze as if taking Anna's measure. "A gamble for us both, I would say, although you appear to be the one who stands to lose the most without my help, wouldn't you?"

"I don't know. I guess that depends on why you kept the note I showed you, the one I found in my coat pocket, the reason I came to Shadow Lake and the reason, I suspect, that my friend Gillian is dead."

Ruth Fairbanks eyed her but said nothing.

"You don't think I'm a murderer," Anna said, surprising them both. "Even with all the evidence against me, for some reason you don't believe it—otherwise, you wouldn't have brought me here."

Ruth looked startled for a moment and then laughed. "You forget. My husband was in politics. I've had much worse than murderers in my home, dear." She turned toward the doorway again. "Dinner is served in forty minutes. Please don't be late."

With that, the woman was gone, leaving Anna dreading

dinner and more than a little worried as to what Ruth Fairbanks was up to.

Anna had no doubt that she was being used. But to what end?

WALKER LOOKED AT HIS FRIEND and surprised himself by saying something he'd been thinking for some time.

"I'm not sure the body pulled from the lake was Jack Fairbanks." He felt an instant stab of relief to have finally voiced his suspicion.

Billy sat up abruptly in his chair. "And you didn't say anything at the time?"

"Hell, at the time there was no reason to suspect it wasn't Jack. He'd gone missing weeks before, after being last seen on the lake. When a decomposed male body was found…"

"Who identified the body?"

"Jonathan, through dental records." Walker didn't even want to think about the chance that he'd helped that damned Jonathan cover something up.

"So what are you saying? That Jack faked his own death? How could he do that without help?" Billy let out a curse. "Jonathan would have had to be in on it."

Exactly what Walker had been thinking. "There's no way Jack would go along with something like this, let alone team up with Jonathan." But even as he said it, he feared that is exactly what Jack had done. Conspired to fake his own death. But why?

"If that's the case, then they got away with it," Billy added with a grin. "I'll be damned. That is, they got away with it until Jack saved Anna Collins's life."

"It's nothing but speculation," Walker said, reaching into the cooler to get them each another beer.

"Yeah," Billy agreed. "But I guess we'll know soon enough. Once Jack's body is exhumed and the DNA tests run…"

"Clearly I'm not the only one questioning if Jack is alive," Walker said, hoping to hell they were all wrong. He'd known

Jack all his life. This wasn't the kind of thing he would ever do. "Why would Jack go along with something like this?"

"You're assuming that Jonathan was behind the deception."

"Hell, yes," Walker said. "You can bet he gains something by this."

"But if that's the case then why, as you said, would Jack go along with it?"

That was one of the questions that had been haunting Walker all evening. That, and how Anna Collins and her rescue at the bottom of the lake fit into all this.

"What worries me is why Ruth Fairbanks wants Anna Collins to stay on the island," Walker said.

"Well, if you're right about Jack faking his death with Jonathan's help…" Billy let out a curse. "You think the old lady knows? Damn, I advised Anna not to go out there, but she's determined to find out why she had that note in her pocket from Gillian Sanders."

Walker lifted a brow. "You're representing Anna Collins?"

"Don't worry, I didn't take her on as a client. I told her all I could do was give her some free advice."

"Obviously, she didn't take your advice."

Billy shook his head. "It's pretty clear to me that someone set her up to take this murder rap, and if the Fairbankses are involved…" He took a drink of his beer as the pizza arrived. "I hope you didn't order anchovies again. Hey, where are you going? The pizza's here."

Walker was on his feet, his car keys in his hand. "The bastard never planned to call in the state CID."

"Who?" Billy said.

"Nash. I wondered why the state boys haven't been all over this case. The Fairbankses. Nash must be trying to protect them. He and Ruth go way back. I've got to go."

"Wait, where are you going? Tell me you aren't about to do something where you're going to need a lawyer."

The Jack Fairbanks Walker knew wouldn't have faked his death. Not unless he was in some kind of terrible trouble.

Which would mean, if Jack was alive, he was in even worse trouble now that he'd blown his cover.

"Pay for the pizza, I'll catch you later," Walker called to Billy as he sprinted for his car.

WHEN ANNA STEPPED INTO THE Fairbankses' dining room, the tension was so thick it was like wading through quicksand.

Dinner was going to be hell.

Ruth was already seated at the head of the table, Jonathan to her immediate left and Pet in the next chair.

A serving attendant pulled out the chair to Ruth's right for Anna and unfolded her white cloth napkin to place it on her lap.

The large room, massive table and all the extra chairs made the family gathering seem too small and intimate given the hostility coming from the opposite side of the table.

"Wine?" the male server inquired.

Anna nodded, thinking it might be the only way she could make it through the meal. He poured her a glass, then filled Ruth's, Jonathan's and Pet's.

"I hope you enjoy the wine," Jonathan said sarcastically. "I see Mother picked our most expensive bottle."

Anna took a sip. She noticed that Pet had already downed her glass and had motioned to the server for more.

Anna was reminded of earlier, when she'd seen them both upstairs. She wondered whose room they'd been in and would make a point of checking when she got the chance.

As the courses were served, there was little or no conversation, with Ruth speaking only to give the waitstaff orders or occasionally asking Anna if she preferred one dish over another.

They ate in the choking silence. Anna tried to keep her eyes on her plate, but she could feel Jonathan glaring across the table at her. By the time dessert was served, she wasn't sure how much more of this she could take.

"Apparently, we're all trying to ignore the elephant in the room," Jonathan said in disgust, throwing down his napkin, his dessert untouched.

Anna wasn't surprised. He'd hardly touched his meal. She'd forced down what she could out of politeness—and to heed Dr. Brubaker's warning about taking care of herself. She needed to get her strength back, especially staying in *this* house.

"In case you haven't figured out why you're here, my mother is obsessed with my brother's death." He let out a sharp, cold laugh. "Just as she was obsessed with Jack when he was alive."

"That is only natural when you lose a child," Anna said quickly.

"You don't understand," he said, scowling at her. "One minute my mother is hiring psychics to hold séances to try to reach Jack on the other side and the next she sees some homeless derelict on the street in Seattle and she's screaming for the chauffeur to stop the car because she's convinced it's Jack."

To Anna's amazement Ruth continued to eat her dessert as if oblivious to this.

"For weeks before his body was discovered, my mother believed that Jack had stumbled out of the lake not knowing who he was. Amnesia. But then I hear you'd know all about that."

Anna let the remark pass without comment, since it was clear Jonathan Fairbanks was looking for a fight. Next to him Pet tagged the male server and took the second wine bottle from him to refill her glass. She waved the server away when he reached for the bottle.

"Mother has completely ignored the fact that it was Jack's idea to take the sailboat out that night," Jonathan was saying.

"It was Mother who insisted *I* go along. Now, why was that, Mother? Because you *knew.*" He swung his gaze from his mother to Anna. "Want to know the big family secret?"

"Jonathan," Ruth said, her voice low.

"Jack didn't fall off the sailboat that night and drown."

"Jonathan." His mother's voice was sharp now, but he didn't seem to hear.

"He *jumped!* That's right. Her precious Jack killed himself and *that* is what my mother can't live with. That and the fact that I couldn't save my own brother." Jonathan awkwardly got to his feet.

Anna caught a glimpse of Ruth Fairbanks's face, high color in her cheeks, the stormy gray eyes a thunderstorm of anger and pain.

Jack had committed suicide in the lake?

"Jack *drowned?*" With horror, she realized why everyone had responded the way they had when she'd told them that Jack had saved her at the bottom of the lake.

"Don't pretend you didn't know," Jonathan snapped. "Why else would you be trying to take advantage of my family with your outlandish story about my brother saving your life?"

"Stop it!" Ruth Fairbanks barked, making Anna flinch.

"You're right, Mother. This has to stop. It was one thing to bring *psychics* to the island. But now you've brought this…" His voice trailed off as he glared across the table at Anna. "This…murderer into *my* home."

"This is *my* home Jonathan," his mother said almost calmly. "Your father left it to me. It won't be yours until I die."

Anna saw the look that passed between them. No love lost there. It made her ill. Ruth Fairbanks had lost a son. But she still had one. Anna would have given anything to have had a remaining child.

"If you'll excuse me," Anna said, rising.

Ruth didn't acknowledge Anna's impending exit as she,

too, rose to her feet. "As long as I am alive and you choose to visit here, I will decide who comes and goes in this house and you will treat them and me with respect, Jonathan."

"Hopefully, I will be living in an even larger house soon. Unless it gets out that my mother is crazy and brings complete strangers and lunatic psychics into the home where I live. Knowing you, you'd hold a séance in the White House."

Anna had heard that Jonathan Fairbanks was running for his father's open seat on the Senate. Apparently, at least according to the media, he was a shoo-in since he had worked closely with his father for years.

"It wouldn't be the first one," Ruth said. "Lincoln's mother held séances there."

"Yes, and look where that got *her* son."

Anna slipped out the door, thankful to have the dinner from hell finally over and be allowed to escape the malice in that room. But at the top of the stairs, she couldn't bear to go back to her room yet. She thought she'd seen a sunroom at the south end of the floor.

She could still hear voices from below and knew Pet wouldn't be coming upstairs until she'd polished off that bottle of wine. Anna decided to check out something that had been bothering her.

She turned then and hurried down the hall to north end, hoping whoever's room was at the end wouldn't be locked. After seeing Pet and Jonathan at the window when she arrived, she'd been curious.

She reached the end of the hall and looked back. She was alone. No sign of Carol or any of the family. Reaching for the knob, Anna tried the door, giving in to her curiosity.

The door swung inward. The room was much like her own, only larger. It was decorated in soft pastels and on the wall by the door was an assortment of photographs from Jack and Pet's wedding.

The redhead looked gorgeous. Anna could see why Jack had fallen for her. They both looked so happy. Unlike the rest of the family in one of the photos.

Jonathan was scowling at the camera and so was his mother. Only Big Jim Fairbanks was smiling his political smile.

Anna glanced toward the window and the huge unmade bed. The drapes were drawn and she could make out several items of clothing on the floor next to the bed. Anna recognized one item of clothing that had apparently fallen beside the bed.

It was the tie Jonathan Fairbanks had been wearing earlier when he'd met Anna at the front door.

CHAPTER NINETEEN

"THERE YOU ARE," Ruth Fairbanks said, when she found Anna outside Pet's bedroom.

Anna couldn't believe how close she'd come to getting caught. She'd closed the door only an instant before Ruth had appeared. As it was, the older woman was eyeing her suspiciously.

"I got a little turned around," Anna said. "It's such a large house." She could tell Ruth didn't believe that. Did Ruth know about Pet and Jonathan? If Anna was right and Jack was alive, did he know his brother was sleeping with his wife? And how long had it been going on? Before Jack allegedly drowned?

"There's a sunroom down the hall," Ruth said. "Let's go down there. I'm relatively sure it's not bugged." She smiled at Anna's shocked expression. "Everyone in this house spies on me. I'm used to it."

Anna couldn't hide her surprise. Or her concern.

"Oh, don't give me that look," Ruth Fairbanks said with impatience as Anna followed her into the sunroom. "I'm not losing my mind. I've never been sharper. Don't you think I know what Jonathan is? Or that I helped him become what he is today?" She closed the door behind them and turned on a lamp.

The last of the day's light glittered on the lake, the view spectacular from the many windows. The sunroom was filled with wicker furniture, plants and colorful pots. It was by far her favorite of the rooms she'd seen in the house.

Ruth motioned Anna into a chair as she took one across from her. "You said you lost a son. Tell me about him."

The statement took her by surprise. Anna had just assumed Ruth wanted to talk about Jack.

Anna's first instinct was to balk at the order. Talking about Tyler was painful. Her reaction to her son's death had been to curl up in a ball and cry the past two months.

Until the other night, when apparently she'd thrown a suitcase in her car and come racing up to Shadow Lake. The chance to find the driver of the car who'd killed her son had brought her out of her misery long enough to seek vengeance.

"Please," Ruth said, her face softening as she looked at Anna. "I would like to hear about him."

Anna hugged herself, took a breath and was surprised how easy it was. She told of what a sweet baby he had been, how he slept right through the night, how he broke into smiles and giggles whenever he saw her, how he'd grown into this incredible little boy who loved trains.

Anna was surprised how comfortable she felt with Ruth Fairbanks in this room. She knew it was the fact that they had each lost a son and still mourned that loss in a way that was soul deep. Neither would get over the loss. Anna suspected though that they dealt with their losses differently.

"Tyler was…four when he died. He resembled his father, big brown eyes, thick dark hair, an adorable little face and a smile that just melted your heart." She smiled at the memory. "He was smart, too. A good boy."

"How did he die?"

"A car wreck. I was driving." She felt Ruth's hesitant touch, just a brush of a cool hand on hers as she reached across the space between them.

"I'm so sorry. Your only child?"

Anna nodded. "When Tyler was born, Marc got a vasectomy without telling me. He didn't want any more children."

"But you did."

"Yes."

"Men can be such bastards," Ruth said, and looked out toward the darkness, her face set in stone. Silence fell between them for a few moments, then she said, "So whose idea was it to divorce?"

"Marc's, but how did you—"

"I confess I knew most of what you've told me. I wanted to hear it from you, though." She raised a brow. "You didn't think I would ask you to stay here without doing some checking on you, did you? I might be crazy, but I'm not a fool."

No, Anna thought. Nor was the woman crazy. "Marc blames me for Tyler's death."

Ruth nodded. "I understand wanting to blame someone. I blamed God, my husband, especially Jonathan." She sounded pained by that admission. "I would give anything to have Jack back. *Anything.*"

Anna felt the older woman's gaze on her. She flushed, thinking of all the offers she'd made God just to have Tyler back.

"Do you think that's awful of me?" Ruth asked.

Anna shook her head. "No. I made my own offers to God."

"Losing a child, no matter how old they are at the time, is something a mother never gets over. There is no price I wouldn't pay to have my son back."

"Is that why you asked me to stay here? Because you think I can give you back your son?"

"You say you saw him. That Jack saved your life." She held up a hand. "I know. Everyone says Jack's dead and how is that possible. But you *believe* it was Jack, don't you?"

Anna nodded.

"So maybe it was his ghost." Ruth shrugged. "Maybe you saw him on the other side. You did say you were about to die. Because otherwise, if Jack is dead, how do you explain what you saw?"

Anna couldn't explain it.

"Why would Jack have been there, though?" Ruth asked.

"Like I told you when I was here before, I believe that my friend Gillian Sanders was meeting someone named Fairbanks that night at the rest stop on the edge of town."

"Jonathan swears he didn't know her and had no plans to meet her."

"Do you believe him?" Anna asked.

The older woman said nothing.

"I don't know what happened at the rest stop, but I believe that whoever was meeting Gillian there saw my car go into the lake and saved my life."

"That couldn't have been Jonathan."

"No," Anna agreed.

"You are convinced that your friend wanted to talk to this person about the hit-and-run?"

Anna nodded. "You read the note. It's the only thing that makes any sense. It would explain why I came to Shadow Lake that night. Also why Gillian is dead. She must have found out something that someone wants kept a secret."

"You aren't insinuating that Jack killed her."

"No. Whoever killed Gillian, and tried to frame me, wouldn't have turned around and saved my life."

"Yes, assuming he is alive and didn't want anyone to know it, he has now exposed that fact by saving your life," Ruth said.

"That's what worries me," Anna said. "Whoever saved my life was at the rest stop or close by. He must have seen who killed Gillian and tried to frame me."

Ruth Fairbanks seemed to give that some thought for a moment. "If that person was Jack…"

Anna nodded. "His life could be in danger—if it wasn't already."

WALKER DROVE BY THE NASH house first, to make sure the chief was at home. His patrol car was in the driveway and all the lights were on inside the house.

He'd had a little time to think on the drive over here and made a decision. He'd damned well investigate this murder on his own. If he was right, Nash was trying to protect the Fairbanks by not calling in the State on this. To hell with that, Walker thought as he drove on past the chief's house.

The Cadillac was right where it had been. As far as Walker could tell, no one had been here. What the hell was going on with Nash? Walker could understand the chief wanting to keep the case. Shadow Lake was short on murders. The chief might want one big case before he retired.

But Nash didn't seem to have any interest in it.

Whatever the reason, Nash had thrown the Gillian Sanders murder case into his lap. Because he thought Walker would fail to solve it without help?

Walker took his time photographing then searching the car, making sure he didn't disturb any evidence. Still wearing the latex gloves, he carefully opened the back door of the Cadillac, slipped the suitcase over into the light and tried the latches.

He'd half expected it to be locked.

It wasn't, which was more surprising when he opened it and the first thing he saw was the .38 Special. Anna's gun.

"Son of a bitch." He took a photo then quickly closed the suitcase without touching the gun.

Whoever had put Gillian's body in the trunk had put the gun in the suitcase. It was the only explanation.

But how had the killer gotten the gun? Anna Collins had it with her. She'd just had a huge fight with her husband. She would have been irrational, grabbing the gun before leaving the house. Was it possible she'd just tossed it on the passenger seat in plain sight?

Seeing the gun could have given the killer the idea of trying to frame her for Gillian's murder.

Walker started to close the car's back door when he spotted

a small pillow on the floor. What caught his attention was the powder burns on the cloth—and the bullet hole in the center.

That, he realized, was what had been bothering him. Why hadn't Anna heard the shot that the killer fired after putting Gillian's body in the trunk of the Cadillac? Because the killer had used the pillow to silence the noise.

Anna must have been close by. Probably looking for her friend at the rest stop. She either hadn't heard the softened sound of the shot—or hadn't recognized what it was. Had Anna been alone at the rest stop with Gillian, she wouldn't have used a pillow to deaden the sound.

Someone was definitely hoping to frame Anna Collins for the murder.

Walker would have the lab boys come up from Pilot's Cove and dust the car, the suitcase and the gun for prints. Not that he expected to find any fingerprints on the gun.

Locking up the garage, he drove down to the station and got on the computer. There was a connection between Jack Fairbanks and Anna Collins and he was determined to find it. Anna thought it had something to do with the death of her son. That was as good a place to start as any.

Taking out his notebook, he checked the date of Anna Collins's hit-and-run collision that killed her son Tyler and put Anna in a coma for six months. August 30.

Jack had drowned September 7.

Eight days later.

Coincidence?

His heart began to pound a little faster as he read through the police report on the hit-and-run looking for a connection. Anna had been driving a small car. According to the only eyewitness, a woman in her eighties who was out walking her dog, the Collins car had been hit by a large dark SUV. She hadn't gotten a license-plate number. But the paint chips found at the scene and on Anna's car matched that of a newer model black Lincoln.

His heart was pounding now. Jack Fairbanks had driven a black Lincoln Navigator, but then a lot of people in this area did.

The case was never solved. Even state criminal investigation division hadn't been able to track down the vehicle or the driver. No area body shops reported a customer with a large dark SUV needing that sort of repairs. The case had ended up in the cold-case file.

Walker made a copy of the file and was starting to put it aside, when something caught his attention. The accident had taken place along a two-lane road south of Seattle in the hills not far from Renton.

On a hunch, Walker checked the address and came up with a hit. The spot where the SUV had struck Anna's car was only a half mile north of the home of Gillian Sanders. The Collins car had been headed southbound. Was it possible Anna Collins had been on her way to Gillian's?

Walker wasn't sure why that seemed important, but something told him it was. Anna Collins had said her friend Gillian had been doing her own investigation, trying to track down the hit-and-run driver. Gillian was so close by she could have been one of the first people on the scene. Had she seen something? Or had she been able to get more out of the eyewitness than the police had?

He copied down the name and phone number of the eyewitness. Elsie Mathews, according to the report, was in her eighties. He hoped to hell she was even still alive after all these months. She'd said she'd seen the two cars collide and the large black SUV then back up and speed away. The SUV, being so much larger than the car, had sustained damage, but not enough that it didn't allow the driver to leave the scene.

Walker tucked the name and number of the witness into his pocket, his hand shaking. He told himself again that a lot of people drove large dark SUVs. But Walker couldn't ignore the fact that Jack Fairbanks had driven a black Lincoln Navigator—that was, until it was reported stolen.

Walker called up the police report Big Jim Fairbanks had filed. Just as he'd feared, Jack Fairbanks's black Lincoln Navigator had been reported stolen on August 31—the day *after* the hit-and-run.

However, Senator Big Jim Fairbanks had made the report saying that the SUV was believed to have been missing for at least two days prior to that. The Lincoln had been parked near the marina in Shadow Lake and to Big Jim's knowledge hadn't been driven by anyone in the family since August 27. Jack always left the keys on the floorboard and never locked the rig, according to his father.

Jack's Lincoln Navigator was never found.

When the phone rang, Walker jumped. He picked up, glad to hear it was his friend with CID.

"Heard about the murder up there, but was told Chief Nash would be handling it," his friend said when Walker asked what was going on.

"Nash didn't call and ask for any help?" Just as Walker had suspected.

"No, in fact, when my boss offered him some men, Nash turned him down."

At a sound, Walker looked up to find Chief Rob Nash standing in his office doorway.

"I'm going to have to let you go," Walker said. "Chief Nash just walked in."

RUTH ROSE AND WALKED TO the window of the sunroom. The sky beyond the glass was dark and black.

"What happened to Jonathan's leg?" Anna asked.

The older woman stiffened and, for a moment, Anna thought she wouldn't answer. "A boating accident when the boys were in their early teens. Jim had bought them a ski boat for Jonathan's sixteenth birthday. It was much too big and powerful. I'd told Jim that, but he was determined that his boys would have the fastest boat on the lake."

She turned to face Anna. "Jack was pulling Jonathan waterskiing. Jonathan fell. Jack went to go back to get him, hit a wave, lost control of the boat." She shook her head. "The propeller..." She dropped into the chair again as if her legs would no longer hold her.

"I'm sorry. That must have been horrible for both boys," Anna said.

Ruth looked up at her, tears in her eyes. "Yes. Jonathan never saw that, of course. He never understood that Jack was a victim, too. Jack never forgave himself. Nor would Jonathan ever let him forget it," she added bitterly. "Jonathan used it against Jack the rest of Jack's life. But then you would understand that, wouldn't you?"

"Yes." Anna traced her scar without even realizing it.

Ruth reached into her pocket and held out the half piece of envelope with Gillian's handwriting on it. "You'll need this. But thank you for showing it to me. I know I sound foolish, but for a little while it made me feel closer to Jack. I never saw him again after that night he and his brother went sailing. His body wasn't found for weeks and by then..." Her eyes brimmed with tears.

"I've only brought up painful memories for you," Anna said. "I'm sorry."

Ruth Fairbanks pulled herself together with an ironlike will that Anna had already glimpsed at dinner. "Pish posh. I love talking about Jack," she said, standing again to go to the window. "His brother tries to forbid me from doing so." She took a ragged breath. "Jack was kind and gentle, everything Jonathan is incapable of being. I suspect Jonathan has wished on more than one occasion that his brother had never been born." She stopped abruptly as if she'd revealed too much.

Anna felt a chill as if the room had suddenly turned colder.

"For a long time, I've felt as if Jack wasn't gone," Ruth said, her back to Anna. "I thought it was his spirit, so I tried to reach him, to ask him…" She shook her head again. "You think I'm crazy."

"No. Sometimes I feel that Tyler is still with me," Anna whispered. "Maybe we're both crazy."

"I've never told anyone this, but I always knew that the lake would take Jack." Her focus was on the water. Or maybe the past. "He almost drowned when he was little. He and Jonathan were swimming by the dock and all of a sudden Jack was gone." She shuddered. "Maybe this lake *was* his destiny. Just as Jonathan's is the White House."

Anna shifted in her chair. It was dark out and suddenly she was tired.

They sat in silence for a moment.

"Knowing about my son, you must understand why I have to find the hit-and-run driver," Anna said.

"You want retribution," Ruth said simply, her back to Anna as the older woman continued to look out into the darkness.

"No. I need to know what happened that night. I need to know if I was somehow responsible. I need to know the truth, especially now that I fear Gillian was killed because of her involvement. She'd been trying to find the hit-and-run driver for me for the past eight months."

"Why would you think her death has anything to do with the accident after so long?" Ruth asked. "Because of that hen-scratch on an old envelope? Who knows when she even wrote that? It could have been about an entirely different matter altogether."

"Maybe it wasn't about Tyler's death," Anna said. "Maybe I'm just clutching at straws. But how do I explain Gillian's death then?"

She saw Ruth stiffen at the window. "It's late," she said, turning to look at Anna.

Anna rose from her chair. Earlier, in the shared loss of their sons, she'd felt close to the woman. But now she felt a distance she didn't understand. Maybe Ruth felt she'd revealed too much to a total stranger.

Ruth's cell phone rang. She drew it from her pocket, checked caller ID and turned toward Anna. "I'm sorry, but I have to take this. We'll talk more tomorrow."

Ruth left her alone in the sunroom. Only one lamp fought off the darkness outside the windows.

Anna turned it off and stood in the blackness waiting for her eyes to adjust, thinking about what she'd learned tonight. Not much, and yet she still didn't know why Gillian had gone to the rest stop to meet one of the Fairbankses—or even if she had.

As her eyes adjusted to the darkness, she stepped to the window where Ruth had been standing earlier and looked out. She could see the lake past the back of the house and the stand of dense pines that ran from the lawn to the water.

That's when she saw him. A man standing in the shadow of the pines looking up at the house. One of the yard lights reflected on his dark hair and just enough of his face. Jonathan. What was he doing out there? Spying on her and his mother?

Suddenly he seemed to realize that someone was watching him and he stepped back into the trees. She felt her pulse jump. The man hadn't limped.

CHAPTER TWENTY

RUTH FAIRBANKS TOOK the cell phone call on the way to her room. "Yes?" She'd already checked the caller ID and knew exactly who was calling and why.

"I have the information you asked for, including everything that could connect this woman with your family. But I've got to warn you, you aren't going to like it," the voice on the other end of the line said without preamble. The man was one of her husband's former "associates." He sounded annoyed, probably more with her husband than her. Big Jim had foolishly thought her so ignorant of his ways that he didn't dream she knew about this particular "associate."

She stopped in the empty hallway. "Just get me the information. I'll be the judge of what I'll like or not like."

"I'm sending it out by boat. I assume you won't want my man coming to the main dock."

"You assume right. How did you handle this sort of thing for my husband?"

"There is an old building on the north end of the island."

Ruth smiled, not in the least surprised. Big Jim used to often take a walk after dinner, saying he needed a cigar. He would disappear down the path toward the north end of the island. The pines were thick at that end, the old cottage barely visible. Near there was the only spot a boat could come in that wasn't rocky shore.

"When shall I meet him there?"

"I figured you'd want it done the same way I did with your husband." There was an edge to his voice. "My courier is probably already there. He will leave the information in the wood box outside the cottage."

So that was how Big Jim did it. Sometimes she was amazed at the things she had learned about her husband after his death. Big Jim had more secrets than she would ever have imagined. Was it like that in all marriages? Or was it because she'd married an overly ambitious man involved in politics?

Her husband had certainly never known *her*. He would have dropped dead of a heart attack sooner if he'd had even a clue as to what she was thinking ninety percent of the time. But then she might have felt the same way had she known everything her husband was capable of.

She thought of her son Jonathan. He was so like Big Jim. He truly believed nothing mattered but the outcome. The means to the end. She liked to believe he got that from Big Jim—and not from her.

"How shall I reward you for your services?"

Silence, then, "Your husband would leave a plain white envelope in the wood box with an appropriate number of bills."

"Why reinvent the wheel when it sounds as if my husband's methods worked so well."

The other end of the line was silent. As perverted as it was, she was for the first time thankful Big Jim had been the way he had. If nothing else, he'd taught her that she could get anything she wanted—for the right price and a little leverage. They agreed on a sum, then she said, "I'll let you know if there is anything else I need."

She would use him again. Just as Big Jim had. She'd learned long ago that once someone had their hooks in another, only death could free him. Obviously, her husband's associate understood that as well.

Sadly, it was human nature, she thought, as she snapped her phone shut and opened the door to her room and froze.

He was standing silhouetted against the evening sky, his back to her. *Jack?*

GIVEN THE HOUR AND THE FACT that Walker should have been off duty, Nash knew exactly what his subordinate was doing.

"Walker," Nash said as he closed the door behind him. "What's going on?"

"You didn't call in the state boys on the Gillian Sanders murder case," Walker said without getting up.

Nash shook his head. "You and I can handle it."

Walker gave him an incredulous look.

"I admit I haven't been of help so far," Nash said, as he pulled out a chair across from the desk and sat down. "The truth is I just found out that Lucinda is pregnant." He nodded at Walker's surprise. "I'm going to be a father. Imagine, at my age. The news has really thrown me for a loop, but I couldn't be happier."

"Congratulations," Walker said after a moment, as if not sure what to say.

"So tell me how the case is going. Anything new? Did you find a connection between Anna Collins and the Fairbankses?" He saw Walker hesitate.

"I've requested phone records on all of them." Walker nodded knowingly. "Judge Gandy must have called you. That's why you're down here."

Nash knew that Walker was smart and had great instincts. He just hadn't realized how sharp he was. "No chance of getting phone records on the Fairbankses unless we have something we can take to the judge to convince him."

Walker nodded.

Nash reached over and turned the computer screen to face him. "I see you have the report on Anna Collins's hit-and-run." His pulse quickened. He frowned as he leaned forward and tapped the keyboard to bring the report he'd glimpsed behind it up on the screen.

He lifted a brow as he looked at Walker and tried to keep his voice level. "Jack Fairbanks's stolen-vehicle report?"

Walker said nothing.

Nash's cell phone rang in his pocket. He'd told Lucinda to call if she needed him. He stared at Walker for a moment, then dug out his cell and checked caller ID. Lucinda.

He snapped the phone open and stood, turning his back to Walker. He was shaking inside, scared even before he heard Lucinda's voice. She was crying.

"What? Lucinda, I can't understand you."

"I'm *spotting,*" she repeated between sobs. "I think I'm losing the baby."

His heart stopped dead in his chest. He'd built this house of cards and they were all coming down around him. "I'll be right there."

RUTH FROZE AT THE SIGHT OF the man silhouetted against the yard light shining into her dark room. Jack. All her hopes and dreams rushed together in an instant of blinding gratitude.

Then the man turned.

"Jonathan." Her voice betrayed her. She could see it in her son's face as he turned.

"Mother." His voice reeked of contempt. He'd heard her disappointment when she'd realized it wasn't Jack. He limped toward her and for a moment she thought he might strike her. "I can't take any more of this. It has to stop. Now."

She had no idea what he might be referring to since there was so much divergence between them. But if she had to guess, she would have surmised it had something to do with Anna Collins.

"Jack is dead," Jonathan spit. "It's time you faced that as well as *why* he's dead."

"I don't want to discuss this with you," she said, suddenly feeling weak. She moved to one of the chairs and lowered herself into it, even though it gave Jonathan the advantage when he moved to tower over her.

"Jack wanted to go sailing that night knowing there was a storm coming in," he said, his voice rising. "You knew he'd been despondent—"

"No." She glared daggers at her son. "Jack didn't kill himself."

"How could you have not seen it, Mother? He had no purpose in life, no ambition, no aspirations. He knew he'd never have to work a day in his life. Every day had become the same and he could see the next fifty years stretched out in front of him, living on this island waiting for you to die, the son of Big Jim Fairbanks his only claim to fame." Jonathan leaned down, placing his hands on the arms of her chair. "He was *miserable* and if anyone was to blame it was *you.*"

"That's not true. Pet was the one making him miserable. Her greed. My God, Jonathan, the woman spent thousands of dollars on a face-lift. A face-lift at her age. Jack had to know she was doing it for some other man. Why do you think he was divorcing her?"

"If anyone destroyed his marriage it was you, Mother," Jonathan snapped. "You babied Jack, turning him into a mama's boy. You always took his side even when…" His voice broke. "Even when he did this to me!" He brought his hand down hard on the artificial leg, the thump loud even in the large room.

Her eyes flashed with anger. She could feel her blood pressure rising like hot acid in her bloodstream. "It was an *accident.* You know that. He would have never meant to hurt *you.*"

She saw Jonathan flush.

"Are we back to that, Mother?"

She turned away, trying to hide the fact that she still believed the swimming "accident" by the docks when the boys were young and Jack nearly drowned had been anything but an accident.

"You really believe that I could kill my own brother?" Jonathan demanded as he limped toward her. "Say it, Mother. Come on, let's get it all out in the open."

She lifted her face to meet his eyes. Eyes so like her own. Eyes like Jack's. "You were always jealous of him even when he was an infant. Later you used the loss of your leg against him, to control him. Yes, I think you'd kill your own brother."

The moment the words were out, no matter how truthful, she wished she could call them back.

Jonathan smiled ruefully as he passed her, but she could see the hurt in his face. "Thank you, Mother. I can't tell you how your faith in me warms my heart."

A part of her cried out that this was her son. The only one she had left. What if all it took was her love to transform him into the caring man Jack had been?

But as she started to reach out to him, she drew back her hand. It would take more than love to change Jonathan. It would take a miracle.

"I overheard what your father said to you the day before he died," she said, steeling her heart against the hatred of her only living son as he reached the door to leave. "I heard him say Jack's name. Your father knew you'd done something to your brother, didn't he?"

Jonathan stopped and turned, seemingly surprised. For just an instant, concern flickered in his eyes. Then he smiled. "I don't know what you're talking about, Mother. And who is going to believe a woman who not only professes to see dead people, but also blows thousands of dollars paying a charlatan to talk with them?"

"Don't threaten me, Jonathan."

His smile faded. "Threaten you? Mother, really, I insist you see a doctor. I'll have Pet make you an appointment. I fear you have Alzheimer's, since you're talking as crazy as Dad did before he died." He turned on his heel and left her alone in the room.

Ruth Fairbanks drew her wrap around her shoulders as a chill settled into the room that had been unusually warm earlier.

AFTER SEEING THE MAN ON the beach, Anna found the back stairs, moving quietly down them until she found a way out of the house. She'd seen the man in the thick stand of pines just off the lawn. He'd been watching her and Ruth, she was sure of it.

She hurried across the short expanse of grass and was instantly swallowed up in the cold darkness of the pines. The wind rustled the boughs high over her head. She stood without moving, listening, waiting for her eyes to adjust to the blackness.

Now that she was here, she felt a chill ripple over her skin and the first real tremor of apprehension. This had been foolish. For all she knew, she was standing just feet away from the man who had killed Gillian.

A rustling of pine needles. Someone moving just ahead of her. She took a step, swallowing back her fear, determined to know the truth. That was why she'd come here. A branch brushed across her shoulder, making her jump.

She stopped and held her breath. He had stopped, too. She thought she could hear him breathing—he was that close in the darkness.

"Jack?" Her voice broke. She cleared her throat and said more loudly. "Jack, I know it's you."

She heard him move next to her. He'd been even closer than she'd thought. She caught his scent. Not Jonathan's too-sweet cologne. Not Jonathan.

Fear paralyzed her as a dark shape stepped into her path.

The gasp was involuntary. She must have blinked, because in an instant he was gone.

Her pulse drummed in her ears. She stumbled back, suddenly wanting only to be out of the pines. Turning, she ran, branches slapping at her.

It wasn't until she was almost to the beach, far from the pines, that she stopped and looked back. The pines were etched black against the dark sky. She had the feeling he was watching her, pleased that he'd frightened her, as that had been his intent. She was shaking, her heart thundering in her ears, her mouth dry.

Jack Fairbanks was alive.

Or someone wanted her to believe he was.

WALKER HAD JUST TURNED OFF the light to leave his office when he heard the fax machine in another room.

He snapped the light back on and walked down the hall as the first faxed page whirred out. Walker snatched the sheet from the basket when he saw what it was. The phone records he'd requested.

While he hadn't been able to get phone records on the Fairbankses, these were the rest he'd requested.

He sat down at his desk again, studying each page. Anna Collins's calls were almost all to two numbers. He checked in the reverse directory, not surprised to find that Anna had called Gillian Sanders repeatedly along with another number belonging to David and Mary Ellen Harper.

The friend she said had told her that the divorce hadn't gone through? Mary Ellen Harper.

The other number Anna had called was listed to Collins Realty, owner Marc Collins. Walker remembered Marc Collins saying something about business being down. Is that why Collins had called off the divorce? It crossed Walker's mind that a husband who couldn't afford a divorce might decide there was a better way to get rid of his wife—like framing her for murder.

He checked the calls Gillian had made, surprised how few he found to Marc Collins's office or his cell. If the two really had been having an affair—

On the day Gillian was murdered, she made a call to Marc's cell that lasted five minutes. The call had been made at 4:03 p.m.

Walker quickly flipped through Marc Collins's phone records. Sure enough Marc had called Gillian back after that initial call at 4:15 p.m. That call had lasted three and a half minutes. At 4:12 p.m. Marc had called his wife.

Is that when he'd told Anna he wasn't divorcing her and to get dressed for dinner?

Walker swore as he saw the next *two* calls Marc Collins made. The first was right after his call to his wife. Collins had called a divorce lawyer. No doubt to actually stop the divorce.

From the order of the calls it would appear that whatever he and Gillian Sanders had said to each other it had precipitated his calling off the divorce.

But it was the second call that had made Walker curse in surprise. The number was from a local cell phone. He dialed it.

The line rang four times before voice mail picked up.

"Jonathan Fairbanks is not available. If you wish to leave a call-back number—"

Walker hung up, heart racing. He'd been looking for a connection between Anna Collins and the Fairbankses.

But the connection he'd found was between *Marc* Collins and the Fairbankses. Marc had called Jonathan Fairbanks's cell phone on the day Gillian Sanders died. No chance of a wrong number. The call had lasted six minutes.

RUTH FAIRBANKS WAITED OBVIOUSLY until she was fairly sure everyone had retired to their rooms, then she dressed and quietly slipped out of the house.

She wore all black and felt like a cat burglar as she kept to the shadows of the pines until she was far enough away to turn on her flashlight.

The air was cold and had a bite to it, but she barely felt it. Her fight with Jonathan had only made her more anxious to know what her source had uncovered.

Jonathan was afraid. That alone worried her.

It had been years since she'd ventured out at night on the island. Even more years since she'd been to the north end where her old family cottage still stood.

She felt stronger and in control. It was a good feeling, one she'd had to hide around her husband when he was alive. Big Jim liked to believe he was running everything. Just like Jonathan.

After her talk with Anna Collins tonight, Ruth was all the more anxious, afraid to give voice to her fears.

She moved through the trees and picked up the path along the lake, careful to watch her footing as the path rose along the cliffs. Following the thin beam of the flashlight, she listened to the night as she had as a child, back when this island was as familiar to her as her own face.

She stopped when she reached the crest of the hill, turned out her flashlight and stood in the darkness for a moment, listening. Of course she hadn't been followed. Jonathan couldn't navigate this path. It was much too steep for him with his injury. And Pet—by now she would be too intoxicated. Nor would Carol or any of the servants have the nerve to follow her. They might take orders from Jonathan, but when push came to shove, they knew whose house it was.

That left only one other person. Anna Collins.

Ruth heard nothing but the wind at the tops of the pines, a low moaning sound, and the lap of water against the cliffs below her.

Snapping on the flashlight, she hurried down the path,

anxious to get the information waiting for her and return to the house before anyone discovered that she'd left.

She hadn't been near the cottage in years. For so long it had reminded her of the poverty of her youth. She'd often wondered if that was why Big Jim hadn't had it torn down. He wanted her to remember what he'd saved her from.

Now though, the cottage looked benign. She'd put enough years between her and the misery that it was only a dim ache inside her.

The manila envelope was exactly where her new associate had said it would be. She stuck it under the waistband of her pants beneath the thick sweater she'd worn and took out the smaller white envelope she'd brought, exchanging one for the other. Then she closed the wood box.

She stood in the darkness, the flashlight extinguished again, not listening for the footfalls of the living but those of the dead.

Was it possible Jack was alive and he hadn't contacted her? She welcomed the anger that came with the thought, letting it fill her to overflowing. It was the self-pity that she abhorred.

She looked out at the lake, just as she had as a girl, and remembered the promise she'd made herself to escape this island, this prison of poverty.

Well, at least she'd accomplished the latter part, she thought as she clicked on the flashlight again. Oh yes, she knew why her husband had built on this island, why he hadn't demolished what was really just a shack. He wanted her to never forget that she owed him her life. He'd left this shack standing as a tangible reminder of what she'd be if she ever got out of line.

Ruth had been too smart for that. She smiled to herself as she walked around to the front of the dilapidated old building, the beam of the flashlight bobbing over the ground at her feet. For so many years, she'd resented that the shack of her child-

hood home had stood on the island. But now she saw that her
childhood had made her the woman she was—good or bad—
she could live with that.

As she started to turn away, the light caught on something.
She lifted the flashlight to the door of the cottage.

The padlock she'd insisted be put on the front door was
missing. She stepped closer, tried the doorknob. The door
swung open and, even before she lifted the flashlight to shine
it inside, she knew. Someone had been staying here.

CHAPTER TWENTY-ONE

WALKER MADE A half-dozen calls, cashing in every favor owed him. He needed the Collins's financial records, both Anna's and Marc's. It hadn't been easy to get what he'd needed given the hour. The banks had been closed.

But he could be persuasive and when he finally had what he needed, he picked up the phone and called Marc Collins at Pinecrest Cabin Court and told him he was coming out.

"Kinda late for a visit, isn't it?" Collins said.

Walker could hear that the man was high on something.

"What's this about? Has my wife been arrested yet?"

Walker couldn't believe the guy. He just seemed to be hanging around waiting for his wife to be arrested. His attempts to have her committed had gone awry when Ruth Fairbanks had gotten involved. So now what would Marc Collins do when he found out what Walker had learned about him?

"I'll be there in five minutes," he told Collins.

"Can't you just tell me what this is about over the phone? I'm kind of busy."

Walker didn't bother to answer. He hung up and headed for his patrol car. Collins was a prick. But a murderer? Walker had his doubts. One thing was for certain. Marc Collins was guilty as hell.

Five minutes later, Collins opened the door of the cabin with his usual cocky grin. Walker caught the distinct scent of alcohol on Collins's breath, but from the looks of the man's eyes, alcohol wasn't the only thing he was on.

For all the bravado, Walker detected a wariness in the Realtor as he stepped aside to let him enter the cabin.

"If you don't mind, I'm going to tape this," Walker said showing him the small tape recorder. "I already have your other statements from before. I just have a few more questions."

Collins had come by after visiting his wife at the hospital and had made a sworn statement, repeating pretty much everything he'd already told them about his affair with Gillian; stopping the divorce, trying to reconcile with Anna, their fight after he confessed about the affair, Anna leaving with her gun, threatening to kill Gillian.

Collins nodded but looked nervous. "Why not?"

Walker took the only chair, a worn recliner in the corner. After a moment, Collins sat on the edge of the bed.

"So what do you want to know about Anna?" Marc asked, making it clear he thought this was about getting the goods on his wife.

"Just trying to clear some things up," Walker said as he opened his notebook. "You had an argument with Gillian Sanders the morning she died."

Collins's head came up. He hadn't expected this. "What?"

"The receptionist at Gillian Sanders's law office told me that you were furious. That you threatened her."

Collins let out a weak laugh. "Is that what this is about? That was just a little disagreement between lovers."

Walker positioned his pencil over his notebook. "This affair you had with the deceased, when did it begin?"

Collins waffled. "I can't remember the exact date."

"Oh come on, surely you can recall. Your wife was still in a coma, right? You must have receipts. I assume at least you took Gillian out to dinner."

"We went back to her place." Collins rubbed his nose.

"Those months are a blur. Gillian and I comforted each other. That's all it was."

"Really? During that time there must be receipts for dinners, flowers, something, right? I mean if you really had an *affair*…"

Collins bristled. "What are you getting at?"

"The truth. How long did this affair last, because I can tell you right now, once the state CID gets on this case your life is going to be an open book."

"It was one time," Collins said, looking away. "One night. Right after Anna came out of the coma."

Walker didn't think he could feel more disgust for this man, but Collins had proved him wrong. "Why did you tell your wife then that it was an affair, which implies it was ongoing?"

The scumbag shook his head.

"You had to know that Gillian was going to tell her the truth."

"It was my word against Gillian's," Collins said.

Walker studied him. "What was it you were really afraid Gillian Sanders was going to tell your wife, Mr. Collins?"

"I don't know what you're getting at."

"Sure you do. You had to have a reason to lie about your *affair* with your wife's best friend. I'm betting it was to discredit Gillian. So I have to ask myself, why?"

Collins shot to his feet. "It's my wife you should be questioning, not me."

"The thing is, I've found witnesses who will testify that you threatened Gillian Sanders the morning of the day she was murdered," Walker said.

"What about my wife's threat to kill her?" he cried.

"No one but you heard your wife threaten to kill Gillian, and quite frankly, you aren't a credible witness since you've already lied to an officer of the law."

Collins looked around the motel room as if searching for a way out of this. "I'm thinking I should call my lawyer."

"That's probably a good idea since, according to the receptionist's sworn statement, your argument with Gillian Sanders was more than a little disagreement," Walker continued. "Gillian threatened to call the police if you didn't leave." Walker glanced down at his notes. "She stated that you called Gillian 'a meddling bitch' and threatened to 'fix her' if she didn't stay out of your life."

"It was just a disagreement. Gillian was angry at me because I never called her after that first time at her house."

"The *only* time," Walker said, not believing a word of it. "Doesn't sound much like a lover's quarrel. In fact, I asked the receptionist if she knew about your affair with Gillian Sanders and after she quit laughing, she was quite adamant that Gillian wouldn't…let me get this right," he said, checking his notes. "That Gillian 'wouldn't have poured water on you if you were on fire.'"

"That bitch," Collins spit out. Perspiration began to stain the armpits of his expensive dress shirt and a muscle in his jaw twitched. Meanness shone in his eyes. His lip curled in contempt. "Gillian was a man-hating bitch. She was always telling Anna what she should do and Anna, who has the backbone of a jellyfish, listened to her."

"What was it Gillian had advised her to do?"

"Divorce me, for starters."

"I thought you were the one who wanted the divorce."

"No, I mean, yeah, I filed, but I didn't want Anna to sign the papers. I just wanted to scare her."

"*Scare* her?"

"She killed my son. I was pissed. I wanted to…I don't know. Make her pay."

"Is that why you seduced her best friend?"

Collins shook his head. "I would have done anything to get that bitch out of our lives—even get her drunk and sleep with her."

"Even kill her?"

IN LUCINDA'S HOSPITAL ROOM, Chief Nash watched his wife sleep, one hand on her rounded stomach and, for the first time in his life, he prayed.

When he finished, he was convinced that the reason Lucinda might lose the baby was because of what he'd done. Not just the night he'd taken her so roughly when he'd thought she was having an affair.

No, this was happening because he'd burned evidence. All the years he'd been a good cop had been canceled out by that one act.

He knew Walker thought he was crazy for not calling in the state CID. At first he hadn't done it because he didn't want the case getting away from him. He'd reasoned he would need to be able to quash any evidence that might hurt Lucinda.

Now he couldn't call them in because he had to make things right. He couldn't get back the evidence. But he could go back to being a good cop. He could end his career right. He could make amends for what he'd done. He knew even then Lucinda might lose their baby.

Either way, he had to do this. For himself. For his wife. For their baby.

He left Lucinda sleeping and went out to his patrol car to make the call to the penitentiary. He tracked down the warden who was a friend of his and set up a call with Leon, the former car thief and Lucinda's ex-partner in crime.

He was told he wouldn't be able to talk to Leon until tomorrow afternoon. Nash thanked the warden and hung up, remembering the other night when he and Lucinda had sat talking about the future and names for their baby.

He covered his face with his hands, his body heaving with the aching pain of the sobs. Hating this weakness in himself, he pulled himself together, wiped his face and went back to his wife's bedside to take her hand.

Her eyes opened and he knew she'd heard him crying, but

had pretended to remain sleep to not embarrass him. He thought he couldn't love her more than at that moment.

"The baby's going to be fine," she said, squeezing his hand. "You'll see."

All he could do was nod and pray that he could make things right.

WALKER WATCHED MARC COLLINS as he realized what he'd said and quickly backtracked. "I didn't kill *anyone*. I only told Anna about Gillian and me so my wife wouldn't listen to the bitch anymore." He snorted. "Hell, I didn't think Anna would *kill* her."

"What else did Gillian advise your wife to do? You said divorce you, 'for starters,'" Walker pointed out, checking his notes. "What else?"

Collins looked nervous, as if trying to remember how much the receptionist might have overheard of his argument with her boss. "Gillian was determined to find the driver from the hit-and-run accident who killed Tyler."

"I would think you'd want that, too."

"Like that would bring Tyler back," Collins muttered. "I just wanted the whole thing to be put behind us. The cops hadn't found the guy, so what made Gillian think she could? I'd already had months of waiting for the guy to be caught."

"But Gillian continued to search for the hit-and-run driver?"

Collins nodded. "She kept Anna's hopes up. I wanted her to stop. I could see what it was doing to Anna and I couldn't take any more. The pain, you know."

Collins looked up, his eyes shiny with the stimulants he'd consumed. If there was pain there, Walker couldn't see it.

"So you thought you'd protect your wife by telling her you had an affair with her best friend."

Collins had the grace to look sheepish. "Yeah, well, maybe I was desperate. I told Anna not to take Tyler with her that night. So I'd been drinking a little and she didn't want to leave him with me. Taking Tyler to protect him from his own father, what a bunch of bullshit. And look how that turned out."

"Where were you from the time your wife left you at the house the night Ms. Sanders was murdered?" Walker asked.

Collins was ready with an alibi. "I went straight to a little bar in Ballard. The bartender or any of the regulars who were there that night will testify that I was there until it closed at 2:00 a.m."

It was all Walker could do not to wipe that smug look off his face.

"I don't know why you're questioning me," Collins said. "It seems pretty clear-cut. When Anna left me, she took her gun and headed for Gillian's house. I tried to stop her, but there was no reasoning with her."

"You could have called the police," Walker pointed out.

Collins shrugged. "A man never thinks his wife is capable of murder. How was I to know she'd drive over to Gillian's house and shoot her, then stuff her in the trunk and head for the mountains?"

Collins thought Gillian had been killed at her house? Maybe the man really didn't know the truth. Or maybe he was lying through his teeth.

"Is there anything else you'd like to tell me?" Walker asked.

Collins seemed to relax a little. "No."

"Okay." Walker reached over to turn off the recorder, but stopped just short of it. "One more thing. Why did you place a call to Jonathan Fairbanks's cell phone the day Gillian Sanders was murdered?"

Collins took the question like a blow. He staggered back, the edge of the bed hitting him in the calves. He sat down, eyes widening for a moment before narrowing. "You know, I think that's all the questions I'll be answering without my lawyer present. You might recall I asked for an attorney earlier."

Walker sat for a moment, then rose from the recliner and turned off the recorder. "Don't leave town, Mr. Collins."

RUTH FAIRBANKS TOOK THE report on Anna Collins to her room, locked the door and settled in to read it.

She hadn't encountered anyone as she returned to the house. She'd used her key and quickly turned off the security alarm before it could sound. She wouldn't have been surprised if Jonathan had tried to follow her or, at the very least, was sitting in the foyer waiting for her when she returned.

He'd been acting oddly lately. She'd meant to ask him earlier why he was spending so much time on the island. It wasn't like him. He much preferred life back East. He lived and breathed politics, working as Big Jim's aide, and had been gearing up for the primary here in Washington hoping to retain his father's seat.

At first she thought it had something to do with Pet. She'd seen the two of them talking once in the hallway when they hadn't known she was there. They were much too friendly toward each other.

But while Jonathan might dillydally with the tramp, there was no way he'd let her within fifty feet of his political aspirations. Pet wouldn't make him a good politician's wife. Jonathan would only want her—because at one time Jack had wanted her, Ruth thought bitterly.

No, ironically, Jonathan needed someone more like Anna Collins, she thought, as she opened the report and began to read. Anna came from old money, a respected family, good social bearing.

Distractedly, Ruth poured herself some of the tea that Carol left for her every night. She took a drink, needing the warmth after her walk. She was anxious to read the report. What in it wasn't she going to like?

She couldn't shake her worry after the fear she'd seen in her oldest son's eyes earlier tonight in this very room.

What if something had come back to haunt Jonathan?

What if that something was his brother, Jack?

Anna had lost both parents when she was young, Ruth noted. Married after getting a dual degree in business and child development at the top of her class. No dummy, that young woman. Married below her station though and had lived to regret it.

Ruth rubbed her eyes. She hadn't even read past the first page and she found herself fighting to stay awake. She took another drink of the tea. The lettering on the paper swam before her eyes.

The tea.

Jonathan. He'd put something in her tea. She glanced toward her bottle of sleeping pills beside the bed, barely able to keep her eyes open. The bottle still looked full. Apparently he didn't intend to kill her. Just put her out for the night?

Fighting to stay awake long enough, she hid the papers to read in the morning and stumbled to her bed. As sleep took her, she worried what it was that Jonathan feared she was going to find out. And to what extremes he would go to stop her.

CHAPTER TWENTY-TWO

Dr. Brubaker found the chief of police slumped in the chair beside his wife's bed sound asleep the next morning.

Like Doc, Nash had stayed the night at the hospital. Brubaker just hoped he didn't look as bad as the chief of police did.

Nash stirred as Doc checked his patient. Lucinda was sleeping peacefully. The spotting had stopped. The baby was fine. At least for the moment.

As Nash opened his eyes, he whispered, "The baby?"

Brubaker motioned Nash to follow him. He said nothing until he reached his office and closed the door.

"Have a seat," he said to Nash.

The chief of police looked nervous as he took the chair across from Brubaker's desk.

"How long have we known each other, Rob?"

"What kind of question is that? All our lives." Nash ran a hand over his face. "I just want to know how my wife and baby are."

"Fine. For the moment."

"She can't lose this baby." Nash covered his face with his hands for a moment.

"If you want this baby, Rob, then you have to start taking care of your wife."

Nash nodded, head down. "I want this baby." He raised his head. "I love my wife. I would do *anything* for her."

"She needs bed rest. No stress. Did she get the vitamins I

told her to start taking?" He could see that Nash didn't know. "Maybe you could hire someone to come in—"

"No," Nash said. "I have vacation time I can take until my retirement papers go through."

Brubaker raised a brow. "What about this murder case?"

"Walker is handling it."

If that was supposed to give him comfort, it didn't. The doctor had seen how Walker was handling it. "I thought you would have called in the state by now."

"Walker's more than capable," Nash said. "The state will provide any resources he needs."

Doc nodded. "Is there anything you'd like to tell me?"

The chief of police frowned. "Like what?"

"I don't know. You seem distracted, upset, worried."

"I'm worried about my wife and baby," Nash snapped. "That's all."

"Okay. Just make sure you don't do anything to upset Lucinda."

"I'll take care of Lucinda," Nash said. "I'd protect her and the baby with my life."

ANNA WOKE THE NEXT MORNING to gray sky. She'd slept fitfully even after locking her bedroom door and putting a chair under the doorknob. She hated feeling scared but this family, with all its dysfunction, would make anyone uneasy.

She showered and dressed, still tired but too restless to try to sleep. This morning she felt even more confused and frustrated. She had hoped Ruth Fairbanks would provide her with the answers she needed. But apparently the Fairbanks matriarch was as much in the dark as Anna herself.

Nor was Anna at all convinced this morning that the man she'd seen in the woods last night was Jack Fairbanks. If Jack was alive, why would he hang around in the shadows? Unless he really did have something to fear. Something more than the repercussions of having let everyone think he was dead.

She stepped to the rain-streaked window only to find the lake cloaked in clouds.

Anna felt the weight of her life as she tried to fight off the depression, the grief. She'd thought she could finally find justice for Tyler, but instead all she'd found was more misery.

What had ever made her think that finding the hit-and-run driver would give her any peace? Gillian would still be alive if Anna had just let it go.

She turned away from the window. That had been her problem her whole life—her inability to let go once she'd set upon a path. She should have left Marc years ago, right after Tyler was born. How different their lives might have been.

No changing the past. Nor did she want to think about her future. She didn't want to think at all and couldn't bear another moment inside this room.

Grabbing her jacket, she headed for the door, hoping not to run into any of the Fairbankses yet this morning. Cautiously Anna cracked open her door and peeked down the hallway. The sconces lit the wide gleaming hallway with a faint golden glow. Hallway empty. She pushed the door all the way open and then, after closing it quietly behind her, headed for the stairs.

There was a tangible gloom that hung over the house. Was this what Jack Fairbanks had tried to escape? Had escaped until he rescued her?

She shivered as she recalled the dark figure in the trees. But nothing unnerved her as much as Jonathan Fairbanks. She'd lived with a bitter man, so she recognized the barely contained fury beneath even the most congenial demeanor. What had caused such anger? she wondered. The accident that had crippled him? Or his jealousy of his brother, Jack?

Anna was still frankly shocked that Pet was sleeping with

her deceased husband's brother. Did Pet know something? Is that why she drowned herself in alcohol?

At the top of the stairs, Anna stopped to peer down. No sign of anyone, but she could hear the rattle of pots and pans coming from the kitchen. Tiptoeing down the stairs, she made her way to the front door. But when she reached it, she saw the security system light was on. She knew that if she opened the door she would set off an alarm and wake the whole household.

Disappointed, she did the next best thing. She'd glimpsed a library as she was being hauled out the first night she'd come here. Did she dare venture down there for a book to read?

Her biggest fear was running into Jonathan, but she didn't want to see Pet or Ruth, either. Not even the servants who seemed to be busy at the back of the house. She knew better than anyone that money couldn't buy happiness. Marc used to say she should be grateful for all she had, meaning him and the luxuries their lifestyle afforded.

But no matter how nice, a house became a prison when the people who lived there were unhappy.

Was that how Jack had felt?

The library door was like the others in the house, thick solid wood. Anna hesitated before turning the knob. The room was dark, the thick drapes on the windows closed. But as she stepped in, groping for the light switch, she saw a wedge of light coming from a floor lamp on the other side of one of the bookshelves at the far end of the massive room. Someone was already in here.

Anna took a step back, trying to ease the door shut behind her without attracting notice.

But before she could escape, she heard someone let out a gasp, which was immediately followed by the sound of glass breaking. The light went out. Anna froze, too shocked to move until she heard what could only be a body hitting the floor.

ELSIE MATHEWS LIVED IN A small ranch-type house south of Seattle. Bright yellow daffodils filled all the flower beds along with a half-dozen ceramic yard ornaments that Walker thought at first were supposed to be elves.

As he rang Elsie's doorbell, he looked down and into the face of one them and realized they were trolls, their faces leering eerily out from behind the flowers with almost evil intent.

Inside the house, a small dog yapped and he heard a woman's voice reprimanding, "Baby, be quiet." A moment later a short, round, elderly woman opened the door holding a tiny black poodle. The dog's eyes gleamed above a protruding pink tongue.

"Yes?" the woman asked.

Walker had called ahead to make sure Elsie Mathews was going to be home and she'd said she would be happy to talk to him. "I'm Officer Walker from Shadow Lake," he reminded her.

"Well, come on in then."

He pulled off his hat and followed her into a room filled with flowered furniture, wallpaper and pillows. The effect was chaotic.

She motioned for him to sit down as she lowered herself and the dog into a large recliner aimed at the television in the corner. The TV was on, the sound turned down.

"As I told you on the phone, I wanted to ask you about the hit-and-run accident that you witnessed about eight months ago," Walker said.

"Can't imagine why you'd be asking about that," she said, glancing at the television for a moment. He feared one of her soap operas might be on, but it appeared to be only an infomercial for exercise equipment. "It's been months since that happened."

He nodded, concerned this trip had been a waste of time. "I know it's been a while, but could you tell me what you saw that night?"

"I suppose I could, although I don't see what good it will

do. You folks didn't catch them the last time I told you. Can't see how you think you will now." She sighed deeply. "I was out walking Baby. Baby's my dog," she said, giving the canine on her lap a pat. "This big black SUV practically ran me over, going way too fast as it went past me. I walk Baby on the edge of the road. We don't have any sidewalks out here, you know."

"The SUV was black?" he asked quickly, hoping to derail her from taking off on a discourse about her lack of sidewalks.

"Black or some dark color. Anyway, I saw the lights of a car coming from the other direction and picked up Baby an instant before that big SUV ran right into that car. There was a terrible crash. Baby was trembling in my arms."

"Are you saying the SUV crossed the center line?" Walker asked.

"It looked to me as if the driver swerved right in front of the car with that woman and child," she said.

"Did you tell the police that?" He knew she hadn't.

"I was so upset that night, I'm not sure what I told them. But after I thought about it, I wondered if the driver hadn't been drinking. He was driving way too fast and rather erratic."

"Earlier you said 'they' passed you. Was there a passenger in the car?"

She frowned. "I suppose I did say that. Maybe there was. I might have seen someone. You know it's funny you would ask that. I had the impression there was someone else in the car when it went by. I think the windows were down because I recalled voices. Like two people arguing. But then when the rig came roaring in reverse at me, I thought I only saw the driver. I didn't mention it to the police at the time. Thought they'd think I was nuts."

"What happened then?"

"Nothing for a moment, then there was the roar of the SUV's motor as the driver reversed and came racing right at me. I jumped back, afraid he didn't see me. But just before he reached us, he shot forward and took off, throwing up gravel from the edge of the road, scaring me and Baby half out of our wits."

"The driver was a man?"

"Only a man would take off without trying to help that poor woman and her little boy," Elsie said emphatically.

"Can you describe the driver?"

Elsie shook her head. "I never saw his face."

"How about the vehicle," Walker said, leaning toward her. "Was there anything on the windows or the side of the vehicle?"

"You mean like one of those signs?" She shook her head, then frowned. "There was something on the bumper. One of those political stickers."

"Do you remember which one?"

She nodded. "My neighbor had one of the fellow's signs in her yard for weeks before the election. I think they should outlaw those eyesores, don't you?"

"Was it a candidate I might have heard of?" he asked quickly.

"Fair-something or other. I didn't vote for him. Didn't like the looks of the Senator."

"Jim Fairbanks?"

"That's the one. But it's odd when you think about it."

"How is that?" Walker was wondering how many cars had Senator Fairbanks stickers on them. Hundreds? Thousands?

"I don't think the man who owned that SUV voted for him, either."

"Why would you say that?"

"Well, if you wanted other people to vote for your candidate, why would you paste something over the name to make it look silly?" she demanded.

Walker didn't know what to say. "As quickly as all this happened, you were able to see what had been pasted *over* the bumper sticker?" *And in the dark,* which he didn't add.

"I *saw* the bumper because it was right in my face," Elsie

said indignantly. "He practically forced me and Baby into the ditch when he backed up like that. That bumper came so close to me that I would have had to be blind to not see it. But it was when he sped off that I saw the fish."

"The *fish?*" Walker mentally kicked himself to think he'd gotten up before daylight to drive all the way over here for nothing.

"It glowed. Couldn't miss a thing like that. My granddaughter has the stars on her bedroom ceiling," Elsie was explaining. "I think they're silly. Who needs something that glows in the dark when you turn the lights off? Do you know what I'm talking about?"

Walker felt his breath rush from his lungs. He knew exactly what she was talking about—and where he'd seen just such a fish.

ANNA SNAPPED ON THE OVERHEAD light and lunged into the library. As she rounded the end of the last bookshelf, she saw the broken glass scattered on the floor surrounding the fallen floor lamp. Next to it, Ruth Fairbanks lay crumpled on the floor.

"Ruth. Oh God, what's wrong?" she cried, rushing to her. Ruth was gasping for breath, holding her chest, her eyes wide.

"Take," she whispered. "Burn them." She clutched at Anna's jacket sleeve and thrust two sheets of half-folded papers at her. Anna saw that Ruth had a small fire going in the fireplace and that several other sheets of paper had been thrown into the flames and were now ashes.

Anna tried to pull free to go to the phone to call 911 and alert the rest of the household, but Ruth was insistent that she take the papers first.

When Anna did, Ruth let go of her sleeve and collapsed back on the floor, unconscious.

Anna rushed to the desk, grabbed up the phone on the desk

and dialed 911. Before emergency services answered, she shoved the papers into the pocket of her jacket, wondering what could be so important that Ruth had been so insistent that she burn them before even calling for help.

After talking to the 911 operator, she pushed the call button and Carol came swiftly into the room. Anna saw at once that the maid had been expecting to see Ruth Fairbanks in the library—not her guest.

"It's Mrs. Fairbanks," Anna said, going to Ruth's side. "I've called nine-one-one. They're sending the chopper to take her to the hospital."

Carol's eyes widened. "I'll alert the family." She spun on her heel as Anna pulled an afghan from one of the deep leather library chairs and put it over Ruth. She took the older woman's hand in hers and checked for a pulse. It was weak, the papers in her pocket forgotten in her concern for Ruth.

A moment later Anna heard the elevator, then Jonathan's distinctive limp as he rushed into the library. "What have you done?" he demanded, shoving Anna out of the way.

"I found her like this," Anna said, wringing her hands as she looked down at Ruth Fairbanks's pale face—and thought about the papers now stuffed in her pocket. "I've called nine-one-one."

Pet rushed in, her red hair looking as wild as her eyes as she wrapped a thin robe around her nearly naked body. "What's wrong with her?" she asked as she stopped to stare down at Jonathan and her mother-in-law.

"How should I know?" Jonathan said.

Anna heard the helicopter, and moments later Carol opened the door to let the paramedics in.

Anna stood back, watching the scene unfold around her, afraid that it would turn out that she was responsible—just as she knew Jonathan suspected.

CHAPTER TWENTY-THREE

WHEN NASH'S CALL WAS finally put through to the prison inmate line, he wasn't surprised that Leon Markowitz sounded like the punk he was.

"I don't know you," the convict said. "Why should I talk to you?"

"Because I know *you,*" Nash said. "I want to know about a car you stole."

"You got to be kiddin'. You think I remember every car I stole, man?"

"Jack Fairbanks's black SUV."

"Jack Fairbanks is dead, so who gives a shit?"

"I do. And so will you if you don't answer my questions," Nash said.

Leon laughed. "You think you can make my life here more miserable?"

"As a matter of fact, I *know* I can. Where did you boost the car?"

Leon sighed. "Ballard, out by the locks."

Nash frowned. Why had Big Jim reported the car stolen from Shadow Lake? To cover up the truth. "Why that car?" he asked, taking a different tack.

"An expensive black SUV, you jokin'?"

"I know it wasn't your usual heist," Nash said.

"Then why you callin' me and askin' a bunch a questions?"

"Tell me the deal you made with Jack."

"I didn't make no deal with Jack." Leon chuckled. "I don't know Jack, you get it?"

"You keep bullshitting me and—"

"Look man, Jack's dead. I'm doing time. So what the hell, I'll tell you. I didn't steal the car. Jack's brother called me. Before you go askin', we had mutual friends. Ain't goin' there though, so don't even ask."

Drug-buying friends. Someone had been supplying Pet for years. Nash had thought it was Jack. Apparently it was his brother.

"He'd heard I did favors for guys who needed their cars lifted. Ya know, can't make the payments, need to get out from under it. The car disappears."

"Jack could make his payments. What was his reason?"

"He'd gotten into a little fender bender."

"Like hell. The whole right side must have been smashed up pretty good." Based on the fact that the registration in the glove box had been bloody, Nash figured the passenger must be dead. "What did you do with the body?"

"There weren't no body. Are you crazy? I don't do that shit."

"But there had to be blood everywhere."

Leon sighed again. "Man, if you know so much about this, then why are you raggin' on me?"

Nash swore under his breath. "Didn't you wonder what was up with all the blood?"

"Sure, man."

"So what did Jonathan Fairbanks tell you?"

Leon laughed. "How dumb you think I am? Like I'm going to ask *that* dude."

"He didn't give you any indication?"

Leon swore. "He *indicated* he wasn't interested in talking about it. Come on, man, I'm going to be late for my meds. But I can tell you this. The dude called me from the hospital."

"Which one?" Nash asked.

"I can't remember the name. That one in Ballard."

AFTER DOC HAD RUTH FAIRBANKS in the ICU and all her vitals stable, he went to find Anna. He'd seen how upset she'd been when she'd arrived at the hospital shortly after the helicopter had brought in Ruth and her son.

Anna was now huddled in the waiting room nervously tracing her scar, her knees pulled up to her chest, her chin resting on them, eyes closed. She looked like a child and he felt a wave of tenderness toward her. He could have so easily had a daughter her age if Gladys had been able to conceive.

"Is she all right?" Anna said, shooting to her feet the moment he entered the room.

"She just sent for her lawyer and Judge Gandy. I guess we're about to find out if she's all right. She's demanded a competency hearing."

Anna felt her heart sink. "She must think she's going to die."

"Then wouldn't you send for a priest? Or your family?" Doc asked. "Instead, she wants guards at her doors and she's put Jonathan and her daughter-in-law on an absolutely-no-admittance list. No, I believe Ruth is well aware that she's going to live and wants it on her terms."

"What about her heart?" Anna asked.

"She didn't have a heart attack, although I can't convince her son of that," Doc said. "I'd say she had a panic attack. It's so not like Ruth Fairbanks. I guess that's why Jonathan has insisted a cardiologist be called in, since his mother has refused to be flown to a Seattle hospital. Not that panic attacks can't be dangerous, especially in a woman her age."

"This is all my fault," Anna said, sounding close to tears. "I should never have gone out there."

He steered her to the couch and sat down beside her. "This had nothing to do with you."

Anna was shaking her head. "When I found her, she was burning these." She pulled two sheets of folded, slightly crumpled paper from her pocket and handed them to him. "She wouldn't even let me call for help until I took them and promised to burn them. She'd already burned a number of the pages in the fireplace."

He frowned as he unfolded the papers, glancing from the first few lines to Anna. "Ruth had you *investigated?* And that makes this *your* fault how exactly?" He couldn't hide his anger. This was so like Ruth Fairbanks.

"She was trying to burn the report when she collapsed. I heard her gasp, then knock over a lamp as she fell. Something in that report about me had to have caused her attack."

"Did you read it?"

She nodded. "The first two pages. The rest she'd already burned."

"Is there something in there that would have been that traumatic?"

"Not that I can see, but read the report and see what you think," Anna pleaded.

Brubaker nodded and, adjusting his glasses, read what was written on the two pages. When he'd finished, he re-folded the pages and handed them back to her. "There's nothing there, Anna. If Ruth's panic attack has something to do with that report, then it must have been in the pages she'd already burned."

His beeper went off. "I told the nurse to call me if Ruth started making more demands."

He headed for the door, then turned to look back at her. "You aren't going back to the island, are you?"

"Not likely."

"I have a big old house and could use the company. The front door is always unlocked. You'd be doing me a favor. The place has been rather lonely since Gladys left. The guest room has a great view." He seemed to hesitate. "Gladys wouldn't object. In fact when I go by to talk to her today, I'll tell her you might be staying for a while."

IT HAD BEEN ONE OF THOSE DAYS. Walker was still reeling from what he'd learned.

If he was right, then the vehicle that hit Anna Collins eight months ago was Jack Fairbanks's Lincoln Navigator. It was too much of a coincidence that Jack's SUV was stolen around that time and matched the description right down to the fish sticker on the bumper.

Back at his office, he went over the financial reports he'd ordered on the Collinses. He shouldn't have been surprised to learn that Anna had real wealth, apparently handed down from her family.

Marc Collins, on the other hand, had made some bad investments in a depressed housing market. But for the past six months he'd been banking ten grand a month on the fifteenth of each month; that sent up a red flag.

From what Walker could tell, the money hadn't been coming from Collins's wife or any other source that he could find. It reeked of blackmail.

When Chief Nash called from the hospital, he said Lucinda might lose the baby.

"I'm sorry. Is there anything I can do?" Walker had asked.

"I just wanted to let you know that I have complete faith in you when it comes to this murder investigation," Nash said. "I'm not going to be able to help."

Walker swore under his breath. He understood what was going on. Jonathan Fairbanks had gotten to him. No CID. *Let that officer of yours handle the murder trial.*

"You can't expect me to handle a case of this size—"

"Walker, I know you. If anyone can solve this case, it's you. Who's working today?"

"Tillman."

"Good. If you need, call in the others. They normally would start the first of May anyway. What's a week early? I'm sure they can use the money. I would appreciate it though if you'd keep me abreast of any new developments."

"Sure." Walker couldn't believe this. Nash was throwing him to the wolves, gambling that Walker couldn't come up with anything that would hurt the Fairbankses. Meanwhile Nash had distanced himself from it.

"How long will Lucinda be in the hospital?" Walker asked, trying to keep an angry tone out of his voice.

"Doc doesn't know. The baby's all right. At least so far. I'm staying with her. As you know, I've been thinking about retiring for some time. I will be announcing my retirement once this murder case is over and recommending you as the new chief."

Walker mumbled a thank-you and got off the phone as quickly as possible. Nash had thrown him a bone, knowing that his chances of being Shadow Lake police chief were nil if he went after the Fairbankses.

He'd barely hung up when Doc called from the hospital.

"I suppose you heard that Ruth Fairbanks was brought in," Doc said. "She has asked me to see about hiring someone to guard her while she's in here."

"Bodyguards?"

"Apparently she has reason to fear for her safety," Doc said.

Walker let out a low whistle. "Okay. I know a couple of guys who might want the work. How soon do you need them?"

"Immediately."

Walker hung up. He hurried down the hall to the fax machine. It didn't take long to find what he'd been looking for. Marc Collins had called Jonathan Fairbanks's campaign office just over six months ago shortly before he was called on his cell by the politician himself. There were several more calls just before the fifteenth when the first ten thousand dollars appeared in Collins's personal account.

Walker picked up his hat. It was time he paid another visit to Marc Collins.

ANNA STEPPED OUT OF THE hospital and took a gulp of the cold, damp air. The day, like all of the rest since she'd been here in Shadow Lake, was dark with clouds and the promise of rain.

She shivered and rubbed her arms through her jacket, thankful that Ruth hadn't had a heart attack. Still Anna couldn't shake the feeling that what had caused the woman's panic attack was something she'd read in the investigator's report. What had been in the other pages—the ones Ruth had saved?

"I've been looking for you," said a male voice behind her, jerking her out of her thoughts.

Anna turned to come face-to-face with Marc. She hadn't seen him since his visit to the hospital. She was surprised he was still in town and wondered what he'd been doing, since little was open for the season.

"I thought you would have left town by now." She'd hoped he had. He was the last person she wanted to see.

"I have a business deal going. Just waiting on a call to finalize it. This seemed as good a place to wait as any other."

She wondered why he was being so cryptic. This deal he had going didn't sound like a real estate one. But she really didn't care one way or the other.

"I also thought I should stay around in case you needed me," he added as an afterthought.

She couldn't help but smile at that. "What? Haven't you done enough to *help* me?"

"I just told the truth."

"Right." She started to walk away.

"We need to talk," he said, and indicated his car parked down the block.

The last thing she wanted to do was talk to him let alone get into his car with him. His eyes seemed too bright, his demeanor odd. She didn't get the impression he'd been drinking, but he appeared to be high on something.

Anna shook her head. "I think we've said everything we need to say to each other. When this is over, I'll be filing for divorce."

He bristled at the news. "You're that confident you won't be going to prison?"

She turned to leave. He grabbed her arm, but she jerked free.

"Please, Anna, I'm sorry. This isn't how I want to leave things between us."

"Sign the divorce papers then, Marc."

He looked off toward the lake, then back at her. "Okay. I just wanted to tell you that I have a buyer for the business. I've decided I need some time to get my head straight. I'm thinking of doing some traveling. I'm not sure when or if I'll be coming back."

That surprised her more than him selling the business.

"It's time I got on with my life," he said belligerently. "I'll be free to do anything I want. I'll have money and nothing but time." He grinned, the grin too big, the eyes glittering. "You sure you don't want to come with me, just skip town before you get sent to prison?"

"I'm sure."

He shrugged. "If you change your mind, I'm staying at the Pine-something Cabins on the lake. It's just down the road on the left. Cabin nine. I'll be there until tomorrow."

She didn't bother to tell him she wouldn't be changing her mind. She waited until he drove away before she walked toward Dr. Brubaker's house.

As she passed the marina, Anna remembered that she hadn't paid for her boat trip to the island. A breeze came up off the water as she neared the small building. She could hear someone inside it moving around and the occasional *tink-tink* of metal on metal.

As she rounded the corner, she saw the same young man who'd taken her out to the island that first night. "Hi, Eric," she said when he looked up.

He smiled bashfully. No doubt he'd heard that the Fairbankses had called the police on her.

"I hope I didn't get you in trouble the other night," she said. "I still have to pay Harry."

"That's him now," Eric said.

She heard the boat motor and turned to see a fishing boat come in off the water. As it pulled to the dock, a heavyset man wearing a Panama hat tossed out a stringer of fish onto the dock.

Eric hurried to tie up the boat as Harry bragged about the day's catch. From the older man's boisterous laugh, she could only assume, even given the hour, that he'd consumed a few of the beers that had once been in the aluminum cans now crumpled and piled in the bottom of the boat.

Eric said something to him and Harry looked her way. "Clean those for me, will ya, Eric?" Harry said jovially, then punched the kid playfully in the shoulder. "Just kiddin'."

"Hello," Harry said as he came up the dock toward her. "Eric says you want to give me money? Always love to get money from a pretty lady." He laughed.

"Eric was kind enough to give me a ride out to the Fairbankses' island the other night," she said. "I'd like to pay you." She held out her credit card, the only one she still had after losing her purse in the lake. "You do take cards, I hope."

Harry lifted one furry brow as he took her card. "A popular place, that island, lately." He looked down at the card, saying, "Always take credit cards. Collins?" He glanced up at her. "You related to Marc Collins?"

She couldn't hide her surprise. "You know Marc?"

"He rented a boat from me. Like I said, popular place that island lately." He stepped into the small building, working his way to the back where he pulled out an old-fashioned credit-card machine and ran her card through it.

"Marc went out to the Fairbankses' island?" she asked, thinking Harry must be mistaken.

"That's right. I gave him the directions myself," Harry said as he came back out with her card, a pen and the receipt for her to sign.

"When was that?" she asked as she scribbled her name.

Harry frowned in concentration. "Two or three days ago? I know, it was the morning before you borrowed my helper here to take you out to the island."

Marc had gone out to the Fairbankses *before* she had? Why wouldn't Jonathan or his mother have told her that?

IT TOOK A WARRANT TO GET the name of the patient brought in the night of August 30 eight months before.

Nash knew a judge in Seattle who'd run against Big Jim Fairbanks in a primary years ago. He'd been happy to sign a warrant even though Nash had told him he doubted little would come of it.

When Nash finally had the patient file in his hand, he'd known at once that even if he'd kept the bloody registration, he could never have brought Jonathan Fairbanks down with it.

The patient, who'd been treated for extensive facial lacerations, had been whisked off immediately by private jet to sunny Southern California for plastic surgery by the state's leading face-lift doctor.

Patricia "Pet" Fairbanks, according to the medical record, had been the only passenger in a one-car rollover. There was nothing about who had brought her to the hospital. Nothing about any drug use. Or record of the accident.

News like this involving the daughter-in-law of Senator

Big Jim Fairbanks would have made national television. Except it hadn't. Nash knew it had taken more than Jonathan to keep the lid on this. It had taken Big Jim himself.

Nash left the hospital and called Jonathan Fairbanks from a pay phone down the block.

"It's Chief Nash," he said. "I'm at the hospital in Ballard."

Silence on the other end of the line.

"I know about Pet's 'face-lift' after her one-car rollover August 30, the same night a woman named Anna Collins was injured and her four-year-old killed in a hit-and-run. The same night a car thief named Leon picked up Jack Fairbanks's black Lincoln Navigator and made it disappear."

"What is it you want?" Jonathan asked his voice cold as stone.

"Nothing. As far as I'm concerned, you and my family have no connection whatsoever nor will we ever again," Nash said.

"I can live with that," Jonathan said.

Nash bet the bastard could as he hung up.

He didn't need Jonathan Fairbanks to tell him that he would have had hell making a case against him. Leon, a felon doing time in the pen, wouldn't make a credible witness against a man like Jonathan Fairbanks, nor would Lucinda even if there had been proof.

Even with the bloody registration, Nash would only have had proof that Pet had been in an accident that was never reported.

But the fact was, Jonathan Fairbanks had paid twenty-five thousand in blackmail money to Lucinda for papers from the car. And Big Jim Fairbanks had reported the black Lincoln Navigator stolen, lying though his teeth to protect his sons.

As Nash drove back to Shadow Lake, Nash told himself that it was over. But he knew he would always wonder who'd been driving the SUV that night. Jack? Or Jonathan?

THE PATROL CAR'S HEADLIGHTS swept through the rain and fog to pick up number nine in the Pinecrest Cabin Court.

Walker was relieved to see that Marc Collins's car was still parked outside the cabin. He pulled in, cut the engine and let the rainy day settle around him.

Through a crack in the curtains, he could see a light on inside the cabin. He considered for a moment how to handle Collins. It would be hard to get him to talk, especially given the disgust Walker felt for the man.

Collins had blackmailed the killer of his child. The minute the eyewitness had told him about the glow-in-the-dark fish pasted over the Fairbanks campaign bumper sticker, Walker had known the hit-and-run vehicle belonged to Jack Fairbanks.

He hadn't wanted to believe it. Not Jack. Jonathan, sure. But Walker couldn't imagine Jack doing something like that and living with the guilt.

But Jack hadn't, had he?

Walker shoved away thoughts of Jack. He couldn't deal with that right now. Later, when he had enough evidence against the Fairbankses, then he would deal with it.

Right now, he had to get Marc Collins to talk. Walker knew the Realtor would have lawyered up by now. Somehow Walker had to get Collins to roll over on the Fairbankses.

He opened his car door and stepped out into the rain. Cabin number nine was cloaked in cottonlike fog. For a moment, this felt like a dream. A bad one.

Stepping under the tiny porch roof, he knocked on the door and waited. He could hear faint music inside the cabin. Probably the television. Herb had installed satellite TV after years of fighting it.

"People say they come up here to get away and then they want to know why they don't have HBO and Cinemax," Herb would say and shake his head. "Next thing they're going to

be demanding is a swimming pool and one of them hot tubs."
Everyone in town knew how Herb felt about hot tubs.

Walker knocked a little harder. He could smell the lake
through the rain. It drew him as it always had. He was a man
who was destined to always live close to water.

Collins might be in the shower. Or asleep.

He knocked again, louder this time, a niggling feeling
worming its way through him.

All his instincts on alert, Walker tried the door. The knob
turned easily in his hand, the door swinging open with a
groan. He already had his weapon in his hands by the time
the door stopped groaning.

Blood. It was everywhere. And Marc Collins was right in
the middle of it, a gun and a bottle of pills spilled on the floor
next to his body.

Sprawled on the bed, half-naked, one arm flung over the
side was a redheaded woman.

It wasn't until Walker checked for a pulse that he recognized her. Pet Fairbanks.

CHAPTER TWENTY-FOUR

ANNA HADN'T GONE TO DOC'S house. She'd walked through the rain unaware of the cold or her wet clothing. She'd known about Marc's failings. Not at first, but a woman couldn't be married to a man for very long without knowing what kind of man she'd married.

It was hard to think of her marriage to Marc as a mistake though. She would never have had Tyler. Even for four short years.

She didn't hear the car pull up next to her. Didn't notice it at all until she heard the whir of the passenger-side window come down and Officer D.C. Walker's voice calling her name.

She stopped walking as the patrol car came to a stop next to the curb. She knew even before she bent down to look inside that he'd been looking for her.

"Would you mind getting in?" Walker asked. "We need to talk."

She hesitated, not out of fear that he planned to arrest her, but because of his demeanor. There was a gentleness in his voice, in his brown eyes, that she'd never seen before and it frightened her. "It's about Tyler, isn't it?"

He nodded, reached across the seat to open the passenger-side door, and she did the only thing she could. She slid in.

WALKER HAD PLANNED TO TAKE her to the station, but when he'd seen her wandering down the street, drenched to the skin, looking lost and scared and freezing, he'd driven straight to his place.

She didn't say a word as he ushered her inside, led her to the bathroom and turned on the hot shower. He stripped off her jacket and boots and then put her in the shower clothes and all. Through the glass door, he watched see her slowly come back to life. It was a terrible thing to see, the way she hugged herself, curling around her soft middle, sobbing as the hot water beat down on her. He watched until he couldn't stand it anymore and shut off the water and dragged her into his arms.

He pulled her down to the tile floor of the bathroom, both of them now soaked to the skin and held her until the sobs subsided and she lifted her head and asked him to leave her for a moment.

Reluctantly, he rose and left the bathroom. He heard the shower come on, the glass open and close. He stood outside, his back to the door, wondering how much more the woman could take.

As the shower shut off, he knew he was about to find out.

ANNA SAT BEFORE THE FIRE wearing one of Walker's T-shirts and a pair of his sweatpants. Both were way too large. He'd given her a blanket from his bed to wrap up in until the chills went away and built a fire in the rock fireplace before going into the kitchen to make them both coffee.

Now she cupped the warm mug not for the heat but to keep her hands from shaking.

Walker told her simply. Marc was dead. An apparent suicide after the companion he was with overdosed on drugs. There was a note at the scene. Marc confessed to killing Gillian to keep her from telling Anna about his real affair—which was with drugs, according to his suicide note. The companion found dead in the cabin with Marc had been Patricia "Pet" Fairbanks.

Anna nodded, staring into the flames, and waited to feel something at this news. Anything. But she'd been unable to dispel the numbness she'd felt earlier when she'd learned that Marc had been out to the Fairbankses.

"You don't really believe any of this, do you?" she asked finally. "Marc and Pet Fairbanks? Pet was having an affair with Jonathan. She wouldn't risk losing all that money and power for a man like Marc."

Walker's brown eyes soften with sympathy, the last thing she needed. "I suspect Jonathan sent her there to pay off your husband. Everyone knew she was on drugs. For all we know Jonathan got her hooked. I think both of their deaths are part of a cover-up. If I'm right, it started with a hit-and-run accident on a narrow two-lane road south of Seattle."

She listened as he told her about the eyewitness seeing a bumper sticker and a glow-in-the-dark fish.

"Billy Blake gave Jack that fish. I was there the day Jack stuck it over his father's political bumper sticker. Billy and I laughed about it at the time."

She heard the pain in his voice, pain not unlike her own. "What are you trying to tell me? That the man who saved my life took my son's?"

"Yes. I suspect Jack Fairbanks was driving the car that killed your son and put you in a coma. Pet may have been with him. That was about the time she disappeared, California, I think, and came back after having plastic surgery. The rumor was it was a facelift but it was a hell of lot more than that."

Anna realized Ruth had mentioned Pet's facelift. Now it made sense.

He went on to tell her about Jack's stolen SUV report, then about finding Gillian's car near the rest stop, the bullet hole in the trunk, the lack of blood and the conclusion that Gillian had died of blunt force trauma from a blow to the head. That she was already dead when someone put her in Anna's car trunk and fired a shot into her temple.

"Somehow your friend Gillian stumbled onto some information that led her to Fairbanks," Walker said. "She might have found out that Marc was blackmailing Jonathan."

Anna felt sick. "That would explain why I was so angry with Marc the night I headed toward Shadow Lake."

"It appears she was meeting Jonathan Fairbanks at the rest stop," Walker continued.

"But Jonathan wasn't the one who saved my life," she reminded him.

Walker shook his head. "It is as hard for me to accept that Jack is alive as it is for me to imagine Jack having any part in Gillian's murder. You didn't know Jack. I did. He couldn't hurt anyone. If he was driving the SUV the night your son died…he would have wanted to turn himself in."

"But he didn't."

"No. Jonathan got to him. Believe me, if Jack faked his death, then Jonathan forced him into it."

Anna had already pieced a lot of it together for herself. Gillian's call. She'd found out something about Tyler's death but what she wanted to tell Anna was about Marc.

That was the shock that had stolen her memory. She hadn't wanted to face what Gillian had told her.

As Walker told Anna about what he believed was a blackmail scheme by Marc, Anna felt the pieces fall into place. Gillian had found proof that Marc had not only known who the hit-and-run driver was but she'd suspected the bastard had been blackmailing the Fairbanks. *That* was what Marc had feared Gillian would tell her. That's why he hadn't gone through with the divorce, that's why he'd pretended he and Gillian had had an affair. He'd wanted to discredit Gillian.

The night Anna went into the lake, she must have known that Gillian was heading for Shadow Lake to confront the man who killed Tyler. Anna would have wanted to go along, but she knew that her friend would have said she would handle it. Gillian had been in a hurry because she was meeting the man.

That's why Anna hadn't taken the time to change her clothing or kill Marc, although she was sure she would have wanted to do both.

Gillian would have been gone by the time Anna reached her house. She must have found the scrap of envelope that Gillian had written on and remembered her friend mentioning Shadow Lake.

"The gun was in your car," Walker was saying. "When you reached the rest stop you would have seen where Gillian had driven around the barrier. You drove in, saw her car, got out to look for her. You would have been afraid when you couldn't find her. You would have searched, then gone to get help."

Anna could see herself driving fast out of the rest stop headed for Shadow Lake—and the police department.

"You'd requested directions to the police department earlier, at the same time you'd asked your in-car system for directions to Shadow Lake."

"The deer," Anna said.

He nodded. "You lost control of your car, ended up in the lake."

"And Jack?" she asked.

"Jack," he said on a sigh. "I know someone came to the rest stop by boat. There is a cove just below the rest stop where a boat had been pulled up onto the shore."

"Jonathan."

"Jack had to be with him or at least close by," she said, seeing how hard this was for Walker to accept.

He nodded.

"I'm trying to make sense of all this. Jack had to be going through hell over what he'd done. He would have wanted to go to the authorities. Jonathan had to be desperate to shut him up. I still don't know how Jonathan talked him into faking his death, if that's what he did…. You know Jonathan lost his leg because of Jack—and he never let him forget it."

"Why would Jack save my life and expose himself?"

"Guilt. He would have known who you were since your husband was blackmailing Jonathan. Or maybe Jack didn't think. He just did what would have come naturally to him before Jonathan got his claws into him." Walker swore under his breath. "The Jack Fairbanks I knew couldn't live with what he'd done. I guess that's why when a rumor surfaced after Jack's drowning that he'd taken his own life, I believed it. I knew something was bothering him."

"It sounds like you believe Jack's alive."

Walker raked a hand through his hair and looked toward the fire for a moment before he answered. "How can I not, given everything I've learned? At least I believe he was that night. I'm not sure he is now. Jonathan has to get rid of Jack for good. He can't take the chance he'll surface again. If I'm right and Jack can't live with what he's done, then he will surface—and he'll take Jonathan down with him. But I fear it's too late and Jack is already dead, and gone for good this time. Jonathan would see to that."

She shivered as she heard him voice her own fear. "But Ruth is having Jack's body exhumed."

"Not anymore. She's canceled it. Apparently she has realized that opening that casket will jeopardize both of her sons' lives."

"Can't you get a court order—"

"Anna, even if I tried to get an exhumation now, the Fairbankses would fight it for years. As far as anyone is concerned, the case is closed. Marc Collins killed Gillian Sanders. Open and shut. Chief Nash has already made a statement to the press and has stepped back in to see that nothing new surfaces."

"You think that is Jonathan Fairbanks's doing?"

"Yeah. Chief Nash has retired."

She could tell he hated to admit that Nash might have helped Jonathan get away with murder. Clearly, Walker had liked and respected the police chief.

"Even if Ruth would agree to the exhumation, it wouldn't prove that Jack faked his death or that he was driving the car that killed your son," Walker said. "Everyone involved who knew something is dead."

"Except Jack and Jonathan."

He nodded solemnly. "Jack's got to know that he's next. Jonathan will never be able to trust Jack to stay dead." Walker looked out the window toward the lake, his expression forlorn.

"If Jack's the man we think he is, then he can't take the chance that Jonathan will ever rise so far in politics as to be president," she said.

Walker turned back to her, surprise in his expression. "You think he'll get Jonathan before Jonathan gets him? Still it has to end badly. Jack knows that."

She saw how hard this was on him. Jack had been his best friend. "What does D.C. stand for?" she asked.

Walker smiled almost sheepishly. "Dennis Charles. See why I go by Walker?"

She smiled back at him. Dennis Charles Walker was handsome when he smiled like that.

"Some year this one has been," he said. "I would imagine you're anxious to leave Shadow Lake, get back to Seattle, put all this behind you. If you can."

She could only nod. Seattle was the last place she wanted to go. There was nothing there for her anymore. Gillian was gone. Mary Ellen…well, she no longer thought of her as a friend. "What will you do?" she asked.

He shrugged. "Shadow Lake is my home. You should see

it in the summer. It's beautiful here and the fishing—" He laughed. "I would imagine you don't fish, huh."

"I grew up on the Sound. Of course I fish."

A silence fell between them. Walker had taken Jack's alleged death hard. He'd taken his betrayal even harder. Jack must have thought that faking his death would make this all go away. Maybe, she realized, the same way that Marc had thought that blackmailing the Fairbankses would be justice for Tyler's death.

"I'm sorry about your friend," she said.

Walker stared into the fire for a long moment, then turned to look at her. "I would think you would hate Jack for what he did."

She smiled ruefully. "From the time I awoke from the coma, all I've thought about is my son's killer. I was obsessed with finding him." She shook her head, thinking of all the loss. Tyler. Gillian. Marc. "And now…Jack saved my life, and by doing so sacrificed his own. I don't know what I feel."

Walker nodded. "You do realize that we can't prove any of this. Jonathan took care of both Marc—and Pet. He had to know that Marc would continue blackmailing him. Pet? I'm betting she found out that Jack had faked his death or was even in on it from the beginning."

Anna listened to the crackle of the fire and the rain falling on the deck outside the window feeling small and insignificant. Tyler was gone. So was Gillian. And now Marc. For months she'd thought she wanted justice for Tyler. She hadn't wanted Gillian to give up looking for the hit-and-run driver.

But she knew that what she really wanted was to know that she hadn't been responsible for Tyler's death. "When you talked to the eyewitness about the accident…"

"It wasn't your fault," Walker said. "The SUV swerved into you. There was nothing you could have done."

She nodded. Marc had led her to believe it had been her fault. Now she knew, thanks to Walker, that he'd been drinking that night. That was why she'd taken Tyler and left. But still, if she hadn't been on that road…

She pushed the thought away, knowing that it would always haunt her. Nothing would change that. Not the arrest of Jack or Jonathan Fairbanks.

"I'm sorry," Walker said. "Sorry I was so suspicious of you in the beginning. I was wrong about you."

"I know how hard that must be for you to admit."

He gave a little quirk of his mouth. "You have no idea."

His cell phone rang, jarring them both. "Walker," he said into it and looked up at Anna. "She's right here. Yes. No. I'll tell her."

She looked up at him and saw the concern in his face. No more, she thought. She wasn't capable of hearing any more bad news. But then who was left in her life? "Tell me it's not Doc."

Walker shook his head. "It's Ruth Fairbanks. She's asking to see you."

WALKER GOT HER CLOTHES FROM the dryer. They were still a little damp. Anna couldn't help feeling anxious. Ruth would have heard about Marc and Pet. She would be relieved Gillian's killer was caught and Anna was free and clear. She would also know it was all a lie.

Walker drove her to the hospital, promising to wait for her even though she told him it wasn't necessary. She was free to leave Shadow Lake. There was nothing keeping her here now and they both knew it.

"Are you sure you're up to this?" he asked her just before she got out of the patrol car. "You don't have to do this."

She nodded. "I'll be fine." Although she wasn't sure of that at all.

Inside the hospital, Anna walked down the empty corridor

SHADOW LAKE

to Ruth's room. The guard outside gave her a nod and reached
to open the door.

Ruth lay in the bed, her face turned toward the window
and the lake.

Anna stepped in, afraid she already knew why Ruth wanted
to see her.

Ruth turned then and held out her hand. Anna moved to
take it. The hand was cool, the skin thin and dotted with age
spots. Anna's own hand was cold and trembling. Ruth didn't
seem to notice.

"I'm glad you came," she said and motioned for Anna to
pull up the chair next to her bed. "I wasn't sure you would."

"How are you feeling?" Anna asked.

"I'll live." Ruth squeezed her hand, those gray eyes of
hers suddenly brimming with tears. "I like you. I wish Jack
had met someone like you. How different things might have
been if…" She let her voice trail off as she shook her head
and let go of Anna's hand to brush at the tears as if angry
with herself.

"No changing the past," the older woman said. "You and
I have learned that, if nothing else." Her eyes brimmed again
with tears. "Your son."

"Tyler," Anna said around the lump in her throat.

Ruth opened her mouth, lips moving, but no words came out.

"I know," Anna said.

Ruth's face crumpled. She turned her face away as if
ashamed.

"You found out," Anna said. "That's what caused your
attack." What Ruth had found in the investigator's report—
not just on Anna, but the connection between her and Jack
Fairbanks. She'd put it together because she'd known her son
Jack, she'd known something was wrong.

Ruth said nothing. What was there to say? Ruth had
guards outside her hospital room door because she knew

what both her sons were capable of now. She would have to live with that.

Ruth brushed the tears from her pale cheeks and finally turned to look at her again. "I'm sorry. I can't bring back your son. Or your friend."

Anna nodded.

Ruth squeezed her hand, pain and compassion in her eyes. "I can't—"

"I know," Anna said. "I know." She'd known where this conversation was headed long before she'd entered this room. Ruth blamed herself for her sons' crimes. But in the end, she was their mother. She couldn't give them up even though clearly she knew more than Anna about what her sons had done.

But as Anna had known, Ruth Fairbanks would take no part in seeing justice done. Not against Jack. And maybe especially not against Jonathan.

With effort, Anna rose and walked to the door. She heard Ruth crying softly as she left the room. She didn't look back.

CHAPTER TWENTY-FIVE

ANNA STOOD ON THE screened-in porch, sipping her coffee. The lake was beautiful this morning, the surface cloaked in a low wispy fog, the sun piercing the thin veil to glow on the slick green water.

It had been over a year since she'd seen Shadow Lake. It had taken that long to see the lake's beauty and not its darkness. She no longer had the house in Seattle. During that time away, she'd rented an apartment in Pilot's Cove that was close to the private nursery school where she had worked. She'd been close enough that she saw a lot of Doc. And Walker.

Not long after she'd left Shadow Lake she'd read about the tragedy in the newspaper. She'd been waiting for it so at least part of it came as no surprise, although Jonathan Fairbanks's drowning sent the rest of the country into shock. He'd won his father's seat on the Senate. There'd been talk of him running for president in 2012.

According to Walker, Ruth was the one who found Jonathan's body washed up on the beach. Walker swore that it wasn't the only body Ruth had found that early morning in July, but that Fairbanks money had kept the truth from coming out.

Jonathan had been buried beside his brother Jack and father Big Jim Fairbanks in the cemetery in Shadow Lake. Anna hadn't attended the funeral, but Walker had. He said that both Jack's and Jonathan's graves had fresh sod on them. "I think Jack is finally at peace."

Shortly after the funeral, Ruth Fairbanks had ordered everything on the island razed, including an old shack at the north end as well as the mansion. She, according to one inside source, was traveling abroad.

Anna hadn't been down to the Shadow Lake cemetery, but Doc still went every day to visit with Gladys. He said the grass on Jonathan's grave was brown year around, while Jack's was always green. Anna didn't believe him. Maybe one day she'd go see for herself.

She'd heard from Doc that someone had seen former Police Chief Robert Nash down in Oregon. Lucinda was expecting again. Another girl.

Anna could hear Doc in the kitchen now making them a sack lunch to take fishing. Summer in Shadow Lake was just as wonderful as she'd been told it would be. She heard Doc go out to meet the mailman, heard their murmured voices as Doc visited for a moment and returned, the screen door banging softly behind him.

Out on the lake, Anna picked up the sound of a boat motor heading this way. Moments later, the bow cut through the thin fog, pulled up to the dock, the motor dying as waves lapped at the shore and laughter drifted up to the house.

"The boys are here," Doc said behind her.

She nodded, smiling as she watched Billy Blake and D.C. Walker playfully pushing each other in a race for the house.

"They're never going to grow up," Doc said, a smile in his voice.

She hoped not.

"Something came for you," Doc said, holding out a piece of mail.

Anna put down her coffee and took the square white envelope. There was no return address. The postmark was Fiji, a place someone might stop when traveling around the world. It was addressed to Anna Walker in care of Dr. Gene

Brubaker, Shadow Lake, Washington. Whoever had sent it knew that Anna and Walker were married and living with Doc. Doc liked the company and said he felt safer with the chief of police living under his roof.

Anna knew Doc needed the company. He still missed Gladys desperately, but he seemed healthier and happier having them there. He now talked of the future as if he had plans to stick around for a while.

Frowning, Anna pried up the flap. There was a card inside with the word CONGRATULATIONS emblazed across the front and what looked like confetti being thrown to the breeze. Only it wasn't confetti, it was tiny colorful baby rattles.

There was no printed greeting inside the card. Just a handful of carefully written words in an older woman's unsteady hand.

As Billy and Walker bound up the steps, Anna covered her swollen round belly, felt the child move inside and read the words.

It was a blessing from the Bible: "The Lord deal kindly with you." *Ruth* 1:8

* * * * *

Melita had been expecting a chaste quick kiss of the generic variety. But this kiss with Sully was the kind that sparked a dying flame to life. The kind of kiss you can't plan for. The kind of kiss memories are built on.

The memory of her murdered lover, Nemo, came to her then and she made a starved little noise in the back of her throat. She raised her arms and threaded her fingers through Sully's hair, pulled him closer. Felt his body settle, then melt into her.

In that instant her hunger for him grew, and his for her. She pressed herself to him with more urgency, and he responded in kind.

Melita came out of her kiss-induced memory of Nemo with a start. "Wait a minute." She pushed Sully away from her. "You bastard!"

She spit two nasty words at him in Greek, then wiped his kiss from her lips.

"I thought you deserved some solid proof that I'm still in one piece." He started for the door. "The clock's ticking, honey. Come on, let's get out of here."

"That's it? You sucker me into kissing you, and that's all you have to say?"

"I'm sorry. How's that?"

He didn't sound sorry in the least. "You're—"

"Getting out of this godforsaken prison cell. Stop whining and let's go."

"Not if I was being shot at sunrise. Go. You deserve whatever you get if you walk out that door."

He turned back. "Freedom is what I'm going to get."

"A second of freedom before the guards in the hall shoot you." She jammed her hands on her hips. "And to think I was worried about you."

"If you're staying behind, it's no skin off my ass."

"Wait! What about our deal?"

"You just said you're not coming. Make up your mind."

"Have you forgotten we need a boat?"

"How could I? You keep harping on it."

"I'm not going without a boat. And those guards out there aren't going to just let you walk out of here. You need me and we need a plan."

"I already have a plan. I'm getting out of here. That's the plan."

"I should have realized that you never intended to take me with you from the very beginning. You're a liar and a coward."

Of everything she had read, there was nothing in Sully Paxton's file that hinted he was a coward, but it was the one word that seemed to register in that one-track mind of his. The look he nailed her with a second later was pure venom.

He came at her so quickly she didn't have time to get out of his way. "You know I'm not a coward."

"Prove it. Give me until dawn. I need one more night to put everything in place before we leave the island."

"You're asking me to stay in this cell one more night...and trust you?"

"Yes."

He snorted. "Yesterday you knew they were planning to harm me, but instead of doing something about it you went to bed and never gave me a second thought. Suppose tonight you do the same. By tomorrow I might damn well be in my grave."

"Okay, I screwed up. I won't do it again." Melita sucked in a ragged breath. "I can't leave this minute. Dawn, Sully. Wait until dawn." When he looked as if he was about to say no, she pleaded, "Please wait for me."

"You're asking a lot. The door's open now. I would be a fool to hang around here and trust that you'll be back."

"What you can trust is that I want off this island as badly as you do, and you're my only hope."

"I must be crazy."

"Is that a yes?"

"Dammit!" He turned his back on her. Swore twice more.

"You won't be sorry."

He turned around. "I already am. How about we seal this new deal?"

He was staring at her lips. Suddenly Melita knew what he expected. "We already sealed it."

"One more. You enjoyed it. Admit it."

"I enjoyed it because I was kissing someone else."

He laughed. "That's a good one."

"It's true. It might have been your lips, but it wasn't you I was kissing."

"If that's your excuse for wanting to kiss me, then—"

"I was kissing Nemo."

"What's a nemo?"

Melita gave Sully a look that clearly told him that he was trespassing on sacred ground. She was about to enforce it with a warning when a voice in the hall jerked them both to attention.

She bolted away from the wall. "Get back in bed. Hurry. I'll be here before dawn."

She didn't reach the door before he snagged her arm, pulled her up against him and planted a kiss on her lips that took her completely by surprise.

When he released her, he said, "If you're confused about who just kissed you, the name's Sully. I'll be here waiting at dawn. Don't be late."

Romantic
SUSPENSE

Sparked *by* **Danger,**
Fueled *by* **Passion.**

Onyxx agent Sully Paxton's only chance of
survival lies in the hands of his enemy's daughter
Melita Krizova. He doesn't know he's a pawn in the
beautiful island girl's own plan for escape. Can
they survive their ruses and their fiery attraction?

**Look for the next installment in the
Spy Games miniseries,**

Sleeping with
Danger
by Wendy Rosnau

Available November 2007 wherever you buy books.

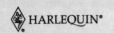

Every great love has a story to tell™

Charlie fell in love with Rose Kaufman
before he even met her, through stories her
husband, Joe, used to tell. When Joe is killed
in the trenches, Charlie helps Rose through
her grief and they make a new life together.
But for Charlie, a question remains—can
love be as true the second time around?
Only one woman can answer that....

Look for

The Soldier and
the Rose

by

Linda Barrett

Available November wherever you buy books.

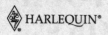

REQUEST YOUR FREE BOOKS!

2 FREE NOVELS PLUS 2 FREE GIFTS!

Silhouette® Romantic

SUSPENSE

Sparked by Danger, Fueled by Passion!

YES! Please send me 2 FREE Silhouette® Romantic Suspense novels and my 2 FREE gifts. After receiving them, if I don't wish to receive any more books, I can return the shipping statement marked "cancel." If I don't cancel, I will receive 4 brand-new novels every month and be billed just $4.24 per book in the U.S., or $4.99 per book in Canada, plus 25¢ shipping and handling per book plus applicable taxes, if any*. That's a savings of at least 15% off the cover price! I understand that accepting the 2 free books and gifts places me under no obligation to buy anything. I can always return a shipment and cancel at any time. Even if I never buy another book from Silhouette, the two free books and gifts are mine to keep forever.

240 SDN EEX6   340 SDN EEYJ

Name	(PLEASE PRINT)

Address	Apt. #

City	State/Prov.	Zip/Postal Code

Signature (if under 18, a parent or guardian must sign)

Mail to the **Silhouette Reader Service™**:
IN U.S.A.: P.O. Box 1867, Buffalo, NY 14240-1867
IN CANADA: P.O. Box 609, Fort Erie, Ontario L2A 5X3

Not valid to current Silhouette Intimate Moments subscribers.

Want to try two free books from another line?
Call 1-800-873-8635 or visit www.morefreebooks.com.

* Terms and prices subject to change without notice. NY residents add applicable sales tax. Canadian residents will be charged applicable provincial taxes and GST. This offer is limited to one order per household. All orders subject to approval. Credit or debit balances in a customer's account(s) may be offset by any other outstanding balance owed by or to the customer. Please allow 4 to 6 weeks for delivery.

Your Privacy: Silhouette is committed to protecting your privacy. Our Privacy Policy is available online at www.eHarlequin.com or upon request from the Reader Service. From time to time we make our lists of customers available to reputable firms who may have a product or service of interest to you. If you would prefer we not share your name and address, please check here. ☐

SRS0

ATHENA FORCE
Heart-pounding romance and thrilling adventure.

History repeats itself...unless she can stop it.

Investigative reporter Winter Archer is thrown into writing
a biography of Athena Academy's founder. But someone
out there will stop at nothing—not even murder—to
ensure that long-buried secrets remain hidden.

ATHENA FORCE
Will the women of Athena unravel Arachne's powerful
web of blackmail and death...or succumb to their
enemies' deadly secrets?

Look for

VENDETTA
by *Meredith Fletcher*

*Available November
wherever you buy books.*

AF38975

At forty, Maureen Hart suddenly finds herself juggling men. Man #1: her six-year-old grandson, left with her while his mother goes off to compete for a million dollars on reality TV. Maureen is delighted, but to Man #2—her fiancé—the little boy represents an intrusion on their time. Then Man #3, the boy's paternal grandfather, offers to take the child off her hands…
and maybe even sweep Maureen off her feet….

Look for

I'M YOUR MAN

by

SUSAN CROSBY

Available November wherever you buy books.

For a sneak peek, visit
TheNextNovel.com

HN88145

HARLEQUIN *Romance*

New York Times bestselling author

DIANA PALMER

Handsome, eligible ranch owner Stuart York knew Ivy Conley was too young for him, so he closed his heart to her and sent her away—despite the fireworks between them. Now, years later, Ivy is determined not to be treated like a little girl anymore…but for some reason, Stuart is always fighting her battles for her. And safe in Stuart's arms makes Ivy feel like a woman…his woman.

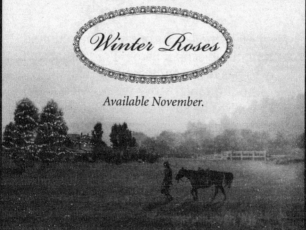

Winter Roses

Available November.